Between and Shadow

By Erik Ballard

Night Of The Amnesiac

A crescent moon dangles above the twinkling stars high in the sky; like a lure cast into an endless ocean of darkness on the tip of a telescopic fishing rod. A palette of Autumn colored leaves rustle against each other. The irritating sound of an air-compressed car horn blares infinitely into the empty womb of the night. Meanwhile, a balding black male with a shaved head has his face planted deep into the wheel of his silver mid-sized, 2009 Nissan SUV. The hood of the SUV has been bent upwards exposing the iron guts of the vehicle after having smashed into the trunk of a massive Thuja Green Giant. Liquid poured onto the Earth from beneath the car forming an oblong shape that drowned a colony of ants that lived in a nearby anthill.

Not far from the site of the accident, at the top of a long, winding driveway was a prodigious mansion. And surrounding said mansion was a beautiful garden with acutely trimmed hedges...but more on that later. For now, we shall stay focused on the man in the vehicle.

Within the next few seconds, this man will awaken and will be cast into a world unfamiliar to him. He will step out of his car and head in the direction of the lovely building built tall enough that it appeared to cut through the sky. Unfortunately for him, inside of this mansion are events and answers that many would agree are better left unexplored…

A dark line of blood seeped out of an inch long cut across the man's right temple. Like molasses, the blood slid down his cheek, dripped from the corner of his jagged jaw, and fell onto his navy blue denim jeans leaving behind a barely noticeable circular stain. The car's left headlight (the right one no longer functioned since a majority of the glass was smashed against the tree) beamed ahead illuminating an abandoned wooded area.

The number of forest animals was scarce. Most had already begun their peaceful journey of hibernation for the Winter. A piercing wind flung hundreds of leaves into the air. A tornado of Autumn nature was formed, dancing in the spotlight created by the individual low beam emitted from the car.

The nauseating smell of gasoline stormed into the man's nostrils. A pair of brown eyes began to slowly appear beneath his rising eyelids.

He pulled his throbbing head from off of the car horn bringing a stop to the annoying sound that wailed into the darkness. His vision was blurry for a few moments until the environment around him started slowly coming into focus. The shattered windshield took him by surprise as he realized that he had no memory of how he had gotten himself into the situation. Still feeling the effects of disorientation, the man patted his hand against the side of his seat until his fingers ran across the seat belt buckle. He pushed his left thumb against the piece of red plastic releasing the harness, causing it to shoot across his body and retract back into its holster in the upper corner of the vehicle. With his index finger, he pulled at the neck of his shirt and could see a blotchy blue and purple bruise slant across his shoulder and down his torso where the seat belt had been fastened.

Blood continued to drip slowly from his forehead. He hadn't taken notice until he tasted iron in the red liquid as it dripped into the corner of his lips. The man raised his hand and placed two fingers against the cut. He winced and quickly pulled his hand away. Touching the wound felt like somebody took their middle finger, tucked it back beneath their thumb, and then slingshotted it forward.

His dark, watering eyes surveyed the interior of the car. Eventually, he found himself staring at his own reflection in the rearview mirror. The dark figure staring back at him looked like a person who had just walked away as the lesser of two combatants from a back alley brawl. The face in the rearview mirror was unfamiliar, but he would have to accept it on his own. There was some swelling around his bottom lip. It came from when his head collided against the steering wheel and he smashed his lower mouth into the jagged edges of his bottom teeth.

The man released a pained groan as he carefully arched his back forward in an attempt to reach behind in his back jeans pocket. The right pocket was empty but the left was home to a thin, brown leather wallet. He flipped the tri-fold wallet open and noticed that most of the slots were empty. A few green dollar bills poked out of the largest compartment at the top. He counted three singles and a ten. Thirteen dollars. He stuffed the money back into place and fingered through the few cards that were within.

The first one he noticed was a punch ticket loyalty card to a Frozen Yogurt shop called Frozen Dozen. Some tiny animals with large eyes (a frog, bear, dog, and cat to be exact) smiled happily, holding hands in the bottom corners of the pink card. *Buy 10 cups of yogurt, get a Small cup FREE on your next visit!* Eight out of the ten boxes at the top of the card had been punched. Only two more to go.

The next card that the man came across was a silver, prepaid Visa debit card. Sixteen braille-like numbers lined beside one another front and center. Card expires 06/23. The expiration meant nothing to the man. He had no idea what day it was, what month it was, or even what year it was. A feeling of frustration melted over him. He wanted nothing more than to find out who he was, and how he had gotten into this situation. Like the money and the frozen yogurt card, he tucked the prepaid Visa back into the wallet.

The final card in the wallet was a green and white library card. It had the words *Library System of Fairfax County* written in cursive along the top. In the bottom left-hand corner was a yellow box with black writing that read: *Access Virginia.*

"Virginia?" the dark man mumbled lightly to himself. He tucked the library card back into the wallet and searched inside one last time, just to make sure that there was nothing that he had missed. Unfortunately, all of the wallet's contents had been discovered. Like he had done to retrieve the wallet, he arched his back forward, lifted his aching ass into the air, and pushed the brown wallet back into his pocket. While doing so, he noticed a phone lying on the floor in front of the passenger seat. He reached across the seat and picked it up.

The man pressed his thumb into the circular indentation that was the Home button at the bottom of the phone, but the slick screen remained black. He pressed it rapidly another ten or so times but still, the phone remained as dark and still as the night that surrounded him. In the top right of the phone, he felt his index finger rub against another small button. He held the button down and was met with the image of a drained battery with a white lightning bolt in the middle.

Dead.

The thought of tossing the phone back onto the floor crossed his mind, but instead, he placed the phone into his front right pocket and proceeded to open the car door. Before exiting, he turned the key that was lodged into the ignition. The totalled car shut down with a dying hum. There was a short debate within his mind over whether or not he wanted to keep the single headlight shining forward, but he chose to turn that off as well. Better to keep himself hidden in the shadows than expose himself in the light. Or better yet, keep the things that lived in the woods hidden. Ignorance was indeed bliss.

The echo of the slamming car door stirred some of the nearby avian inhabitants. The sound of rushing wind being thrown around by heavy wings filled the void between the trees. Branches shook wildly as large black birds were juggled from tree to tree. Brown and yellow leaves that hung from the ends of trees were released, silently floating down, down, down to the earthen ground.

Caw! Caw! Ca-caw!

The crows were vocal about how unhappy they were with being disturbed. They screeched viciously from high in the trees, shielded by darkness. Then, one of the birds discovered enough courage to leave the safety of the tree. Like a gargoyle painted in ebony, it spread its wings and soared through the air until landing on the upturned hood of the car.

Soon another followed.

Then another...And another, until the entire car was overcrowded with bulky winged bodies.

Like an organized military strike, the crows began to attack.

Fueled with rage, they flew at the man and pecked at his flesh. He swung his arms wildly, occasionally striking one and sending it crashing towards the ground. But within seconds, another crow would take its place. It didn't take long for him to realize that he was in a losing fight. He was outnumbered and embarrassingly outsmarted.

Ignoring the soreness that erupted in his legs, the man turned in the opposite direction of the car and ran as fast as he could. The murder of crows were right behind him, cawing and screeching. The wind expelled from their flapping wings brushed against the back of his neck. The further he ran, the more sinister the crows became. Their grating coos lingered in his ears, sounding more and more like the gurgles of someone drowning in their own blood. Soon, he reached a small embankment and climbed. Exhaustion was taking hold of him. Upon reaching the top, the man tripped over a hidden ditch falling hands first onto a gravel road.

His hands trembled uncontrollably as he lifted himself off the ground. Tiny pebbles were lodged into the wet, sticky skin of his newly exposed layer of flesh. The hoarse caws faded off into the distance as the crows returned to the woods.

The man sat on the ground and held his hands in front of his face. If he squinted hard enough, he could see the tiny rocks that glued themselves against his skin. One by one, he removed them. The feeling of skin being lifted every time he pulled a stone away was agonizing. Puddles of salty tears welled in his eyes.

Fifteen minutes passed by. Thirteen pebbles had been removed from both hands.

For the first time that night, the man found himself shivering as he sat there on the rocks. Transparent clouds formed in the air with every breath. The temperature had dropped down into the low forties. He was wearing a simple gray T-shirt with a pocket protector. If his short term memory served him right, he had not seen a jacket while in the car. Regardless, he had no intention of trekking back through the woods and having a second showdown with the maddened crows. He would have to venture forth without one.

Flashes of white light jolted life into the abysmally blank sky. A roar of thunder chased shortly behind. Rain was coming. The man raised up to his feet, careful to not use his hands as crutches. Another lightning bolt sliced the sky in half and was followed by more thunder that boomed like a series of shots set off by a cannon. Hoping to find some form of civilization, the man started to walk along the winding gravel road.

His hands burned tremendously. It felt like he had his palms pressed firmly against the burners of an electric stove. He gently blew on them trying to put out the invisible fire, but all it seemed to do was irritate the nerves further.

In the distance, two vibrant flames waved him closer. The pace of his walking quickened, and eventually became a light jog. The semi-nude trees lining both sides of the road swayed in the nightly wind. The closer the man got to the flames, the fewer trees there were to make eerie mockeries of him in the darkness. Within minutes he entered a clearing, noticing that the flames were encased by two gold plated lanterns attached to a large gate.

Behind the gate was the largest, most beautiful red brick home that he had ever seen (or could remember seeing.) A large semi-circle window stood front and center as the heart of the building. On either side of the central window were five more tall, rectangular windows each with an electric candle perched on the inside sill. Spouting out of the slanted black tiled roof was a towering greystone chimney releasing a thick display of smoke that vanished beneath the starlight. Two brilliantly designed pearl columns formed an archway that acted as an alcove leading up to the mansion's jet black front door. The road smoothed out the closer that the man got to the home.

"Hello? Is anybody there? Hello?" He peeked into the glass of a security booth located on the outer wall of the massive residential gate. An empty chair sat alone inside. He walked around to the side and came across a door in which he turned the doorknob. To his surprise, it was unlocked. Six monochrome screened security monitors were alive and running. Two cameras focused on opposite ends of the gate, one on the front door, one on the back door, one overlooking a gorgeous garden in the front yard, and the last looked over a large wooden deck attached to the home's rear. None of the screens showed movement.

On a table beside the monitors was a black and white composition notebook. Inside were pages filled from top line to bottom with names, dates, and times. The man paged through about three-quarters of the notebook until the names stopped. The final page that had been written listed four names and beside each a time and a date. They read as follows:

Amanda Wilson-----18:24-----10/27/13
Rachel Lewis-----21:44-----10/28/13
Geneva Turner-----18:06-----10/29/13
Angela Ramirez-----22:15-----10/30/13

Each of the names was of a woman, and each had arrived only one day after the name before. The man fingered back a few pages and saw the names of males written as well. He figured the recent names being only female must just be a coincidence. The thing that stuck out to him the most were the dates. If this notebook had been filled out recently, that meant that it was the year 2013. Also, depending on how recent, it was possible that today was Halloween. The thought of it being a day dedicated to sinister activities sent a slight chill down his spine. He persuaded himself to ignore the thought knowing that the dates in the notebook did not confirm anything, and exited the security booth.

A display of several white flashes of lightning lit the sky. Another parade of rolling thunder clapped soon after. An almost silent, calm drizzle began to rain down from above.

The mansion was ominously inviting. The large black, metal gates were spread wide open and the smooth curved driveway allured the man to continue forward. More flashes erupted in the sky, this time arriving without their noisy counterpart. Still feeling dazed and confused, he trudged forward towards the building. Like the flick of an imaginary switch, the rain began to pour as soon as he crossed the property threshold.

By the time that he arrived under the shelter of the pearl archway, his clothes had been drenched.

Water dripped onto the cement beneath his feet giving life to a multitude of tiny puddles. The smell of must and wet grass floated freely through the air.

The man gripped the heavy horseshoe knocker attached to the door and tapped it vigorously.

Knock. Knock. Knock. Knock.

Four times.

Thirty seconds passed without a response. He lifted the knocker once more and slammed it a little harder this time.

Knock! Knock! Knock!

"Excuse me!" The amnesiac shouted, his voice nearly drowned out by the storm coming to life around him. "I seemed to have crashed my car a little way down the road and I was wondering if I could get some help by chance? Hello? Is there anybody home!?" Without much thought, he lifted the knocker again and began pounding wildly on the door.

Knock! Knock! Knock! Knock! Knock! Knock!

Still, there was no response.

He released the knocker and turned around, looking out into the distant darkness that loomed amidst the torrential downpour. Countless spears of water crashed toward the earth from the puffy, dark clouds floating overhead. The idea of trekking back to the SUV entered his mind but didn't stay for long. *Maybe they can't hear me,* he thought. *It is a massive property after all.* His raw hand wrapped around the doorknob and turned. To his surprise, the door began to inch open.

"Hello? Is there anybody here? My name is-" He stopped mid-sentence feeling foolish for not being able to recall his own name. How was he going to explain that to the owner of the home? Perhaps an alias would do? Just for now that is.

As he entered the home his retinas were burned by the bright lights of a crystal chandelier that hung from the high ceiling above. Rainwater leaked from off the man's clothes and down onto the spotless white oak flooring.

Directly in front of where he stood was a gray carpeted set of stairs accompanied by wooden railings that lined either side. To his right was an opening that led into what appeared to be the dining room, completely furnished with a light gray rug that laid beneath a long, black rectangular dinner table; six gray chairs were neatly tucked underneath. A tall, thin vase sat in the middle of the table and within it stood half a dozen skinny green straws that blossomed into pink and yellow flowers. Nailed against the far wall was a colorful water painting of elegant white yachts docked at a port with an orange and purple sunset dipping into the horizon.

His soaked shoes squeaked every time he pressed his foot against the floor. A trickled chain of water traced along the wooden floor mapping out the man's every move.

"Is there anybody home!? I don't mean to intrude, but I need help! I knocked on the door a few times but I figured maybe you didn't hear me since the house is so big! Hello?" The only response was the echoes of his own voice.

The man explored the first floor hesitantly with a nervous hopefulness that he would run into whoever lived in the home. He figured it was a possibility that the owner could help him, but there was also the possibility that they could shoot and kill him for entering into what he imagined has to be private property. Before entering into a room he made sure to boldly announce his presence.

The mansion had so many rooms that each one seemed dedicated to a specific activity. In one room (most likely an office) there was a harvest cherry L-desk and hutch combo with a black leather office chair tucked behind it. On top of the desk was a slim silver Macintosh computer and a clear jar filled with pencils and a variety of pens. A matte black picture frame occupied the corner and inside was the picture of a beautiful blonde with sparkling blue eyes smiling for the camera as she hugged a girl with caramel skin and curly hair. Pinned along the wall was a medium brown bookcase and storage cabinet filled with thick books focusing on business and psychology along with a few pieces of polished fine china. A giant clock with large roman numerals ticked away on a nearby wall. Based on the time displayed, it was one thirty-four in the morning.

The next room (a music room of sorts) welcomed its guests with an ebony satin Estonia 190 grand piano. A book of sheet music titled *A First Book of Classical Music: For the Beginning Pianist* by Bergerac was propped up on the music rack. The lid prop was erected at an angle lifting the piano lid and giving full exposure to the stringy guts inside. A gray sectional sofa lined the far corner of the room and in front of it was a glass coffee table with a single burning Yankee Candle titled Harvest. The smell being produced by the candle was a warming blend of cinnamon, cloves, pumpkin, and sweet apples.

The rain continued to pour outside. The smacking of millions of tiny droplets pounding against the windows sounded like a symphony of typing computer keys. As the man found himself entering the kitchen, a strike of lightning flared beyond the glass of the window. The kitchen light, which was frighteningly left on as was every other light in the house so far, flickered a few times. The amnesiac held his breath and was eased when the flickering stopped, and the flashing bulbs found the power to remain on.

In the center of the kitchen was an island with a black granite countertop and walnut sidings. The island had a sink installed within it and the man tipped the cold water tap upwards. A fountain of running water poured out of the faucet and he placed his damaged hands beneath it. Veins bulged from his neck as he tightly gritted his teeth, struggling to withstand the pain that shot through his hands and up his arms. After a few seconds, he removed his hands and flipped the tap back down bringing an end to the running water.

The microwave, refrigerator, and stove were all sleek stainless steel. Hanging from the ceiling above the island were three chrome Freeport LED light pendants. On the wall beside the refrigerator hung a wall plaque with a bunch of dining words written with different types of typography. Words like kitchen, spice, delicious, appetite and cuisine were listed just to name a few. He then noticed a calendar held against the refrigerator by a magnet that read *You can't scare me, I have KIDS*.

The top half of the calendar was covered with a beautiful picture of three bright orange pumpkins leaning against one another surrounded by a sea of auburn and pecan brown leaves. The bottom half was headed by the word **OCTOBER** with the date of Thursday the 31st circled in red marker.

Halloween.

Next to the calendar was a piece of lined white notepad paper with words written across it in the same red ink that was used to circle the date. **COME UPSTAIRS TO THE GUEST BEDROOM...2nd DOOR ON THE LEFT**. At the bottom of the paper was the drawn image of a smiley face.

"Come to the bedroom?" the man whispered lightly to himself. Surely this note couldn't be meant for him. Possibly it was some promiscuous note left behind by an aroused housewife who fell asleep awaiting the arrival of her husband from work. The note had been written recently. The fumes from the red Sharpie marker still lingered from the paper and into the air.

He exited the kitchen and returned to the main hall with the set of silver carpeted stairs.

"Hello, I...I saw your note taped to the refrigerator." God, he felt so ridiculous calling up to the top of the empty stairs, as if some beautiful woman (perhaps the one that he saw in the picture back in the office who he wouldn't mind going a couple of rounds with) was going to scurry into focus from around the corner and greet him as if she had been expecting his arrival for hours. Still, he stood at the bottom of the steps reluctant to proceed further into the heart of the house that had urged him to come ever closer from beyond the front gates; like a carnival game operator instructing him to step right up and win himself a prize.

The man found himself torn between three options:

1. He could follow the instructions of the note and precede upstairs to the said bedroom. The chances of somebody responding to his calls if he chose to call out from the top of the steps may be higher than what they were from the first floor. Also, there was a smiley face at the bottom of the note which usually meant good things even though at the moment his memory was too hazy to recall any examples.

2. He could remain on the first floor and find a place to relax until somebody either walked through the front door or came down from upstairs. The chances of the homeowner spiraling into a panic from finding a strange man in their house uninvited could result in the police being called immediately and him being detained for breaking and entering, trespassing, or whatever the blue suits of justice would want to call it. He couldn't remember much,

but he still understood the fact that he was a black man in America and his time would more than likely exceed the crime.

3. Lastly, he could turn around, walk out the front door, and leave. Yes, he would be out in the wild beneath the stars and abused by the rain, but there would be no consequences. That is if he refused to view the possibility of catching hypothermia, becoming sick, and dying as a severe consequence resulting from his action.

He decided to go with option number one. Whether or not that was the best option from the list is and forever will be debatable.

The soft carpeting beneath his feet had a soft, welcoming feel as he took his first step onto the stairs. As he arrived on the seventh of sixteen steps, the lights went out. A flicker of lightning seeped through the windows, lighting the house for a short second before leaving the man to stand there alone in the darkness surrounded by the rumblings of thunder. Shadowy marionettes danced along the walls. Seconds passed, but the lights never came back on.

"Excuse me, is there anybody home?! Hello? I saw the note that was taped to the fridge! Is there anybody up here? I honestly don't mean to intrude, I'm just trying to get out of the storm and figure out a way to get some help with my car." The mysticism of the night played foolish tricks on his mind. He imagined deformed monsters with crooked, inverted legs roaming the halls of the unknown. Crazed cannibalistic conservatives who were patiently waiting within the black preparing to strike, kill, and feed from his flesh. Or maybe adolescents plagued with the disease of madness who had killed their parents and couldn't wait to push a blade down deep into his own gut.

The house lit up momentarily as he reached the top of the stairs. The sight of a dark man staring back at him nearly caused him to jump out of his skin. As his body jolted quickly in fear, so did the figure in front of him. Lightning flashed again and the identity of the figure was revealed. He was staring into the deep, dark eyes that were his own. A large, silver antique mirror hung on the wall before him. The cut that tore across his temple had been cleansed by the rainwater. His eyes were dark and dilated. He took his right hand and rubbed his knuckles across his high cheekbones. Tiny stubbles of facial hair pricked his fingers in the way that they do after a few days of not shaving. Not a single feature resonated within him.

COME UPSTAIRS TO THE GUEST BEDROOM...2nd DOOR ON THE LEFT.

An imaginary voice repeated the instructions that had been written on the notepad. The amnesiac stepped away from the mirror and followed the directions. An ivory multi viscose runway rug was laid across the floor. The man walked cautiously down the hallway so as not to run into anything unexpected. He passed a door to his right that was closed. A few steps further he passed the first door on his left which was also closed. Beside the door against the wall was a dark wood console table with a large, glossy red bamboo vase. A couple more steps and he would arrive at his destination.

This door like the others before it was also closed. He grabbed hold of the glass doorknob which burned fiercely against his injured palm. He turned the knob slowly. The door pushed open.

The room was dark aside from the flickering light coming out of the small electrical candle that sat on the window sill. A set of polyester Dreamweaver curtains hung in front of the window. The rain continued to pour, endlessly tapping against the window. Against the back wall was a queen bed covered with a heavy vanilla comforter and sitting on top of that was another note with red scribblings. The man picked up the note and walked over to the candle so that he could properly read it.

REMEMBER HOW YOU LOVE TO PLAY GAMES? THE FIRST ONE TOOK PLACE IN THE BEDROOM CLOSET. SEE

FOR YOURSELF. At the bottom of the note was the same smiley face as the one in the kitchen. He laid the note down on the sill beside the electric candle and stared down at the words on the paper.

"What is going on in this house?" he murmured. He turned around and could see the closet mentioned in the note. Beneath the crack in the bottom of the door, he could see a reddish glow dancing around from within. The man walked towards the closet door and was met with the smell of burning candles. As he got closer, he noticed a strange noise coming from within.

The closet door had been opened.

"Holy shi-" The man couldn't even finish his sentence before a waterfall of vomit pushed itself up through his esophagus and ejected a greenish-yellow blend of stomach bile onto the wooden floor. The muscles in his stomach contracted and he retched a few more times before releasing another spillage of his innards. Strings of saliva dangled from his bottom lip. With a swipe of his hand, he wiped the remaining sick from his mouth and lifted his eyes back up to the sight that began the cycle of events.

Five tall, burning candles were placed in a large circle. The smell of spiced pumpkin overwhelmed the narrow walk-in closet. In the middle of that circle was a woman with black hair tied to a wooden chair with her neck slit. The legs of the chair sat within a thick pool of dark blood. The gash along the woman's neck was stretched wide open as her head hung, falling backward behind the chair. Sections of the wound were beginning to clot. The woman's mouth fell ajar in a crooked, silent scream. Her hands looked like blueberries as a result of the circulation being cut off from the tightness of the thick rope that had bound her wrists. The pearl white color of her satin nightgown had been washed away in a ruby river. Her feet, like her hands, were countless shades darker than her God given skin tone.

The smell of pumpkin spice mixed with the stink of vomit, blending to create an Autumn concoction of sweet, sour, and stale. Add to that the metallic smell of blood and you have yourself an in-home slaughterhouse; a possible scent recommendation for Yankee Candle's Halloween fragrance line.

Sitting on the woman's lap was a sealed envelope with the words **OPEN ME** written on it. The man's heart was pounding. He wanted nothing more than to find a phone and call the police. But who was to say that they wouldn't blame him for the murder? He did enter into a home uninvited that wasn't his. Why should they believe anything that he would say, especially when he wouldn't even be able to tell them who he was?

The only sound in the room was the *pitter-patter* created by the rain hitting against the window. He anticipated a gurgling scream to fly from out of the woman's mouth, somehow miraculously resuscitated just to find herself choking on her own blood, but it never happened. His arms trembled as he reached down towards the woman's thighs and pulled the blood-stained envelope away from the deceased.

His stomach continued to churn. He closed the closet door and rushed over to the window with the electric candle. Before unsealing the note, the man stared into the hallway, hoping that somebody would turn the lights back on and inform him that he was being pranked. That all of this was just some sick person's idea of a joke. That the lady in the closet was nothing more than a damn good actress who was actually alive this entire time.

But nobody came. Even he was able to comprehend that that had been wishful thinking.

He turned the envelope over and held it close to the glowing warmth that buzzed from off of the electric candle. He slid his fingers inside and pulled out a driver's license. The smiling face that stared up at him belonged to the woman whose body was now lying limp in a closet, tied to a chair, and surrounded by a pool of her own blood.

Rachel Lewis:
-ORGAN DONOR

-BROWN EYES

-5 FT, 3IN

-BORN JULY 17, 1990

Just that small amount of information listed on the woman's driver's license gave him the feeling that he knew the woman. Information that wasn't listed would be that she was a daughter. Maybe a sister. Maybe a mother. Perhaps she provided a lot of service in food kitchens helping the homeless and the needy. But at this point, did any of that really matter? Thinking about that kind of stuff left the man feeling a sense of guilt for a crime that he didn't commit.

"You're guilty!" his conscience constantly screamed at him. "Guilty! Guilty!" He dropped the license onto the ground and fell onto the bed as his legs weakened and gave out from underneath him. His eyes immediately darted back towards the doorway. It was as empty as it had been since his arrival. He put his fingers back into the envelope and pulled out another piece of paper. More instructions.

ANSWERS LIE WITHIN THE HOUSE. HEAD TO THE BASEMENT. WHATEVER YOU DO, DO NOT LEAVE. I SAY THIS FOR YOUR PROTECTION.

The man dropped the note onto the bed and felt his eyes begin to swell as they filled with tears. This was quickly becoming the night from Hell.

The note instructed him not to leave, but why shouldn't he? Why should he stay inside of a house where there's a dead woman with her throat slit tied to a chair in a bedroom closet? Then rationale began to speak to him. It explained how his DNA was all over the home by now. How his vomit was beginning to harden against the hardwood floor.

It sounded absolutely insane, but the man was beginning to believe that the notes left behind were indeed meant for him. So the questions were *who exactly left the notes behind?* And *how did they know that he would end up at this house on this night?* He wanted answers, but fear left him paralyzed on the bed. What else would this house of horrors have to offer?

"Do not leave the house, I say this for your protection. Head to...The basement?" He spoke the words quietly as if hearing each phoneme would help him better understand what was being asked of him. As he stood from the bed, the floor beneath him creaked under his weight. The sound left chills running down his spine.

Meanwhile, the rain continued to flood the outside world.

Haunting images of Rachel Lewis' contorted face flashed constantly in his mind. The house was blanketed in darkness, but the images continued to appear under a focused spotlight. As he descended down the steps he could hear the ominous whispering of the wind seeping through the front door. The man could barely see and yet, he was tasked with finding the basement, the one place in the home he would prefer not to explore.

Upon entering the dining room, the amnesiac felt his way around the large table and then exited into a long hallway. A large grandfather clock chimed through the home, almost forcing the man's heart to burst through his chest. The swift beats of his heart raced in stride with his heavy breathing.

Ding! Ding!

The grandfather clock struck twice from an undisclosed location. Two o'clock.

A tapping sound echoed lightly from down the hallway. The man found a way to compose himself and continued his exploration of the home. The further down the hallway he walked, the louder the tapping became.

Tap...Tap...Tap.

He arrived at another door, and behind it came the origin of the eerie sound that crept down the hallway. "Hello?" he said quietly, praying that he didn't receive an actual response. There came no voice, but the tapping continued. He reached his hand forward and felt around until his fingers ran across the doorknob. With the pain still shooting around in his hand, he grabbed the doorknob and turned.

Something heavy was blocking the door. He pushed with all of his strength until the door flung open and he stumbled inside. Right away he was smacked in the face by a foreign object.

The tapping ceased.

Another electric candle sat on the window sill, supplying light to a small area in the back corner of the room. Lightning flared through the window and gave life to the silhouette of a body that hung from the ceiling before him. The amnesiac let loose a bloodcurdling scream and stumbled backward into the hall. Another lightning strike froze the room in time, like a picture captured by an old school analog camera. The dainty woman's body swayed gently back and forth from the tightened noose that was wrapped around her neck.

He remained on the cold wooden floor, whimpering in a way that no grown man would ever admit to his friends or family. There was another one...Another dead body hanging right there in front of him.

A dry, pudgy tongue fell from the side of the woman's mouth. Her eyelids were trapped in a half open position, staring lifelessly down at the ground, or in this case, at the horrified man that grieved before her. Like Rachel Lewis who was tied to a chair in a closet above them, this woman also wore a white satin nightgown.

Taped to the woman's nightgown was an envelope predictably inked with red Sharpie instructing the man to **OPEN ME**. The twisted games continued.

The man batted at the envelope like a kitten swinging playfully at a piece of yarn. It would be a successful moment in time if he could detach the message without having to touch the body. Unfortunately, he failed. After a few failed attempts, the envelope was knocked loose where he crawled beneath the hanging body and retrieved it. He continued crawling until positioning himself inside the bubble of light that illuminated the far corner.

The envelope was torn open and another driver's license dropped to the floor. The man stared down at the square picture on the license' corner. "Why are you smiling at me?" he asked empathetically, aware of the sad future that awaited her. He was shocked by how beautiful she had been; her eyes shone like a pair of tiny blue galaxies and her hair was done up in a tight bun. But now, she was nothing more than warped skin and rigor mortis. It was difficult to tell that the woman in the photograph and the woman hanging from the ceiling were the same person.

Amanda Wilson:
-ORGAN DONOR
-BLUE EYES
-5FT, 5IN

-BORN DECEMBER 2, 1987

Inside the envelope was another note.

TIME IS OF THE ESSENCE. DO NOT STRAY, OR IT WILL BE <u>YOU</u> WHO WILL PAY. THE BASEMENT HAS THE ANSWERS. LAST DOOR ON THE RIGHT SIDE OF THE HALLWAY.

Signed at the bottom was that damned smiley face. The man crumpled the letter and threw it across the room in frustration. He rose to his feet and stumbled towards the doorway, pushing past the hanging carcass of the now identified Ms. Amanda Wilson.

As he traveled down the deep, dark hallway, the amnesiac could feel the souls of the victims clawing at the nape of his neck. Their final cries for help would linger within the walls for eternity. From beyond the grave they watched his every move, and judged his every action. More than anything he wanted to run as far away from this place as he could, but the notes recommended against doing so. Disobeying was an option, but he had seen what the owner of the mansion was capable of. Just a little further now.

The basement has the answers. The basement has the answers. He repeated those five words over and over again in his head. Hopefully, the answers he was looking for didn't come with the steep price of his death.

The man opened the basement door and stared down into the abysmal belly of the beast. It became evident that even darkness had its own variety of shades, and the shade that floated around in the basement was ten times darker than what was on the first and second floors.

On the top step was a tiny, pocket sized LED flashlight with a note that said **TAKE ME** propped up against it. Of course, the message came accompanied by the mansion's marquee signature. He lifted the flashlight, twisted the head to the right, and descended down into what would undoubtedly be Hell on earth.

The basement was cluttered with boxes that were labeled with words like **HOME MOVIES, POTS & PANS,** and **XMAS DECORATIONS,** just to name a few. Thick spiderwebs pinning from one wall to another were ripped apart as the man unintentionally destroyed them with his face. Eight tiny little legs scurried across his neck. He let loose a horrified cry and slapped at his neck. A pale-green longlegged sac spider was flung onto the ground where it quickly retreated into the darkness between a tower of boxes. Trapped within his own paranoia, the man continued slapping his hands against his body, batting away at phantom arachnids that his mind tricked him into believing were crawling beneath his clothes.

The repulsive smell of mildew ruled the area. He waved the flashlight around the basement like an adolescent wizard who had just received his first wand. The beam of light bounced from surface to surface, trembling significantly within his shaky hand. The diminutive squeaks of a family of field mice called to him from within the black. There were twenty-two unwelcome rodent squatters using the basement as their home, but there was no way for him to be aware of that. However, in just a few seconds, that number would drop to twenty-one after one of their necks would be crushed beneath the heel of the man's size eleven shoe. The sudden crunch of tiny neck bones being crushed into dust fabricated the clicking sound of an unfitting key being forced into a keyhole. The light fell to the cement floor and revealed the convulsing body of a light brown rodent. No matter the size of the death, the weight that came with it was always substantial.

The beam of light was locked into place as it focused on a baroque throne chair that sat in front of a bulky thirteen-inch Zenith color television. The TV sat on top of a wood Baxton Studio television stand and beside it was a VCR that flashed a blocky white 12:07 PM (a time which had obviously not been programmed). The back of the red velvet chair stood high and was rimmed with a golden frame, decorated with detailed hand carvings of templar symbolism offering an immaculate scale of grandeur.

The man treaded slowly around the majestic throne. The radiant beam spraying forward from the LED bulb spotlighted a group of mice ripping away at bits of flesh that gave way to an emerging tibia bone. Attached to the decomposing leg was the rest of the body, slumped in a lackadaisical manner. The body was covered in sores and had been mutilated so extensively that the gender was no longer identifiable. A gaping hole was ripped into the side of the person's face; acting now as an alternate route into the mouth while also providing vacancy to a jet black centipede that had it's yellow legs wrapped around this person's tongue. Each decomposing arm seeped swampy pus from out of the countless wounds. Wavy locks of black hair fell down across the shriveling face of the deceased.

The monotonous routine of finding a dead body equipped with a mysterious note was becoming undesirably predictable. The smell though, as many times as he had experienced it within the last hour of his life, seemed to worsen every time. A vanilla envelope had been carefully placed against the body's lap. The mice that were enjoying a carnivorous feast scurried away as the man reluctantly outstretched his arm. For the third time, the envelope contained a note and an identification card rather than a driver's license.

Angela Ramirez
-BLACK EYES
-5FT, 2IN
-BORN APRIL 7, 1994
THERE IS A VHS CASSETTE TAPE
AND A REMOTE CONTROL ON TOP OF
THE TELEVISION. THE TAPE IS TITLED
VIDEO TJR-PY08. TURN ON THE TV. PLACE
THE TAPE INSIDE THE VCR. GAIN
ENLIGHTENMENT.

Smiley face.

The VHS tape and the remote were exactly where the note said they would be. "T...J...R." He whispered the letters to himself. There was something vaguely familiar about them. Crows' feet materialized around the man's ebony eyes as he tightly shut them, trying as hard as he could to remember something, anything. His efforts were in vain.

The flashlight hovered over the remote until the man spotted the red power button in the top right corner. With a simple press of the button, the TV came alive. A turbulent hiss erupted from the ancient electronics. A war of salt and pepper battled across the screen. It was an endless monochrome battle where a decisive victory would never be attained.

He slid the VHS tape labeled *TJR-PY08* into the VCR and watched the buzzing jumble of black and white vanish. Three white fuzzy lines ran vertically down the screen before adjusting into a clear frame showing the red velvet throne. A pair of legs walked into view. The so-called enlightenment that was promised in writing was about to be delivered.

"This video will be titled Thomas J. Ross, project year: zero eight. What you are seeing and what you are about to hear might be a little hard for you to comprehend at first." The man's mouth hung ajar. His eyes quivered in disbelief. A tight pressure seized his chest.

The dark eyes. The creamy caramel skin tone. The receding hairline. Speaking directly to him through the television set in distorted, crackled audio...was himself.

The man (from the virtual world within the television set) took a seat on the throne and crossed his right leg over top of his left. He removed a pair of black reading glasses that sat atop the bridge of his nose and twirled them around between his thumb and index finger. He wore a white button-up dress shirt, with the three top-most buttons unbuttoned, tucked into a pair of navy blue dress slacks. Appearing below his pant cuffs were a pair of walnut calf leather dress shoes.

"At this point, you probably have no memory of who you are, so let me tell you. My name...or better yet, our name is Thomas Joseph

Ross. You are the Chief Operating Officer of a multi-billion dollar corporation called Magari Incorporated. For the past eight years, you have been participating in this ritualistic activity to satisfy the needs of a personal thrill that is simply lacking in your life on other three hundred and sixty-four days out of the year. I mean what better time than Halloween, am I right?" Thomas (the virtual one) let loose a string of cackles.

"A majority of people would probably tell me that I'm sick for the things that I do on Halloween, but they obviously can't comprehend the fine line that divides mental sickness with boredom." Television Thomas pulled a folded piece of notebook paper out of his front pocket and placed the glasses back onto the top of his nose. "Allow for me to break things down for you in bullet points so that I don't miss anything. Understanding is a crucial part of successfully completing the game." He winked at the camera flirtatiously.

"First thing to explain is why you have no memories at the moment." He leaned down beside the chair and lifted a syringe into camera view. "Magari is currently one of the top donors for a sixty thousand dollar drug called Zodiasepinephren which causes short-term effects of amnesia. It is currently being developed to help bring forward repressed traumatic memories for victims of sexual and or physical abuse by temporarily locking away a person's common thoughts and memories. The drug normally wears off between four and seven hours and I will be injecting it into myself at ten o'clock sharp. Also, the drug causes the user to lose consciousness for about half an hour after its initial usage. And just a little side note here, this is the first year that I am doing this after taking the Zodiasepinephran. So just imagine how much planning went into making all of this feel mysterious and exhilarating as well as making sure that we have another successful year!"

"By this time I'm sure that you've noticed the dead girls that are strewn throughout the home, and yes, this is *your* home. Each woman is nothing more than a prostitute, living a lifestyle that eventually would have resulted in their death or their incarceration. I simply sped up the timetable for one of those circumstances. They agreed to return to the home after I promised to pay them twenty thousand dollars for two hours of service. Their names are -" Television Thomas reached forward out of camera view and then sat back with four rectangular cards in his hands. "Let's see...we've got Rachel Lewis. Amanda Wilson, Geneva Turner, and Angela Ramirez." He continued thumbing through the cards after reading off the names. "No big loss. I asked and none of them have any close friends or family members. So, nobody will be looking for them."

"Moving on, you're probably wondering about the cut on your forehead and why you woke up in a crashed car. Well, I...Or should I say you did it all to yourself." Television Thomas dropped the cards onto the ground and refocused his full attention toward the camera. "Man, this shit is a lot more confusing to explain when talking to my future self than I figured it would be." He bared his fangs at the camera like a heartless vampire who couldn't wait to dig their jagged teeth into a chunk of flesh. "There should be a cut somewhere along your forehead. You did that with this razor blade."

He held an inch long blade close to the camera lens. It took a few seconds for the camera to focus in on the new object.

"After using the razor, I'll make sure to throw it into the woods along with the syringe with the Zodiasepinephrin. The SUV that you woke up in is a throwaway car that has been down in that ditch for years. I own over seventy acres of private land so there's nobody walking around those woods to discover it."

"Before I end this recording, I think that it should come as common sense to you just how necessary it is to dispose of the bodies. Bury them in the garden. Make sure that this is done within the next two days because Marie and Isabella, your wife and daughter, will be coming home from vacation, and it might not go over too well if they return to a home filled with corpses." Television Thomas grinned at the thrilling thought of his future kills. "Also, make sure to tear the pages out of the visitors log in the security booth with the ladies' names on it as well as destroy this tape. No need to incriminate ourselves now."

Amnesia Thomas couldn't pull his eyes away from the television set. If everything that was being said was true, he should be regaining his memory within the next hour. He also couldn't believe that the man on the TV screen was him, talking about kidnapping and murdering women like it was a sport.

"Well, that pretty much covers it. Here's hoping that you find your way back home, find the letters left behind, and find this tape." Television Thomas stood from off of the throne and walked towards the camera, fumbling around before dropping his face back into view. "Oh, and I almost forgot! One of the ladies will still be alive by the time that you find this video. I haven't decided which one yet. She will be locked inside of the panic room which is set to automatically unlock and release her at three in the morning. If she escapes, I'm sure that she will contact the police and you'll be charged with multiple counts of homicide. Kill her, or spend the rest of your life in prison. Au revoir."

A piece of paper with a large smiley face drawn on it was held into focus. Seconds later, the tape ended and was automatically ejected by the VCR. The static black and white war taking place within the television resumed.

Thomas clutched the remote in his hand and pressed the power button bringing an abrupt end to the TV's short-lived life. He turned and blasted the rotting corpse behind him with a shot from the flashlight. To think that he was capable of committing such a horrific crime against another human being. He collapsed onto the ground and slammed his back into the television stand. Thomas went on to weep hysterically in the darkness with his legs tucked tightly to his chest. The sobbing and sniffling was muffled as he dropped his head between his knees.

The rain was slowing down. Sparks of lightning still occasionally lit up the night sky but the thunder had moved on. The stinging smell of mold and mildew now comforted the man; it brought about a sense of familiarity. Voices of the past screamed from out of the darkness and flooded over the small sliver of sanity that still existed within Thomas' mind. The feelings of remorse, guilt, and fear were instantly washed away. The black of the basement caressed the man's soul and administered an icy dose of adrenaline into his veins. Thomas' heart pumped faster and faster until the blood rushed into his head so quickly that it created a euphoric high. He lifted his head and laughed madly as the flashlight rolled back and forth across the ground shining across the left half, then the right half of the bodily remains in front of him. Like an infant throwing a tantrum, Thomas kicked his legs and slapped his hands against the ground as he continued to laugh. A concert of chittering mice joined the man as he descended deeper and deeper into the madness that had repossessed his mind.

Ding! Thomas' laughter ceased immediately as he allowed his brain to process the familiar chime that echoed through his home.

Ding! The grandfather clock tolled its commanding bell for a second time.

Ding! The long, black hands of the grandfather clock pointed north and east respectively. The house was silent. Thomas lightly rose to his feet knowing what was supposed to happen when the clock struck three. He listened intently. Loud clicking noises resonated from the second floor and invaded the basement. Thomas' eyes bounced around in the darkness. He tiptoed towards the steps trying not to make any unnecessary noise. Then, there was a scurrying of footsteps that swept across the floor above the man's head. Like a rocket breaking through Earth's atmosphere, Thomas launched himself towards the steps.

The duo of footsteps coincided with one another. The only living female in the house rushed as quickly towards the front door as her body would allow. She arrived at the top of the gray carpeted steps and felt her eyes widen as they studied the door that stood invitingly at the bottom of the descent.

Behind that door was freedom. There was life and opportunity. Outside was the looming dawn of the final day of October where she could offer to take her three-year-old nephew who had picked out a Buzz Lightyear costume Trick-or-Treating. Or the chance to attend community college and make something positive out of her life. Perhaps going back to school could help emancipate her from the sadness and humility that came packaged with satisfying selfish perverts for a handful of twenty dollar bills. But that was only if she could make it through the front door, because if she didn't, her life would be snatched away by a thief in the night.

The woman, (more commonly known as Geneva Turner on a normal day) lunged her arm forward towards the door as her bare feet slammed onto the wet hardwood floor. She grabbed the doorknob and was hurled to the floor by a wicked backhand from the murderous millionaire, Thomas Ross.

"*Tsk. Tsk. Tsk.*" Thomas clicked his tongue against the rigged roof of his mouth while wiggling his index finger back and forth insinuating his disappointment in the frightened prostitute. "Now, where were you planning on going? Last I remember, the money that you shoved into your disgusting pockets acted as the signature to our mutual contract. You know, the one where you agreed to pleasure me?"

"You're out of your goddamn mind!" Geneva screamed, dragging herself backward into the dining room. Trickles of blood slid into her mouth from a cut on her bottom lip, courtesy of the bony middle knuckle on Thomas' right hand. The mad man crept closer and closer. Tears poured out of Geneva's chestnut eyes. "Just let me go home."

"No, I'd rather not." Thomas pounced on top of Geneva and folded his calloused fingers firmly around her neck. She kicked uncontrollably and could feel the life being vacuumed out of her body. Her eyes began to roll into the back of her eyelids. She forced out a few raspy coughs hoping that a backdraft of oxygen would kick back into her lungs. In a desperate attempt, she swung her arms towards Thomas' face and succeeded in connecting a clubbing blow against his left eye. The contact loosened his grip and sent him tumbling to the side. Geneva pulled herself to her knees and then to her feet as she ran off into the shade.

Geneva's hands layered on top of each other, pressing against her mouth in an attempt to deaden the sound of her breathing. She quietly entered into an open room and was tapped in the face by the lifeless foot of Amanda Wilson who still dangled from the ceiling like a piece of strange fruit. Geneva made an uneasy squeal from beneath her hands as she slithered around the body. Amanda's departed eyes seemed to follow her every move as the noose twisted the carcass in circles.

She bent down beside the bed and slid her body underneath. Thomas' rhythmic footsteps preyed upon Geneva's fragile emotions. Tears poured down her face, but she found a way to cry without making any noise.

A kitchen drawer slammed shut sending tremors into the still night. Thomas gripped an eight-inch butcher knife within his sensitive hands. The adrenaline that pumped through his bloodstream nullified any pain that would have sent shockwaves up his arms earlier in the night. He took the tip of the blade and dragged it gently along the wall as he marched up and down the hallway. Geneva's body trembled merely inches beneath the metal bed frame. She listened as Thomas whistled an inaudible tune with a fluttering off-key pitch.

Run! Her conscience scolded. *Run! Get the hell out of here and don't look back!*

The second that the woman decided to listen, a pair of legs stopped in the doorway. The sound of steel slicing through thick, braided strands of hemp irritated the nerves in Geneva's top two front teeth as if she had just bitten down on a freezing block of ice. A loud thump crashed through the room as Amanda Wilson's body collapsed onto the floor. Her eyes, more barren than the widest of wastelands, pierced through Geneva's skin and stared deep into her wavering soul. Amanda's right arm bent awkwardly like a floppy piece of moist Playdoh. Her index finger ironically pointed in Geneva's direction as if to silently say *She's under the bed! Kill her! Kill her just like you killed me!*

Thomas grabbed both of Amanda's legs and tucked them beneath his armpits. As her body was dragged out of the room, the bumping of Amanda's head against the floorboards manipulated her mouth into a cocked smile. Even Death had a sick sense of humor, constructing wicked facial features on the dead with his invisible strings like a master puppeteer. Thomas and the one hundred twenty-four pounds of dead meat faded into the blackness of the hallway.

This is it! Go now. RUN!

There it was again. The mysterious voice that directed Geneva's decisions demanding to be obeyed. That voice begged for her to listen. Begged for her to survive.

So, she did as she was told.

Like a seasoned military veteran, Geneva Army crawled her way out from beneath the bed and darted towards the hallway. The mind-bending illusion that the walls of the home were closing in on her brought life to a minor panic attack. The air felt like it was being sucked out of the building and into a giant whirlwind that she couldn't access. Geneva's vision grew blurry and she struggled to maintain her focus as she stumbled through the hallway and into the main parlor. The front door was fifteen feet away, but it might as well have been fifteen miles. Geneva fought against her own body and surged towards the door with as much energy as she could muster into her skinny legs. A thick mist shrouded her brain. Logical thinking felt like a forced chore.

"Get outside," Geneva whispered softly to herself. "You have to...Get outside." She sucked in small gulps of air like a toddler sipping juice from a sippy cup. Her hand clasped around the doorknob and she pulled. It opened. Freedom was inches away.

Her eyes found themselves lost within the hazy mist that drifted above the massive front lawn. Thoughts of her past raced through her mind. The decisions that she was proud of. The ones that she wasn't. Regrets over how she wished she wouldn't have missed her nephews last birthday party, or her sister's wedding because she was too doped up on heroin with some stranger who had left her with nothing more than fifty bucks on a filthy motel nightstand. The events of her life that she wished she could do over far outweighed the ones that left her standing there in the doorway with a crooked smile poorly drawn across her face.

It wouldn't be long now. She would be welcomed into a celestial haven where the sins of her life would all be washed away. The first ones to greet her would be Amanda Wilson, Rachel Lewis, and Angela Ramirez.

The darkness before her was washed out by the overwhelming presence of a smothering light. The lower her eyes began to shut, the brighter the light became. Time stopped. The soothing melodies of harps, flutes, and trumpets latched onto the woman's spirit and floated away. Geneva Turner's body slumped forward smashing headfirst into the concrete. Five inches of the sharpened kitchen blade stood erect, glimmering against the glow of the descending moon. The other three were submerged into the back of her skull.

Like he had done with Amanda, Thomas grabbed Geneva's body by the legs and dragged her back into the house. A river of blood flowed from the concrete onto the white oak floor. The front door closed, exiling Thomas and the four bodies of the murdered prostitutes from the outside world. The feathery notes of the piano serenaded the home as the night died and gave birth to a distant twilight. The dewey grass glistened beneath the morning sun. What a beautiful beginning to Halloween.

The sound of a car door slamming in the distance traveled around the side of the house and into Thomas' ears. He shoved the edge of the spade into a patch of soft soil and lifted himself to his feet. With a few quick swipes of his hands, Thomas brushed the traces of dirt from off of his jeans. He pushed the pair of black glasses that rode his nose closer to his face and wearily walked towards the source of the sound. He whipped his head back and quickly scanned the quality of his gardening. Shaking his head in a personal nod of approval, he continued on.

"Daddy!" A long-locked, bouncy-haired girl rushed towards him and rushed her head full speed into his lower abdomen. He let out a defeated groan and cupped his hand around the back of his daughter's neck. "Me and mommy got you a present from…" The eight-year-old girl lifted her head and gave off a guilty expression having forgotten where she and her mother had traveled.

"From Paris?"

"Yeah, yeah! Paris. We got you a gift from there. You gotta come see!" As fast as the girl had run towards her father, she darted off in the opposite direction. "Mom, daddy's in the back by the garden." Her tiny, innocent voice carried weightlessly in the wind.

"Ah! There you are." A blonde-haired, blue-eyed woman emerged from around the corner of the massive house. She walked up to Thomas and greeted him with an aggressive kiss on his lips that nearly knocked him off his feet. After a few moments of embrace, she stepped away and analyzed her husband. "Tom, you're filthy."

"Sorry, I know. I was back in the garden pulling out some weeds and checking on the fertilizer. I was hoping to be finished by the time that you two got home but I guess I wasn't moving fast enough." Thomas shrugged his shoulders as he looked embarrassingly down at his clothing. "How was Paris?"

"It was gorgeous. I just wish you would have been able to come. We really missed not having you there." She wrapped her arms around his shoulders and interlocked her fingers around his neck.

"I know, I know. Trust me, I would have much rather been there with you guys than here, but work has just been crazy lately." He leaned forward and gave her three rapid pecks on the lips.

"And I'm very proud of you for working as hard as you do." She leaned in for another kiss and was interrupted by the bossy commands of their daughter.

"Dad, let's go inside so we can show you what we got from Parsa!" The loving couple chuckled to one another and released from each other's grip.

"I think she means Paris." Thomas raised his eyebrows and grabbed ahold of his wife's hand and together they walked around to the front door of the home. Laughter and love escaped the house as gifts were opened and stories were shared. Some of them were true, others far from it.

The buckets of blood that had been spilled in the home only days prior to the return of Thomas' wife and daughter would forever be soaked into the floorboards. The blood-curdling screams would haunt the hallways for anyone who entered and was willing to listen. Bits of a black videotape containing footage of Thomas instructing a drug-induced version of himself to kill smoldered in the flameless fireplace. Four rotting bodies were decomposing beneath the garden that Thomas' daughter would pick fruits and vegetables from come the following Spring.

Those four women whose tragic deaths were described would join dozens of other victims from previous years who had merged with the Earth and had become one with the nefarious property.

Dozens of others were still to come.

For the next two and a half decades, Thomas J. Ross would continue his annual tour of murders. He would never be caught and would continue living within a home that would forever harbor the souls of those trapped on a property located somewhere between light and shadow.

Home is Where the Heart Isn't

A torrential storm had reared its ugly head. Puffy, gray clouds crowded the heavens. Crashes of thunder shook the 1979 station wagon being driven by twenty-four year old Peter, and with him, his twenty-three year old wife, Mary. Thin bolts of lightning illuminated the dark sky as the summer sun fell below the horizon.

The date was August 9th, 1984, and the location of the couple...Lost. They had just returned from their honeymoon in Santorini, Greece the day before yesterday, and were still making their way home. Peter, who was known for being a narcissistic know-it-all, had decided to take a "scenic route" home, and had claimed it would be a fun post-honeymoon road trip of sorts. However, it was not. Little did he know, this so-called road trip would be the worst decision that he could have ever made.

"Pull over and ask for directions." Mary commanded in an unnerving tone. "We've been driving forever. I can't remember the last time we saw a town or even another car." Peter tightened his grip on the leather steering wheel and let out a deep sigh. The concept of marriage was nice, but the reality of it had been nothing but a pain in his ass.

Another flash of lightning brightened the sky. It was followed by a light boom of thunder a few seconds later.

"Do you trust me?" Peter asked Mary in the calmest voice that he could bring himself to ask. She looked him in the eyes as he looked over at her. He then reverted his attention back onto the long, lonely road. Mary nodded her head. "Then everything will be alright. Here," Peter said as he took his right hand and began to play with the car's radio dial, "just listen to something on the radio and relax. And, if it makes you happier, I'll ask the next person we see for directions. Then again, what sane person would willingly be out driving in this mess?"

Mary smiled and began to fiddle with her wedding ring. Peter turned the radio dial and watched the tuner pass over different radio stations, but not a sound came through the speakers.

"Hey, can you turn the volume up? I'm not hearing anything." Peter continued fiddling with the dial, but still there was nothing. Mary slapped his hand away and attempted turning the dial herself. Back and forth she spun the knob. However, the car remained a coffin of silence.

"Still nothing?" Peter asked quizzically. Mary shrugged her shoulders and pressed her head against the passenger door window. Typically the sound of rain calmed her, but tonight, it was enough to drive her insane.

Peter was beginning to notice a set of rough calluses forming at the top of his palms; a result of how tightly he had been gripping the wheel. The wedding band wrapped around his finger still felt foreign to him. With the ball of his thumb, Peter would constantly spin and play with the ring. It was uncomfortable; a perfectly tangible metaphor for marriage.

"Just great," an infuriated Peter said out loud with the intention of speaking only to himself. "I just knew that this car was a piece of crap as soon as we bought it. The price was too good to be true for it only being five years old. And now, we probably need to spend even more money on getting the damned thing fixed." Peter ran his hand through his short hair, down the front of his face, and over top the few short whiskers that had grown since his last shave. "It's fine, it's fine. Everything is going to be fine." His words were an effortless attempt at providing he and his wife with a sense of false hope.

The road seemed to stretch on forever. It was a straight shot of black asphalt that ran beneath an even blacker night.

"Where are we, Peter? Do you even know what state we're in?" Mary's complaining caused Peter to grow even further upset.

"We're close, okay?! I know that much. Just stop worrying for five minutes! Why don't you take a nap or something?" Mary looked over at Peter and gave a disgusted look that went unnoticed. She placed her head back against the window, watching the rain pour down from the Heavens to the Earth.

The car was washed out by an eerie silence. The only noises came from the small pellets of rain and the roar of the engine as Peter pressed his foot deeper into the accelerator. The man couldn't help but think back to the past week when he and Mary were still in Santorini and life seemed to be going perfectly. They were happy, surrounded by a beautiful environment, delicious food, and an unlimited amount of alcohol. The honeymoon had been to die for! But upon returning to the States, life had been anything but ideal. It had not been long, but Peter was already missing the independence and lack of stress that the bachelor life afforded him.

"I'm sorry," Mary said, still looking out the window. "I just want to get home, be able to unpack, relax, and cuddle in bed." Peter took his hand and placed it onto Mary's shoulder, rubbing it up and down.

"Soon," he said, forcing a not so confident smile. "We'll get there soon." The rain began to slow, and just as fast as it had come, it faded. "See," Peter began to say, "things are starting to look a little better already."

The couple continued driving down the lonely road to what felt like nowhere. The car's high beams continued to be their guide. The light from the moon was lost somewhere behind the clouds, trapped in the celestial abyss known as space.

"How much gas do we have left?" Mary questioned. "It's been a while since we filled up." Peter looked down at the fuel gauge and saw the orange needle nearly hovering over the Large E on the bottom left side. Not knowing how to react, Peter just chuckled.

"Oh God, why us?" he pleaded.

"That doesn't sound good," Mary said as she sat up in her seat and peered over to look at the gauge. "What are we going to do?"

"I guess just drive as far as we can get, and then walk and hope we reach either a gas station or a town or something." A loud bang rattled the car as the front two tires were elevated and then dropped to the ground. Immediately after, the back two tires followed suit.

"What was that?" Mary asked with desperation pouring across her face. Suddenly, the car radio which had refused to make any sound began blaring commercial static. Mary covered her ears and yelled for Peter to make it stop as he turned the volume dial both to the right and left.

"It's not shutting off!" Peter yelled over the top of the static. He slammed his foot down on the brakes and turned both of the dials but still, the white noise filled the brown station wagon. The headlights began to flicker on and off. The windshield wipers started quickly swaying back and forth across the windshield.

"Make it stop!" Mary continued to yell.

"What does it look like I'm trying to do? I don't know what's going on," Peter yelled, slamming his left palm into the top of the steering wheel. With the static fogging his ability to think, Peter resorted to pounding on the top of the dashboard hoping that it would cause all of the noise to come to a stop. "Damn it, I don't know!" He looked out through the windshield and briefly within the flickering of the headlights thought he saw a small girl standing in the middle of the dirt road. His mind had to be playing tricks on him. Just as quickly as he thought he saw her, she was gone.

"Honey," Peter mumbled within the noise of the car. "Did you just see a little girl standing in the middle of the road?" Mary gave him a strange look before attempting to peer past the chaotic windshield wipers and through the glass.

"No, I'm not seeing anything!" She strived to make her words louder than the hissing static. Peter gazed back out of the windshield. He didn't see anybody. He then looked out of the driver door window and still, nothing but pitch-black darkness.

"Stay in the car for a second. I'm going to look under the hood and see if I can figure out what's going on." Mary opened her mouth, but before anything could come out, Peter raised his hand in a way that prevented her from speaking. "Just stay here." He opened his car door and stepped out onto the darkest road he had ever seen.

"Pop the hood for me, will you sweetheart?" From inside the car, Mary hit a switch that unlocked the mechanism keeping the hood attached firmly to the front end of the vehicle. A series of haunting musicals were being played by a troupe of crickets that lived in the surrounding cornfields. On this particular night, Peter wasn't a fan.

As a man, and a newly married one at that, Peter felt it was his responsibility to uphold an unwavering fearless demeanor, but the thick fog being born from the heat and balmy rain created an unnerving atmosphere. It felt like spiders were crawling beneath his clothes. Like sinister eyes were stalking him from the unknown.

All of a sudden, everything stopped. The static from the speakers faded, the windshield wipers came to a rest, and the headlights sprayed the road in a glorious glow. Peter looked around with a puzzled look on his face. He had peered beneath the hood of the car but hadn't touched anything. The fix was welcome, but Peter had nothing to do with it.

"What just happened?" Mary asked while opening her car door and stepping outside.

"I don't know, but I think it's time we get home." Peter closed the hood of the car and released a loud sigh of relief and frustration that blended into one contorted, beastly snarl. As he stepped around to the side of the car, the man noticed a thick liquid dripping from off the front right tire. Peter dropped to one knee and rubbed his index finger along the tough rubber. He held his hand out in front of the bright beam that shot out of the headlight. The red substance was clotted with dirt and stone. "Blood?"

"What did you say?" Mary asked, walking around to the side of the car where Peter was kneeling. "Oh my God!" she shrieked, seeing the blood that covered the wheel and front end of the car. The couple noticed a crimson trail that led back down the road from whence they came. At the end of the bloody trail, perhaps 20 meters away, was a mangled figure lying in the middle of the road.

"Oh my God!" Mary repeated again, throwing her hands up and covering her mouth. "You hit something. That must be what the thud against the car was earlier. Oh my God!" She repeated her cry to the Lord over and over. Meanwhile, Peter remained speechless. He stared down the dark road at the barely visible, motionless carcass that lay in a pool of its own blood.

"Get back in the car Mary," Peter said in a stern voice.

"But -"

"Stay there. I mean it!" Knowing that he was serious, Mary opened the car door and stepped back inside. Peter opened the trunk of the car and rummaged around for a couple of seconds before pulling out a flashlight. He flicked the switch on the side and could hear the rattling of the batteries within. A thin source of light appeared, shining against a tall family of corn stalks. Even without eyes, Peter could feel them watching him. Judging him.

Slowly, Peter followed the trail of blood down the road, feeling his heartbeat grow more and more intense until it got to the point that it hurt. He could feel his insides coming up through his throat as he got close enough to identify what it was that lay before him. Through gritting his teeth and clenching his fists, Peter found the ability to keep the urgency to vomit away. Left gasping for air, he waited for his innards to slide back down into the depths of his stomach.

Lying on the ground was the body of a mangled young girl. Streams of blood poured from her mouth and a gentle breeze caused her dress to wave back and forth. It gave the illusion that the girl was still breathing as her cold, lifeless brown eyes stared up at the newlywed. The girl had jet black hair, most of which was flattened into the ground. Her frail arms and legs were contorted. A sharp, milky bone had pierced through her index finger leaving thin slices of flesh to hang. The long, black dress that the girl wore was in tatters, but in excellent condition compared to the multitude of shattered bones that barely held her brittle frame together.

"It's her."

"Is that a little girl?" Mary asked, slamming the car door behind her. Peter thought back to the girl he saw standing in the middle of the road, and although it was quick, knew that this was the same girl. But that was impossible. How could he have seen the girl standing in the road after he had already hit her? It was a horrible thought to have, but one that dominated his thoughts nonetheless.

"How many times do I have to tell you to stay in the car?" Ignoring her husband, the young woman walked gingerly over to the corpse and caught a sense of vertigo after noticing the horrific scene.

"I don't know what to do. I mean, we have to tell somebody, but we haven't seen a payphone or a person in miles! Think about her parents!" Mary ran her hands through her thick, dirty blonde hair and began to pace back and forth.

"I've killed her," Peter whispered. The thought of being a murderer consumed his mind. He began to hyperventilate and nearly fell backward after losing his sense of balance. A flash of white flickered in the sky and was followed by a distant roar of thunder. The rain had stopped, but the storm was still passing over. "We have to hide her body,"

Peter said to Mary trying to calm himself down by breathing deeply into his hands.

"Are you out of your mind? We need to get help! A little girl is dead, Peter!"

"Help from who, Mary? We haven't seen anybody in forever, and even if we did, what am I going to say? Hey, there's a dead little girl back on the road, and oh yeah, I ran her over with my car! I'm sure that will go over just fine. Come on Mary, think for once." Mary rolled her eyes and bit her tongue before walking back to the body. There were words that she wanted to say to her new husband, but knew that now was not the time. The spit attached to them would undoubtedly be filled with venom. "I can't go to jail for this. Please, can you help me move her off of the road?"

Mary stared off into the distance before grabbing one of the girl's legs and gagging. She was against everything that her husband was proposing but figured what choice did she have? At least the body would be out of the road and unable to be hit by other cars...if other cars even existed where they were.

Peter grabbed the girl's hands and dragged the body along the ground before disposing of it in the field of corn. A morbid odor fell off of the girl and glued itself to the couple's clothes.

Mary and Peter returned to the car and sat in silence as they reflected on the last ten minutes of their lives. "This is never to be brought up at any time, to anyone. Agreed?" Peter glanced over at his wife who was still shaken by the events. "Agreed!?" he repeated, this time with bass in his voice. Mary quickly looked over at Peter and nodded her head, unable to look him in the eyes. She was being introduced to a side of him that she had never met before. With a turn of the key, the car's ignition started up, and the couple found themselves once again traveling down the abysmal road.

  The drive became a quiet one, and the young couple preferred it that way. An unfavorable stench of cow manure swept over the area and surged through the inside of the car. It was the rural air freshener that forced itself into every car lucky enough to pass by.

  "Look! Peter, look!" Mary perked up and exclaimed while pointing out to the right of the car. A large billboard stood tall on the side of the desolate road and read: *Small Town of Saturn, 2 Miles ahead. Population: 253. Welcome Home!* "We can finally ask for directions, get gas, and maybe even find a motel to spend the night in."

  Peter nodded his head, but couldn't help but have his mind stuck on the weird behavior of the car and the distorted face of the girl that he had killed just a few minutes prior. Mary's hands were shaking on her lap. Whether it be because of fright, or anticipation of reaching a town to rest, we will never know.

The brown station wagon pulled into a small, eerie town. Nothing was modernized. All of the buildings and surrounding structures took on the appearance of something out of an early twentieth century western film. Peter came to notice that there were no cars within the town which had substituted dirt roads for the more modern asphalt ones. Lanterns hung off the sides of buildings replacing what towns would typically use streetlights for. Nobody was outside. Peter pulled the car deeper into the town, pulled over, and parked next to a building that read SALOON in large red letters painted on white wood.

"Where is everybody?" Mary asked in a panicked tone while lighting a cigarette, placing it into her lipstick stained mouth, and taking a long drag.

"I don't know. People should be around, it only got dark like half an hour ago." Peter removed the car keys from the ignition and placed them in his front jean pocket. "Stay here, and I mean it! I saw a payphone a couple of buildings over. I'm going to call my brother Bill and see if he's ever heard of this place. Maybe he can tell me how far away from home we are."

Peter stepped out of the car and slammed the door behind him. Squinting, he looked around and noticed that all of the buildings were completely dark inside. At this point, he was beginning to suspect that the town might be abandoned. That would explain the lack of modern housing and missing vehicles. That would also mean that the chances of the payphone working probably weren't the highest. Regardless, it wouldn't hurt to try.

After a dozen or so steps, Peter heard a car door open and close. With no other cars in sight, he knew that the sound had to have come from the vehicle that belonged to him. He turned around to see Mary quickly following behind him. Her strides were short, yet nimble. Peter released a heavy sigh while imagining a future filled with these moments where his wife refused to listen.

"Did you really expect me to sit and wait in the car? This place gives me the creeps," she said, wrapping her arms around her chest, pocketbook swung across her shoulder. The wooden swing doors of the saloon creaked as mild gusts of wind blew them back and forth. The old dirt road stunk of rot and ammonia.

Peter opened the door into the claustrophobic phone booth and stepped inside. He pulled the black payphone off of the receiver, then poked his head back out.

"Do you have a dime in your purse? The payphone costs ten cents." Mary rummaged through her tan purse for a few moments before pulling out a silver dime and handing it over. Peter slid the dime into the coin slot and placed the icy phone next to his ear. Mary watched as he punched in a few numbers, looked awkwardly at the phone, then placed it back on the receiver. The dime came tumbling out of the machine. He reinserted the coin and tried again.

"There's no dial tone," Peter yelled as he slapped the inside of the phone booth with the palm of his hand. "Figures." He turned around and could see the concern on Mary's face. "So now -" Peter stopped mid-sentence. "Mary, what's going on?" Peter motioned for his wife to turn around.

Groups of people, some old and some young, were standing between the buildings with long candles in their hands. Their stares were icier than the black payphone receiver. All of their clothes would be considered vintage, plucked out of the distance past and plopped into the present. "Do they live here?" Mary asked quietly, her back pressed against the phone booth.

"I don't know, but it looks like we don't have much of a choice but to find out." Peter stepped out of the phone booth and stepped in the direction of the townspeople.

None of them moved.

Mary followed behind, but Peter immediately turned around and told her to go back. "Just wait by the phone booth, I'll be right back.

And this time, can you please, please listen to me?" Mary reluctantly stayed where she was. Peter continued forward to greet the mysterious strangers.

"Hello!" Peter yelled, his hands held up around his shoulders. "Are you the people who live here? My name is Peter and over there is my wife Mary. We're a little misdirected from where we should be and we were wondering if anybody would be able to give us a little help?" An elderly woman with salt and pepper hair wearing a powder blue nightgown stepped forward and spoke in a hair-raising shrill.

"So are you two lost out here?" There was a lack of emotional concern in the woman's question.

"We're just a little out of our way."

"No, we're lost!" Mary chimed in, obediently standing over at the useless phone booth. "Would we be able to get some directions?"

"Mary!" Peter scolded, his patience wearing thin. "Please, just let me handle this." Peter turned back toward the old woman and shamefully nodded his head. "Maybe we're just a little lost."

"Poor things! You two must be exhausted and frightened beyond your wits!" The woman turned her head and took a few seconds to observe the couple's car. "Oh my! It would appear that you've had a little accident. That wouldn't happen to be blood on the front there, would it?" Panic set in and it wanted to take control.

"Well uh...You see, what had happened was _"

"A deer! We were driving about a mile back and out of nowhere a deer came flying out of the cornfield and hit us. It was terrifying but luckily everything turned out okay. Even the deer just ran off like nothing ever happened. Amazing creatures they are. Truly." Peter turned his head, baffled by his wifes quick thinking. He had spent a majority of the evening scolding her, but it was times like this that he was happy he married her.

"I see. Such a horrible thing must have you kids shaken up. Please, come inside for some tea while I try and figure out the best way that I can help." Peter smiled, thanked the woman, and motioned for his wife to follow. "Oh, how rude of me. Agnus. My name is Agnus."

"It's a pleasure to meet you." Peter held out his hand in greeting, but the woman responded as though he was offering her his head on a platter. He pulled his hand back and shrugged. Meanwhile, the onlookers were beginning to disperse, returning from wherever it was that they had come from. Their candles continued to flicker; their mouths sewn shut with silence. Nobody said a word.

"Sorry about the payphone," Agnus said as they all walked into the old woman's house. "All the power in town has been out for the past hour. Ever since that storm it's been nothing but darkness.

Lightning struck the only generator in town and we won't be able to fix it until tomorrow. So, here we all are living by candlelight until the sun decides to pay us another visit." The woman cackled.

"The storm, of course!" Peter said while nudging Mary. "We both thought that it was a little weird that there were no lights on in any of the buildings. It looked like this place was a ghost town." The decrepit woman flung her head around and gave off a heartless glare.

"A ghost town you say? Now that's ridiculous, we all know that ghosts aren't real! What do you take us for, a band of characters in some old Grimm tale?" Agnus cackled once more. She set the candle down on the kitchen table and motioned for the couple to take a seat in the chairs that surrounded it. "Give me a second to go into the dining room and find a few more candles. It would be rude of me to entertain guests in the dark now, don't you think? Please, make yourselves at home." The old woman hobbled into the shadows and vanished. Mary grabbed Peter by the hand.

"I have a bad feeling here." Mary whispered. "Can we just ask them for directions to the nearest interstate? Maybe buy a little bit of gas if they have it and get out of here? Something just doesn't feel right. I mean, did you see the way everyone stared at us? It was like we owed them something." Peter nodded his head and placed his free hand onto Mary's thigh. The house smelled of mustiness and old flesh. Something similar to a retirement home or a morgue perhaps.

An airy breeze brushed across the kitchen table extinguishing the candle's flame. It had come from an unknown source. Mary released a startled cry as the two were shrouded in darkness; her fingers digging deep into Peter's hand.

"Where did that wind come from?"

"I don't know. Maybe there's a fan running somewhere."

"A fan that creates just one strong blast of air? Because I'm not feeling anything now and I didn't feel anything before it. I'm telling you Peter, we need to just get up and go. No more questions. No more waiting."

"Oh dear," Agnus' voice resonated as she walked through the doorway and back into the kitchen. She carried with her a bundle of white wax candles. "I'm so sorry. I heard you scream and came immediately to see what was wrong. The air from the vents must have blown out the candle. I hope it didn't startle you too much. Here, let me light up a new one."

The couple surveyed the room but never came across the vent that the woman mentioned. With the strike of a match, Agnus lit one of the candles and placed it into the candelabrum on the table. She followed up with igniting another two candles and handed one to both Peter and Mary.

"Sorry to be so direct, um...Agnus was it?"

"Yes, that's right." the aged woman answered back.

"We were wondering if you might have some gas that we could buy off of you. We really don't want to bother anybody. We appreciate your hospitality but if we could maybe get some gas and some directions, we could be out of your hair within the hour." The old woman's face grew stern and she rubbed her index finger across her arched white brow.

"You two can't leave." Peter and Mary nervously looked at one another. The air in the room grew heavy.

"Excuse me?" Peter responded with a bit of hostility in his voice.

"You two can't leave." the woman repeated. "It would be dangerous for such young kids to travel back out into a storm that might not be over. You two did say you were lost, didn't you?"

"Misdirected." Peter corrected, which invited a frustrated stare from his wife.

"Besides," Agnus continued, "I personally don't have any gas so you would have to get it from Robbie. But, I do believe that he has retired for the night. I don't remember seeing his face outside with the others when you two arrived. Then again,

Robbie is one slippery devil." Peter looked over at Mary and they talked quietly amongst themselves for a few seconds. "Is everything alright?" Agnus interrupted.

"So would we have to wait until tomorrow in order to get the gas?" Mary asked.

"That's right."

"Would you happen to know of anywhere that we could stay for the night? Maybe a nearby motel within the town? We have cash on us so the fee for the room shouldn't be a problem." Peter pulled his wallet from his back pocket to confirm his statement.

"Oh, don't be foolish! You two are going to spend the night right here. Please, put your money away. I insist. Besides, we don't have any motels here. No need for them. We don't get many visitors here in Saturn, in case you couldn't tell by everyone's reaction to your arrival." The couple began discussing amongst themselves once more.

"I'm not sure if we have much of a choice. We would appreciate the hospitality if it's not too much trouble." Peter looked at his wife who much preferred the option of taking their chances on the road.

"It's no problem at all. I've had plenty of guests throughout the years and not one has been dissatisfied. The hospitality I provide my guests with is, what's the phrase? Ah, yes...to die for."

The front door of the old home banged shut. Mary released another high-pitched yelp before placing her hand over her heart. From out of the darkness emerged a young girl about the age of seven. She wore her long black hair in pigtails and had on a light blue nightgown that fell to her ankles, similar to the one that Agnus wore.

Peter looked at the girl and stumbled back, falling over the chair and onto the floor. Mary covered her face with her hands and as much as she tried, couldn't remove her stare.

"Oh dear me, are you alright?" Agnus lifted her limp body up from her chair and hovered over the shaken man.

"I'm fine," he said as he stared over at the young girl. "I just tripped over the leg of the chair. This damned darkness has my eyes playing tricks on me. Excuse my French. Maybe I'm a little more tired than I realized." The girl's eyes lacked life. Wisps of her stringy hair fell across the bridge of her tiny forehead.

"Abigail, this here is Mr. Peter and Mrs. Mary. They're going to be spending the night with us, so be sure to mind your manners, okay?" The young girl nodded, never blinking. "This is Abigail. She's my granddaughter. I've been raising her since she was four years old. Both her father and mother died in a car crash and luckily she somehow survived. I couldn't bear to imagine what it would be like if such a precious child were to get killed in a car accident. I'm sure it would be the most horrific scene." Peter and Mary looked at each other, their minds shrouded in fear and confusion. "The poor girl hasn't spoken or even made a sound since their deaths. She's even lost the ability to cry."

"That's terrible," Mary said, trying her best to sound as convincingly sympathetic as possible. The pale girl walked over to Mary and grabbed her hand with her own. The feel of the child's frigid touch against her hand caused Mary to immediately pull back. Abigail stared up at Mary, her soulless brown eyes bellowing for help.

"Okay, well it's getting late." Agnus said quickly. "Abigail, it's time for you to head off to bed. I'll be in shortly to tuck you in." The girl turned around without the slightest response and disappeared into the next room. The walls echoed the tiny pitter-patter sounds of her feet as she marched up the stairs. Agnus returned her attention to Peter and his wife. "And you two can follow me. Allow me to show you to your room."

The couple followed the unhurried movement of the old woman up a set of stairs, around a corner, and into a door on the right side of a narrow hallway. Through the faint glow of candlelight, Mary spotted Abigail peering at them through a small crack left open from her bedroom door.

"To bed!" Agnus scolded. Abigail slammed the door shut. The sound of her tiny feet racing across the room slid beneath the door. "I deeply apologize for her behavior. She's always been a curious girl. I'll handle her disobedience as soon as I'm through settling you two in." Agnus flashed a set of jagged yellow teeth as she donned a wicked smile.

Each of them still carried a candle. Upon entering the guest bedroom, Agnus sat her light down on a large wooden dresser near the entrance. The room appeared spacious due to the lack of furniture and barren walls. Cobwebs covered the room's only window. On the far side was a small, twin size bed and beside that a monstrous chestnut wardrobe.

"I'm sorry that it's not a five-star hotel, but it's the best that I can offer." Peter raised his hands and shook them in a motion that waved off the old woman's comment.

"No worries Agnus, this will do fine. We appreciate everything. Really. We just want this night to be over as soon as possible so that we can get back on the road and finally make it home. It's been one heck of a journey." Agnus grinned and picked her candle back up.

"Well, even if just for a short while, it's a pleasure having you here. I'll leave you two alone so that you can get some rest. My room is right down the hall if you need anything." The couple nodded their heads and Agnus left the room, shutting the door behind her. Mary walked over to the bed and collapsed on top of it. Peter headed over to the window and peered outside after brushing away a few of the cobwebs. The black that blanketed the town prevented him from being able to see too much. However, the house was positioned so that he could see their station wagon parked beside the old saloon just a few buildings down.

"We can't stay here," Peter said to Mary from over by the window. "I don't know how far away the next place is, but maybe we can make it there or close to it with the amount of gas that we have left." Mary sat up on the bed and looked over at Peter. The candle's orange hue danced across his face and clothes.

"You're the one who wanted to stay here, remember? And now it looks like it's our only option."

"I know, I know." Peter replied. "But you were right, something is wrong here." Peter walked over to the bed and sat down beside his wife making sure to keep his voice low. "Do you remember when we were driving here and the car started malfunctioning and all that *other* stuff happened?" Mary nodded her head.

"How could I forget?"

"Then are you thinking the same thing about that little girl that I'm thinking?" Mary dropped her head and nodded. There was a familiarity to the little girl that internally she wanted to refuse admitting.

"They're identical to one another. Twins maybe?"

"Maybe, but Agnus never mentioned another little girl. And if Abigail's parents died when she was young, wouldn't Agnus be caring for them both?" Peter cupped his hands over his face. "Am I crazy for thinking that the girl we hit is sitting in the room across the hall from us?" Mary looked toward the hall, remembering the girl's eyes as she peered through the crack in the doorway.

"I really want to believe that you're crazy, because if you're not, what does all of this mean? We both know that what you're saying is impossible, Peter."

"I know, but I don't think insanity is the answer here. You know it just as well as I do that something feels off here. If you ask me, we need to get the hell out of here as soon as possible." Peter's mouth opened again like he was going to continue speaking but Mary shushed him and pushed her index finger against his lips.

"Listen," she whispered. Mary stood up and walked over to the door. Peter followed. The couple pushed their ears up against the wooden door.

"Don't you ever disobey me again!" Agnus' voice could be heard screaming from what sounded like Abigail's room. Loud whip lashes crashed through the hallway. It was the sound of leather smacking against skin. "Pay for your sins!" the woman yelled as another smack of the whip reached its target. "Pay for your sins!" Sixteen times she repeated those words, and sixteen times a whipping noise followed. The bedroom door swung open and out came the old lady. With leisure strides, Agnus traveled from her granddaughter's room to her own. Peter and Mary were left petrified by what they had just heard.

"Her hands," Mary mumbled beneath her breath. "When I touched that little girl's hand, they were ice cold. It felt like she had been in a freezer for hours and hours. Peter, I'm telling you she was freezing!"

"But it's like seventy degrees outside." Peter placed his hands on his hips and tapped his foot against the floor as he thought. "Listen, after hearing what we just heard, the decision is final. We need to go, and we need to go now. I'm not sticking around any longer. Things just continue to get more weird the longer we stay."

As if the clouds had parted and the shining gates of Heaven had been revealed, a bright golden light flooded into the room through the window. Peter ran over to see what could be causing it.

"No frickin' way!" he said in a panicked voice. "This isn't happening right now. This can't be happening!" Mary stood up from the bed, scared by how hysterical Peter was acting.

"What? What's wrong?" Mary questioned, her legs quivering beneath her body.

"It's our car! They set our car on fire!" Mary ran over to the window pushing Peter out of the way in the process. She was stunned in disbelief. Golden embers floated into the warm night sky amidst a gray plume of towering smoke.

"That's our car!" She turned to her husband and grabbed his wrist. "What are they going to do to us, Peter?" Tears fell from her eyes. Peter grabbed his wife and pulled her close, promising that he was going to get them both out of this strange town.

Again, Peter remembered how perfect the previous weekend had been back in Santorini. They were the typical young newlyweds, happy for the most part and madly in love. Fast forward less than forty-eight hours, and their romantic fairy tale had taken a turn for the worst; they were now characters in a hellish nightmare.

"Come on, we've gotta get out of here." Peter grabbed Mary by the wrist and pulled her behind him. They opened the door to the room and turned down the hallway before racing down the dark staircase. The couple turned another corner and headed for the front door but came to an instant halt as they saw the little girl, Abigail, standing in front of it. They were soft, but tiny whimpers escaped from the girl's lips. Her hair was no longer up in pigtails, but rather fell forward over her face. Pockets of mud stained her clothing. Lines of blood spilled from her mouth and dripped off her chin.

"Is she crying?" Mary whispered. Peter shrugged his shoulders. He had no sympathy for these people whether they be man, woman, or child. His car was outside burning!

"I thought she couldn't cry?" he answered back. Mary was cautious as she stepped towards the small girl. The whimpers grew louder the closer she got. She stopped when she was only about a foot away. Mary knelt down on one knee prepared to console the crying girl.

"Are you okay, Abigail? What's going on? Can you tell me? Can you help us?" Abigail continued to cry, her hair covering her face like an ebony blanket.

"Mary, just push her to the side and let's go! We need to get out of here! Did you not just see our car up in flames out there!?"

"Abigail, what's going on?" Mary calmly asked again. She reached up and parted the girl's black hair from out of her face. "Oh my God!" Mary backed away from the girl and fell into Peter's arms. "What's happened to her?"

Abigail's eyes were no longer present within her skull. Replacing them were dark, endless pits where her soulless eyes had once been. From out of the holes poured streaks of blood like crimson waterfalls. Her neck was twisted and her skin had lost its color. Abigail took a small step forward. Mary clasped her fingers around Peter's wrist. The ghoulish girl cocked her head up toward the ceiling and released a murderous screech that rattled the couple's eardrums.

"We're leaving!" Peter yelled as he rushed past the screaming girl, his wife right on his heels. Abigail's body shook violently; her screams reverberated to the convulsing of her body. The girl made no effort to stop them. She just continued to holler like an angered banshee. Peter flung the door open, stepped off of the small wooden porch, and jogged down the two small steps that led off into the dirt road. The flames rising from the burning car provided more light than the couple had seen all night.

"Where do we go?" Mary asked. The two searched for an escape but they were being surrounded. The townsfolk who had made their presence known earlier in the night had returned. They crept out of their dark homes and into the fireborn light. Like Abigail, their eyes had been gouged out. A harmony of moaning, laughing, crying, and screaming surrounded the area. Peter and Mary were trapped in the center of a human circle that was closing in around them.

"We're trapped!" Mary yelled with tears falling from her eyes and sliding down her cheeks.

"What do you want from us?!" Peter roared. The eyeless ones menacingly inched closer, each one in possession of a burning candle. "We haven't done anything to you! Just let us go!" The man's voice trembled with fear. As the people grew closer, the couple heard a sullen chanting coming from within the pack. Hidden behind the disturbing screams and cries was the recital of two words.

"Welcome home." Such a welcoming phrase had been transformed into an unholy mantra. The words were being bathed beneath the blood that ran from the holes in their heads. Horrid, expressionless faces bound the newlyweds with paralysis. The chanting hastened, becoming more guttural now.

"Welcome home."

"Welcome home."

"This is not our home!" Peter yelled. Laughter from a bunch of small children drifted through the night. The couple watched the children hold hands and dance around the burning station wagon. Their laughs were becoming maniacal.

Abigail exited the home and slithered down the porch steps. She was still wailing at the top of her lungs; her head cocked back so far that it looked like it would snap right off of her neck. The black haired girl beelined to the burning vehicle. Without hesitation, she opened the car door and sat down in the driver's seat. Her screams became flooded gurgles. Abigail turned her head towards the couple as the inferno fed upon her ashen body.

"Help!" the girl yelled in a dispassionate plea. "Help! Help!" The words were robotic. Abigail begged until the skin melted off of her bones; her existence faded, becoming nothing more than a speck amongst the midnight smoke.

"Ring around the rosie…Pocket full of posies…" A children's nursery rhyme being sung by what looked like children, but were something else entirely. The car horn blared as though an invisible force had it's hand pressed against the middle of the steering wheel. The chilling horn enveloped the town and became a part of what was already an overwhelming abundance of sounds. Mary dropped to her knees as her crying intensified.

"Leave us alone!" Mary shouted. Her appearance on the dirty earth was juvenile. She was as helpless as a newborn child. All the while, the evil residents continued treading forward, ignoring her request.

"You should know that it's impossible." The voice came from behind. It was a familiar one. Coming out of the house was Agnus; two black craters where her eyes should be. Her powder blue nightgown was wet with crimson. She approached the young newlyweds until she stood only a few feet away. "I specifically told both of you earlier that you cannot leave. Now, I meant that. And in case you couldn't tell, I don't take too well to those who defy me."

Peter pulled Mary up to her feet and tried to run off, but there was nowhere to run to. The distinct chanting continued along with the ominous melodies of the young children singing the nursery rhyme.

"This is your home now. There's no need to be afraid. Everyone is so happy here in Saturn. So, allow me to be the first person to properly say, "Welcome home!" Agnus approached with a staggering limp. A rotten grin exposed the rows of black and yellow fangs that lived in her mouth. As she grew closer, back facing the fire, her eyes returned to normal.

"Please, just let us leave." This time it was Peter who begged.

"But Saturn is perfect for young couples. We could actually use more people your age. You'd be such a wonderful couple to join us. Welcome home," she repeated, a corrupt smile attached to her words.

The couple turned away from the old woman and made an attempt to run over to the phone booth. Successful, Peter picked up the phone and still there was nothing. "Don't bother children, this town hasn't had power for over 90 years." As the people came nearer, away from the light, their appearances returned to normal. The youth stopped their singing and joined the crowd, chanting in sync with the rest of the undead mob.

"Welcome home." They continued.

"Welcome home." As the population of Saturn surrounded them, two hundred fifty-three cold, clammy bodies began pulling, tearing, and gnawing at their young, warm flesh. Murderous cries of pain filled the starry night, but not a soul heard them. The last words that the newlyweds heard while living were the malicious, yet normally soothing words of 'Welcome home'. Two words that they had been looking forward to hearing since returning from their honeymoon.

"Where are we? This was seriously your idea of a shortcut?" a mature woman asked her husband as they drove down an all too familiar road. Towering stalks of corn waved in the wind, ushering the family forward.

"We'll get there soon, okay? Just relax!" the man responded. The tires of the black Honda Accord flung bits of dirt into the air. The couple's nine year old son sat in the backseat, enamored by the new pokemon game that he got for his Nintendo Switch.

"It's starting to get dark out, and we're running low on gas. Please, explain to me how this was a good idea." The man looked over at his wife and gave her an intense glare.

"Look," he said, pointing out of the window to the right. "There's a billboard over there! I'm sure it says something about us being near something. A gas station or a food joint. Something." The frustrated wife peered out of the window, moving her head back and forth to get a good view. "What does it say? I don't have my glasses on." The cartoonish music from the game did everything but help lighten the mood.

"Slow down, you're going too fast!" the woman instructed. Tightening his grip on the steering wheel, the man slowed down significantly. His wife went on to carefully read each word on the sign. "Small Town of Saturn...Two miles ahead. Population two hundred eighty-three. Welcome Home!" She let out a sigh of relief knowing that there was some form of civilization nearby. "We're stopping in this town and asking for directions, I don't care what you have to say, we're doing it!" The man pushed his foot deeper into the accelerator and sped down the road.

Ten minutes later, the family would find themselves in a horrible hit and run accident. The corpse of a beautiful, black haired girl would be disposed of in the corn fields yet again. Move ahead another half hour and they would be introduced to the tiny town of Saturn and all of its inhabitants. Unbeknownst to them, the town's population was about to grow by three. The first person to greet them was a little old lady with salt and pepper hair. Her name was Agnus. By night's end, the last words spoken within the town would be the same as always.

Welcome home.

Smile

Alexis Tomani had seen her fair share of dead bodies. It was one of the many interesting perks that came with being a forensic analyst. Mangled corpses, trails of blood, vomit, mucus, sweat, disease. But to Alexis, these were all natural occurrences; no stranger than a pre-k teacher helping adolescents tie shoes all day, or a firefighter bravely reporting to an uncontrolled inferno. This was who she was and had been for the past three years, and at this point, the deceased made more sense to her than the living. The dead never had anything to argue about or disagree with her on. All they provided were unique stories that needed piecing together, and that's what she loved about her job. The challenge. The mystery. The solution.

Needless to say, Alexis was not one to become squeamish. It was her job to collect and preserve evidence from crime scenes, mostly homicides, but sexual assault cases would occasionally find their way onto her desk as well. She would collect samples of human tissue, weapons that may have been used in a murder, blood, as well as other bodily fluids that may provide evidence and lead to a culprit. But not even her experience as a forensic analyst could prepare her for the night that lay ahead.

It was October 2nd in modern-day urban America. The emergence of autumnal colored leaves beautifully covered the Manchester, New Hampshire sidewalks. A vibrant orange sun was starting to dip beneath the horizon as mid-evening fast approached. Cars zipped up and down the wide, two-lane road outside of Alexis's three-storied brick apartment building. Occasional car horns and expletives were aimed at a group of teenage boys who were throwing a football back and forth from one side of the street to the other. And inside, on the second floor of 341 Amherst Street was Alexis, standing in her bathroom wearing a pair of tight black jeans and her favorite red lace bra from Target which she had eagerly purchased for the sale price of $11.98.

"How long has it been? Three, four, maybe five years at the least? Look excited, or this guy is never going to be into you. You're getting to that 'gonna die miserable and all alone age'." Alexis looked down at her phone and stared into it with an unamused look. Jackie, Alexis' best friend since the second grade, was on Facetime providing her with some advice before going out on a dinner date.

"If I'm meant to die miserable and alone, then it is what it is. Besides, you know how hard it is for me to try and build a relationship with this job. For the past month I've been working sixty hour weeks. I mean, I just don't have the time to dedicate to some guy." Alexis raised her head, changing her focus from the phone to the full mirror in front of her. With careful flicks of the wrist, she continued applying mascara to her right eyelash.

"You used to be so much fun! It's hard to believe that in college, *you* were the one that we would have to pull away from all the creepy, desperate guys at the parties. And now, your personality is more dead than the victims you see at work." Alexis provided Jackie with a courtesy laugh while putting the mascara back into its slick black tube. She took a step back and examined her face.

"I'm trying, I really am. Unfortunately, not all of us are lucky enough to find the right guy in college who we then go on to marry." Alexis made the comment jokingly, but behind her words were hidden feelings of envy.

"The moment Matt told me he was majoring in mechanical engineering, I made sure to lock him down. I knew that the money was going to be nice!" High pitched yips from a tiny white poodle echoed through the phone. "Hold on one second, I need to let Lacy out before she decides to piss all over the rug again. I don't know why, but it's become a thing lately." Jackie rolled her eyes and placed the phone onto an unknown surface.

While Jackie dealt with getting her dog to properly use the bathroom, Alexis resumed dolling herself up. She dabbed her blush brush into a pinkish powder labeled "Heat Wave" and applied the makeup to her cheeks. Normally she allowed her dirty blonde hair to hang across her shoulders, but tonight decided to pull it into a bun allowing a few strands to dangle loosely around her ears. To complete her outfit, Alexis grabbed a red long-sleeved V-neck top off of the bathroom counter and pulled it over her head; her eyes twinkled in the mirror's reflection as she stared at herself.

She was beautiful. This was something that Alexis had forgotten about herself. She seldom took the time to put on makeup for work. Sometimes, it was because she was too tired. Other times it was because she wanted to attract as little attention as possible from the sleazy, conceited men whom she called her coworkers. But, it was nice to know that the gorgeous girl who couldn't keep the boys off of her in college still existed beneath the overworked woman she had evolved into.

"Hey, sorry about that. Are you still there?" Jackie's voice snapped Alexis out of her daze.

"Yeah, I'm still here. Just finishing up actually."

"Wow Lex, you look amazing! Rick isn't going to be able to keep his hands off of you!" Alexis rolled her eyes. "How many times have you gone out with him now? Like five?"

"This will be the third." Alexis picked up her phone, turned off the bathroom light, and exited into her bedroom.

"Aaaaaaaand…"

"And what?"

"You know...Have you?" Alexis hoisted the phone close to her face making sure that Jackie could clearly see the unamused expression she had on.

"No, nothing like that has happened. We can't all just give it up on the first night." Jackie laughed in a way that demonstrated pride in her promiscuity.

"Some of us know what we want, when we want it. What can I say?" Alexis could only shake her head in disappointment.

Three light pumps of Stella McCartney perfume shot out of the glass bottle and onto Alexis' neck. One more pump was sprayed against her left wrist, which she then rubbed in a circular motion against her right wrist.

"Has he ever been back to your place? Or have you gone over to his?"

"No, we've gone to the movies once and had dinner once. Afterwards we just say goodnight and go our separate ways. Who knows though, tonight might be the night. I really do like him."

"Girl, I think it has to be. You keep playing hard to get and he's going to get bored and find himself someone else." Jackie lifted her eyebrows and pushed the phone screen close to her face. A stern look was projected through the phone. "Invite him over!"

Alexis lowered her phone as she could feel her face growing red. It had been a long time since she had been intimate with a man and just the thought of something happening between the two of them made her nervous. Obviously, nothing like that *had* to happen, but there was that inkling of fear that made Alexis wonder if maybe Jackie was right. Rick was a good guy, and not once had he come across as overbearing. If she brought him back they could watch a movie, make some popcorn, and if she wasn't comfortable there wouldn't have to be anything beyond that. Plain and simple.

"Maybe you're right," Alexis answered, elevating her phone back into a position where Jackie could see her face.

"That's my girl! And you already know that I want to hear all…" Jackie cut off mid-sentence and was overcome with a horrified look on her face. "What is that behind you?" The intensity in which Jackie asked her question left Alexis frozen. The hairs on her arms and the back of her neck stood up.

Maybe she had an overactive imagination due to all of the gruesome murders that she had seen from work, but something in the back of her mind told her that there was going to be some large figure who had broken into her apartment standing behind her just waiting to partake in her demise. Images of her bloodied, lifeless corpse mangled across the bedroom floor flashed before her eyes.

"Hellooooo? Alex, I asked you a question."

"Behind me?" Alexis asked quietly with caution. Her voice trembled.

"Yes! What is that all over your wall?" Alexis turned around and was showered with instant relief upon learning that there had never been any sort of killer standing behind her. Instead, there were rows and rows of polaroids that Alexis had taken at various crime scenes from a current case dealing with what the police believed may be a local serial killer. It wasn't uncommon for Alexis to bring her work home with her. Severed limbs and mutilated corpses played an important role in her life. On most nights these horrendous polaroids were the last things that Alexis stared at before falling asleep. Some people count sheep; Alexis counted corpses.

"It's work. Just a bunch of evidence from various crime scenes. "

"Girl, you can not bring him back to your place with all of that taped across your walls. He will think that you're some sort of psycho!" Maybe she was. Alexis never said it out loud, but she often debated it. Anybody who can stare at photos like those and not have some sort of sickening feeling develop deep within the pit of their gut has to have something wrong with them.

"I can't take them down, Jackie."

"Well then, it sounds like you're going to his place tonight. Keep your phone close by so you can keep me updated." Alexis smiled into the phone while a scratching noise came through the speaker. "Ugh! That's Lacy at the backdoor begging to come back in. I'm gonna let you go so you can finish getting ready. Text me, okay?"

"Believe me, you will be hearing from me very soon." The two women said their goodbyes. Alexis threw her phone onto her bed and went back into the bathroom to give herself one final look over before leaving. Her hair looked good. Her makeup looked good. She even did a quick whiff beneath both underarms to make sure that there was no foul smell and was pleased to be met with the lavender aroma of her Dove deodorant.

"You got this," Alexis whispered to herself as she picked her keys up from out of the silver bowl on the table next to the front door. Even though this would be the third date between them, her nerves were working overtime. She was nauseous and had that lumpy feeling in the bottom of her throat that generally acted as a prelude to vomiting. But, the more she procrastinated walking out the front door, the worse her nerves became.

Finally, she built up the courage to open the door and walk outside.

The chilly Autumn air that playfully swiped against her face helped relax her. The boys who had been causing a ruckus with their teenage antics were gone. Night was fast approaching. Alexis tapped the home button on the bottom of her phone and the screen lit up revealing a photograph of Alexis and her six-month-old niece, Darcy. Displayed across the top in white was the time. **6:43 PM**. She dropped the phone into her black purse, walked down the steps of the apartment building, and traveled across the street to her 2016 silver Hyundai Sonata. By seven o'clock she was at the restaurant.

"So what made you pick this place?" Rick asked as he twirled a few pieces of angel hair pasta around his fork, making sure to carefully aim the food into his mouth without smearing alfredo sauce all over his face.

"A friend of mine recommended it actually. I've never been here myself but she said that I had to come and check it out, so here we are." The two attractive adults were sitting at a square, dark wood table inside of an Italian restaurant known as Mangia. Dimmed bulbed lights lined the walls and windows making for an intimate atmosphere for a restaurant tucked away in a beautiful location.

Rick smiled. Alexis had forgotten just how attractive Rick was. It had been almost three weeks since their last date and seeing him dressed up in a two-piece royal blue suit was very attractive. Confidence was something that most guys lacked anymore, but Rick was not one of them. Alexis liked that about him. Dark, prickly stubble covered the lower half of Rick's face. His hazel eyes gave off a gentle warmth while simultaneously being dark and mysterious. He was ex-military, but the thought of being paired up with a soldier did something to her.

"Well, she was right." Rick acknowledged. "The food is wonderful. This is my first time here as well. Let your friend know that she recommended a wonderful place."

"I'll make sure to let her know," Alexis said with a smile. She took her knife and cut off a corner of her chicken parmigiana. The two talked and laughed for nearly two hours, sharing past memories and work experiences. Alexis was timid at first to share her work with Rick, but found a bit of confidence in sharing the less gory details with him after he persuaded her that what she did for a living was fascinating to him.

"So how long has it been since you've dated somebody?" Rick immediately paused after speaking as if to evaluate the words that had just left his mouth. "That is, if you're comfortable sharing that information. I mean I don't want to -"

"No, no, it's fine. I'd say it's probably been about four years. I can't remember the exact timeframe, but it's definitely been a little while." Alexis finished the sentence off with a nervous chuckle and a less than classy gulp of her pink Moscato wine. She was more than willing to allow the liquid courage to guide her through the night. "How about you? How long has it been?"

Rick lifted his eyebrows in a way that said *'here comes a doozy'* before replicating Alexis' previous action and taking a small swallow out of his own glass of cabernet sauvignon.

"It has been seventeen months."

"That's pretty specific," Alexis responded jokingly.

"Well, once upon a time I was married. Wonderful girl. But, we married young. I was twenty-one and she was twenty. At that point in my life, I saw myself in the military for the long haul. You know how it goes, put in my twenty plus years of active service, retire with a nice pension, all that good stuff. And for the first five years or so, everything was going great, just as we had planned. Then one night she went out to get a few things to make for dinner, and she never came back." Rick's voice cracked beneath his words. It was apparent that speaking about his ex-wife was uncomfortable for him. Alexis sat quietly on the opposite end of the table, lost for words.

"She was killed in a hit and run accident. They still have no idea who it was. The officer told me that she died instantly, so she didn't suffer. But, I don't know if I believe it or not. When I arrived on the scene, the driver's side door was smashed in far enough that it could almost touch the passenger seat. I just remember seeing blood everywhere."

"I'm so sorry. I had no idea. I shouldn't have asked." Alexis grabbed Rick's hand and cradled it within her own. She could feel his heartbeat throbbing through his wrist against her palm.

"Please, don't be. It's been almost a year and a half. I'm going to have to learn how to talk about it sometime."

"So then what happened with the military? Actually, nevermind. Forget I asked. I'm prodding too much." Rick again assured her that the questions were welcome.

"I was discharged. They believed that mentally I wasn't in the position to defend our country, so they let me go. And just to be clear, when I say mentally it was because I had fallen into a deep depression, not because I became some sort of psychopath or anything like that. Please don't think that I was out shooting rifles at ghosts in the woods or something." Both of them laughed. Alexis couldn't help but think of how nice it was to see Rick smile after seeing how emotional he had become in the last few minutes.

"Sorry to interrupt, but here is your check. I'll place it right here on the corner of the table. Feel free to pay whenever you're ready. There's no rush." Rick and Alexis both thanked the young waiter. It wasn't until then that Alexis realized that she was still holding onto Rick's hand after all this time. Embarrassingly, she removed them right away, trying not to do it so harshly that it alarmed Rick of her awkwardness. Without much of a response, Rick dug his hand into his rear pocket and pulled out a brown leather wallet. He placed his Discover credit card onto the check holder and motioned to the waiter that they were ready to pay.

"Would it be appropriate if I said that I didn't want this night to end yet?" That nauseating feeling that had hit Alexis as she was preparing to leave her apartment unexpectedly returned. Jackie had warned her about this though. It was their third date after all, and not a single thing had happened between them. She also really did like him, more than she was willing to admit, even to herself. Then, she thought about the pictures that were hanging across her bedroom wall. Images of gore and death lived in her bedroom, waiting for her to come back home like silent two-dimensional children that craved her attention. If there was anything that

Jackie was right about, it was that Alexis could *not* bring Rick back to her apartment. It didn't matter how fascinating he believed her job was.

"Maybe we could take this back to your place?" Rick seemed to think for a few seconds before giving his answer.

"Yeah, sure. I don't see why not." Alexis smiled and placed the mint that had been brought back by the waiter with Rick's credit card into her purse. Usually Alexis studied forensics and the dead, but even she knew that something didn't seem quite genuine about Rick's approval of them going back to his place. He was a fantastic guy, but there was still that nagging voice pecking at the back of her mind screaming *THIS IS A MISTAKE!* She wanted to listen, but ultimately decided to ignore it.

"So, I'll just follow you?" Alexis asked as they walked in opposite directions to where their respective vehicles were parked.

"Sounds perfect." Alexis slipped into the driver's seat as gracefully as one wearing a tight pencil skirt could and reached into her purse to get her phone. Three text message notifications collapsed down her screen, all from Jackie. The first read **Well…**, while the next one said **Helloooo???**, followed lastly by **Bitch r u dead!?**. Alexis put the key into the ignition of the car and turned her headlights on so that Rick didn't think that she was stalling. As fast as she could, Alexis started typing out her response.

No, I'm not dead! Going to his place...Wish me luck!! [winky face emoji].

In her mind, the emoji wasn't necessary but knew that Jackie wouldn't be satisfied unless she gave her a reason to believe that things were going to be raunchier than what they really were. She sat her phone into the circular cup holder beside her and pulled out of the parking lot behind Rick.

Alexis turned the volume of the car stereo up hoping to hear a familiar song that would help soothe her nerves. Instead, what she heard was the WGIR radio host talking about a topic that was all too familiar to her.

"From what the news stations are saying, the death toll is up to seven. The cops believe that each of these killings is connected to whom they are now calling the Manchester Mutilator. I know...Rolls right off the tongue. Over the past few weeks bodies have continued turning up with what police are saying have either dismembered and or missing body parts. Well, apparently another one was discovered last night bringing the total to seven. This is all very disturbing, and something that I never imagined would be happening in our backyards. So, I urge all of you to please be careful and do not go out alone at night. Be wary of strangers and any suspicious activity that you -"

Alexis turned the radio off and decided she would rather sit in silence than listen to another word about this serial killer. Her entire life revolved around investigating these crimes and for the first time in years, tonight would not be about work. Tonight was about her.

Alexis pulled up behind Rick into a driveway that ushered up to a lovely two-storied house with light blue panel siding. The car let out a dying hum as she turned and removed the key from the ignition. Alexis opened the car door and was assisted by a gust of wind. As she stepped out of the vehicle, a sudden chill ran up and down her spine. Rick noticed Alexis shivering and acknowledged the fact that the temperature had seemed to plummet in the twenty minutes that had passed since leaving the restaurant.

"Come, let's get inside before you freeze out here." Alexis thanked him and followed Rick up the porch steps and into the front door of the house.

The first thing she noticed was how the home smelled. It wasn't bad, just different than her own. There was a male-dominated musk in the air; a mix of cologne, fresh cut venison, and oak. It was alarming at first, but Alexis adapted quickly and soon found herself quite fond of the aroma.

"Take a seat," Rick said, pointing towards the grey sectional couch in his living room. "Do you want me to get you a drink? I can't guarantee anything as fancy as what the restaurant had, but I'm sure I have something hidden away."

"A drink would be great!"

"Awesome, just give me one sec." Rick entered the dining room and then made a right into the kitchen. She could hear cabinets being opened and slammed shut, followed by the opening of the refrigerator door and the clinking of glass bottles being pushed around. "I hope you're a beer girl because that might be all that I have."

"Beer is fine!" Alexis assured him. Rick returned with two bottles of an IPA that Alexis was unfamiliar with called Voodoo Ranger. The two used a bottle opener to pop the tops and each took a few gulps of the golden pale ale. It was bitter, but there was also a refreshing tropical taste mixed in that helped it go down easy.

"What do you think?"

"It's actually not too bad," Alexis answered before raising the glass bottle back to her lips and taking another few sips. Rick put his beer down onto the coffee table that sat in front of the couch and slid a few inches closer to Alexis while trying to remain as inconspicuous as possible. He wanted her, but also did not want to come across as only wanting that one thing. She was beautiful, well educated, had a career, and most importantly, she tolerated him. Something a woman hadn't done in far too long.

Alexis noticed Rick's subtle advancement, but was cautious not to elicit a reaction. There was still some uncertainty lingering in the back of her mind on how far she was willing to allow the night to take her. She wanted these decisions, whether good or bad, to be hers and hers alone, not based around the pressure that she felt to satisfy her friend.

Rick leaned in and Alexis did the same. Her body had moved on its own. It had been a long time since she had felt the arousal of nerves on her mouth initiated by a kiss. The motions of her lips and tongue felt natural. Within the compartments of her mind, she was now able to file away 'Making Out' in the same folder as 'Riding A Bike'; a folder she had subconsciously labeled: **ONCE YOU LEARN, YOU NEVER FORGET**. Alexis pulled away as she felt something brush up against her lower leg. Startled, she looked down at the floor and was pleasantly surprised to see a chubby, orange and white cat pacing around the base of the couch.

"I would have never imagined you to be a cat guy." Alexis teased.

"That's Garfield, real original I know. He's been around for about eight years now. It was my wife's...Ex-wife's idea to get him. I personally wanted a german shepherd, but like most disagreements I have with women, I ended up losing. So, instead of a german shepherd, I have

Garfield." The cat looked up and let loose a soft meow as if to inform the two adults that it knew that they were talking about him.

"He's probably hungry. I can't remember if I fed him or not today. Lucky for you, you're getting to see the cat dad of the year in action." Alexis giggled at Rick's sarcasm. He leaned down and stroked the cat from the peak of it's head down to the tip of its tail. "Do you want anything else while I'm in the kitchen?" Alexis lifted her bottle and shook it around as to measure the amount of alcohol that was left inside.

"No, I think I'm still good. Would it be okay if I used your bathroom though?" Rick nodded his head.

"Yeah, of course. It's straight up the stairs and will be the second door on your left." Alexis gave her thanks, grabbed her purse, and headed over to the beige carpeted staircase. "I wasn't aware that you would be coming over, so please don't mind the mess! It's honestly a little embarrassing. Just try not to explore too much. Remember, second door on the left!"

"It's no problem! And I got it!" Alexis shouted back into the kitchen from midway up the stairs. "Second door on the left!"

The first thing that stuck out to Alexis as she reached the top of the stairs was a beautiful white console table. Sitting on the table was a dark blue vase with a bundle of pink and white roses poking out of the top, giving the hallway a much-needed splash of color. Alexis leaned in to smell them but was shocked to discover that they had no smell at all. She pinched one of the pink petals between her thumb and index finger and rubbed in a circular motion against the artificial flower. She was one of the rare women who preferred artificial flowers to the real ones anyway. Less hassle and they couldn't die on you. Death was plenty present in her life as it was.

Beside the vase was a framed picture of Rick and another woman whom Alexis assumed must be his late wife. She was stunning. So beautiful in fact that it made Alexis question why Rick would have any interest in her? Alexis was pretty, but this woman could have been a model. She had long, golden hair with bright blue eyes and a pearly white smile. It was hard for Alexis to admit to herself that she was indeed envious of a dead woman.

Alexis closed the bathroom door and sat down on the toilet. She removed her phone from her purse and pressed her thumb against the round home button and watched as the screen lit up revealing one new text message from Jackie. Alexis used her thumbprint to unlock the phone and as usual, couldn't help but roll her eyes after looking at the message. No words, just two emojis. [**Eggplant**

emoji. Okay hand sign emoji.] Her thumbs hovered over the phone as she debated in her head over how to respond. She decided that in this instance, the best response was no response.

The phone slid nicely back into Alexis' bag which also housed her credit card, a tube of "Rose Matter" lipstick that had never been opened, and a Buy One JR Whopper, Get One Free coupon for Burger King. For now, she had been advised to give off the facade that she enjoyed these fancy Italian restaurant dinners (which she did), but on an average day, Alexis was a fast food, chicken nuggets and french fries kind of gal.

She ripped off a few squares of toilet paper, folded them up, and finished her business. She flushed the toilet and stared at herself in the mirror. Her hair and makeup still looked presentable. It wasn't as good as it had been at the start of the evening, but by her standards, it was passable.

Alexis stopped at the white table once again and felt her gaze drawn back down to the picture of Rick and his ex-wife. *What are you so jealous of? Stop being like this! It's weird!* Her thoughts wrestled about in her mind, disorienting her thinking to the point that she could have sworn she heard the sound of clanking chains smacking against the floor in the adjacent room. She stood there silently, waiting for the noise that sounded so much like chains rattling to happen once more. Silence.

Alexis tiptoed toward the closed room and gently pressed her ear against the door. She held her breath and listened quietly.

"Hello?" The sound clattered from within the room again in response to her voice. Alexis jumped away from the door and pressed her back against the wall next to the bathroom.

Something was inside the room.

"Hey, are you doing all right up there? You didn't fall in did ya?" Alexis opened the bathroom door and yelled back a response while pretending as though she was still handling her business.

"No, no, I'm fine. I um...I'm just fixing my makeup real quick. I'll be down in a minute!"

"Okay well, don't be too long!" Alexis shut the bathroom door with just enough force to make sure that Rick would hear. If he thought that she was in the bathroom, he wouldn't be tempted to come upstairs to check on her.

Alexis' hands perspired and felt clammy as she reached for the door. She wrapped her fingers tightly around the silver doorknob. With the turn of her wrist, she slowly pushed the door open and was left petrified.

"Oh my god." Alexis' heart sank into her stomach. The sound that she was hearing was indeed real. Sitting in the dark room with no light except for the God rays that beamed in through the window was a bony, blonde haired boy. He wore a plain white T-shirt and a pair of shorts that were covered in brown stains and fell no farther than his upper thighs. His ankles were shackled to a bedpost so tight that the skin above both feet was raw and covered in sores. A musty, sewage-like odor crashed into Alexis like an invisible wave. The smell very quickly dominated the upstairs hallway.

"Are you okay? I'm going to get you out of here." Alexis entered the room and uncontrollably began heaving and gagging from the revolting smell. She closed her eyes and took deep, slow breaths. After composing herself, she reopened her eyes and cautiously moved forward. Behind the shaggy-haired child was a metal bucket filled to the brim with urine and feces. Dozens of flies buzzed around the room while an even higher number of creamy white maggots wriggled across the floor and up the bucket.

Alexis dropped to her knees and pulled at the chains. Her eyes surveyed the shackles for a way to remove them.

"Are you okay?" she asked the boy again.

The child did not answer her. Instead, he kept his large eyes locked onto her with a wide crooked-toothed smile. His expression was vile and haunting. He was nothing more than bones wrapped up in sore covered flesh.

Alexis tugged at the chains a few more times until she noticed a keyhole on one of the shackles. She stood up and flung her head from side to side.

"Is that it? The key?" Alexis asked the boy, pointing to a tiny key placed on top of a dresser that stood upright against the far side wall.

He kept smiling. He did not speak. His eyes followed her every move but they lacked expression. The grin that he wore across his face looked unnatural. It was as if his mouth had been stitched open and he could no longer relax his lips.

Alexis hurried over to the dresser, grabbed the key, and quietly rushed back to the boy's side. She picked up the shackle and pushed the key into the opening. With just the slightest twist of her hand, the shackle loosened. Alexis pulled the cuff apart from around the leg of the bed.

"Just one more now," she whispered. Her dialogue was directed at the child, but she was yet to get a response out of him. The only thing he offered in return was that unsettling smile.

Another twist of the tiny key resulted in the other restraint loosening and being removed. "Come on, stand up. We're going to get you out of here." The boy stared at Alexis for a few seconds before slowly obeying her command. She knew that the child's robotic demeanor was likely a result of whatever trauma he had been exposed to, but that didn't make the hollow smile sprawled across his face any less unnerving. "Good boy," she encouraged. "Come on, hurry now." Alexis grabbed the boy by his spindly wrist and turned towards the hallway.

"What have you done?!" Standing in the doorway blocking their exit was Rick. Alexis expected him to become aggressive and hostile, but it was he who had the appearance of fear displayed throughout his body. His hands and legs quivered as he stared down at the chains sprawled across the bedroom floor. "What have you done?" Rick repeated, this time in a much softer tone.

The boy clapped three times. He still did not speak, but he did continue to smile. The soulless articulation exhibited by the boy's eyes remained, but the quick claps wordlessly demonstrated his excitement to see Rick and to finally be free from his confines.

"I think *I* should be the one asking the questions here. This boy and I are leaving, and I'm calling the cops!" Alexis pulled the child behind her as she cautiously moved in the direction of the hallway.

"No listen, you don't understand. You need to leave him there. He's dangerous!"

"He's dangerous?" Alexis questioned as she pushed through Rick while exiting the room. "He was shackled to a bed and was left to rot next to a bucket of piss." Rick reached for Alexis' arm, but she immediately pulled away. "Do not touch me!"

"Adam is not normal. Please, just take him back into the bedroom and let's talk about this." Rick spoke in a calm and quiet tone. He was doing his best not to alarm her, but Alexis wanted to hear none of it. She had seen too many homicides in her lifetime and was convinced that this was the making of another.

"Don't come any closer or I'll scream as loud as I can." Rick took a large step back and raised both of his hands to his chest with the flat of his palms exposed. He was surrendering before there was even a fight.

Adam smiled.

Meow! Garfield bounced his fat stubby body up to the second floor hopping from one step to the next. Stray traces of wet food were still sprinkled around the cat's mouth.

"Come on Adam, we're leaving." Alexis tugged on the boy's arm but he did not budge. She pulled again, but still, the boy refused to travel any further. Instead, Adam dropped down on all fours and looked at Garfield. His arms and legs spread widely giving him the appearance of a human arachnid. The cat paused, debating on whether it was safe to move ahead towards the malnourished child or not.

MEOOOOW. The cat's cry was long and high pitched.

Adam smiled.

Garfield wobbled in Adam's direction. With all the charm of a domesticated feline, Garfield purred and rubbed himself against the boy's outer arm. Rick grew anxious as he nervously watched as his cat trotted happily around Adam. He took a few quick steps forward in an attempt to grab his cat, but he was too slow.

Adam swiped Garfield between both of his hands and held the cat by its face with an intense force. The cat forced out a plangent sound as Adam crushed its skull within his grip. Garfield flailed his body in the erratic way that a cat in danger does, catching Adam's arms with a few deep scratches that drew blood.

"Adam, stop! Put him down!" Rick screamed. Adam continued to smile as he shook the cat violently back and forth before slamming it repeatedly onto the wooden floor. Blood drained from out of every orifice in Garfield's head. The right side of the cat's cranium had been flattened like a pancake. His skull was crushed to dust. Alexis looked on in horror. She was speechless to the atrocity that was playing out in front of her.

"What have you done?" For the first time, Adam separated his teeth. He lifted the cat's body up and shoved its bloody head into his mouth before chomping down. Sounds of what remained of Garfield's skull breaking between Adam's jaws emulated that of a handful of dry twigs being snapped in two. A blend of hair, liquid, and brains seeped through Adam's teeth. A crimson mask stained his mouth which he confidently displayed as he continued munching away.

Adam tossed the headless carcass against the wall which hit with a loud *thud*! He tightly clenched his teeth and smiled. The red that filled his mouth could have passed for a portal to the underworld.

Like he had done when Rick first appeared in the bedroom doorway, Adam clapped his hands three times, proud of his accomplishment. Then, as if possessed by the soul of the animal that he just murdered, the boy took off on all fours like a beast from Hell. Down the stairs he went, his arms and legs uncomfortably contorting in ways that made him look like some perturbed humanoid crab. His loud, raspy breaths resonated up the stairs until he had traveled too far for them to continue being heard.

"What the hell just happened? He just...Ate the cat!" Alexis had her back pressed up against the wall. Her lips fluttered with fear as she spoke.

"What did I tell you? I told you not to let him out of the room and you didn't listen! Now we're both dead."

"I don't understand," Alexis mumbled inaudibly to herself. "Who…Or what, is he?"

"He's Adam, my son. But he's not like normal little boys. All he does is kill. He has no empathy and doesn't know how to show love. He is death in the form of a child, and you have released him." There were hundreds of questions that Alexis wanted answers to, but more than anything she wanted to leave. To walk straight out of the front door, get into her car, and drive off under the moonlight, back to her apartment to live peacefully among her own strange perversions. The photos taped onto her bedroom wall was child's play compared to whatever was going on here.

"Listen, I'm just gonna go. I won't involve the police because I can't even begin to comprehend what's happening here, but I can't have anything to do with this." Alexis tucked her hand purse firmly against her waist and stepped down onto the first step. Then, from around the corner, Adam reemerged. He had abandoned the animalistic movement for a more human one. The boy was back up on two legs. Squeezed inside of his right hand was a box cutter with a two-inch blade. Adam stood at the base of the stairs with a savage blood coated smile. He raised the tool and stabbed it into the wall repeatedly. His focus was directed at the woman who stood at the top of the stairwell.

"Adam," Alexis said softly while taking a slow step down with her left foot. "Please, put the weapon down. I don't want to hurt you. All I want to do is walk right past you and out the front door. That's it." She took another step, this time descending with her right foot. Adam continued to stab the wall which was now filled with inch deep vertical cavities.

"Alexis, I think you should come back upstairs." The woman raised her hand up by her shoulder in a motion that was intended to inform Rick that she had the situation under control. She was used to taking the lead in unusual situations.

Left foot. Right foot. Left foot. Right foot.

Slowly, Alexis descended down the steps. She was about halfway now. Adam stopped stabbing the wall and stepped off to the side of the railing as if to invite her to walk past him; his entire being shook with excitement.

"That's it, Adam, you have nothing to be afraid of." She was almost at the bottom now. Her heartbeat banged inside her chest like a drum. Adam raised his arm and held it out in the way that a host does when inviting a guest into their home for a holiday party.

Only two more steps now. Rick watched with a sense of insecurity from the top of the stairs. He was visibly more shaken and disturbed than the woman who had no idea what she was getting herself into. Then again, he knew what the boy was capable of, and more frighteningly, what he wasn't; compassion and understanding being two of those things.

As Alexis lifted her leg to take one final step from off of the carpeted stairs, Adam lunged his body forward and stabbed the knife once again into the wall missing her face by mere centimeters. Alexis threw her body backward, letting out a painful cry as her spine slammed against the edge of one of the steps. An electric jolt shot through her neck. Some of the connective tissue in her spine ripped, misaligning her backbone. A tingling feeling vibrated down her calves and into the soles of her feet.

Adam bent down and started crawling up the stairs. Alexis tried to get up but had lost all feeling in her legs. With both arms, she pushed and lifted herself high enough to move up to the next step. Unfortunately, the boy was able to crawl forward much faster than she was able to drag herself backward.

Adam leaned his head down intimately close above hers. From beneath the boy's lower lip down to the point of his chin was a thin film of blood and saliva that dripped onto Alexis' blouse. A sour odor leaked from between Adam's teeth and onto the woman's face. Her eyes were bottled with tears. Her breathing hastened. Faster now. Heavier. This continued until she was to the point of hyperventilating. Adam watched as the woman struggled for air with a detached look.

The bloody-faced boy raised the box cutter into the air and stabbed it down into Alexis' shoulder. He then pulled it out and slammed it down again, this time driving it into her bicep muscle. Then again. Alexis howled in pain as blood poured onto the carpet. As Adam continued to plunge the knife into her flesh, Alexis noticed for the first time signs of joy in his eyes. Low pitched croaks broke free from out of Adam's throat in glee. A sparkle came alive within his pupils as he brought Alexis closer and closer to death. He found euphoria in the pain of others.

Even with the attempted murder currently being her own, Alexis couldn't help but analyze everything about the child on top of her. Up until moments ago, all signs of emotion were nonexistent. Now, like a child scoring his first goal on a youth soccer team, there was evidence of pleasure and excitement. There were symptoms of arousal and accomplishment that only a psychopath could experience from the adrenaline that was stemmed through the means of killing. The adrenaline that most normal wired humans felt during activities such as rollercoaster rides, or skydiving, or sex. But this boy...No, this killer, was the embodiment of everything that she had been investigating throughout the past few months. Although he was ripping her life away from her, there was a small sense of bliss that came from the fact that in Alexis' mind, she understood him.

"That's enough!" Rick tackled Adam off of Alexis and the two tumbled down the bottom few stairs before hitting the ground hard. Adam pounced in the direction of the blade which had been dislodged from his hand during the fall, but instead was met with a size twelve boot to the ribs. The boy rolled onto his back and then sat up as if nothing had happened. He then jumped at Rick and wrestled him to the floor, his jagged, dirty fangs biting down at Rick's neck like a rabid beast.

Rick did everything he could to hold the boy back, but in time felt his arms start to weaken. With every passing second, Adam's teeth came closer to gnashing away at Rick's jugular. The veins around his throat bulged, filled with red ether.

Then, came the blood. Alexis watched the father and son rumble across the floor until the larger of the two conceded the fight from exhaustion. Adam bit down into his father's neck and whipped his head back, ripping and pulling a chunk of flesh with him. Rick's neck transformed into a geyser that spewed out a fountain of blood that covered the floor, Adam, and himself. The man pawed at his neck, trying to stunt the bleeding. His eyes locked with hers. The two stared at each other as they inevitably waited for death to come and usher them into whatever afterlife awaited.

Meanwhile, Adam found a way to keep smiling, even as he chewed ferociously on the piece of skin that halfway hung out of his mouth. After properly chewing, Adam swallowed and lurched down for another go. The boy's jawline was fully extended, but he never clenched down. Like a malfunctioning machine, Adam hovered motionlessly over his father's neck.

Adam's body became limp and fell to the floor. The blade stood erect out of the boy's ribcage from where Rick had just stabbed him. For a few more seconds, Rick held both hands over his neck until his veins ran dry. He was dead.

Alexis, barely conscious, slid her body down the steps and grabbed her black purse. She unzipped the bag and pulled out her phone. Bloody fingerprints marked the screen over top of the 9 and 1 on the keypad.

"Nine-one-one, what's your emergency?" The voice on the other end of the line was angelic.

"I've been stabbed, and I'm bleeding really bad. I need an ambulance."

"Okay ma'am, try and stay with me. Where are you? What address should I send the paramedics to?"

"I don't know," Alexis grunted as she dragged herself down to the bottom of the stairs.

Rick and Adam both lay motionless on the red-coated wood in front of her.

"That's fine. I can use the location displayed by your cell phone. The ambulance will be there shortly. In the meantime I need you to stay on the phone with me. I need you to keep talking with me, okay?"

"Yeah...Yeah okay." Alexis dragged herself toward the front door, her legs sliding behind her like useless dead weight. Somehow, she was able to find the strength to prop herself up and turn the doorknob with her one good arm. Like her legs, Alexis had practically lost all feeling in the arm that she was stabbed in. The front door opened, and Alexis leaned out onto the front porch.

"Do you mind telling me your name ma'am?" The voice startled her. Alexis had nearly forgotten that she had somebody speaking with her on the phone.

"Alexis Tomani. My name is Alexis." Her voice had grown soft and breathy.

"Okay, Miss. Tomani, is the person or persons who hurt you still there with you?"

"No. Well, yes but he's dead. I think. It was a little boy, he -" Alexis rolled down the front porch steps and looked up into the night sky. It was freezing out. Her breaths formed shapeless, gray clouds. "He killed his father, and then his father...Killed him."

"Miss Tomani, I don't know if I'm hearing you right. Do you think you could explain the details a little clearer? Are you telling me that a father and son killed each other?" Alexis dropped the phone beside her. Long, wailing sirens screaming into the night echoed in the distance. "Hello? Miss. Tomani, are you still there?"

Alexis didn't answer. A smile formed across her face as she listened to the ambulance and cop cruisers draw closer. She allowed her head to drop to the side and inadvertently looked back at the house of horrors.

Inside the window, glaring down at Alexis with a cold smile, was Adam. She stared back at him as he clapped in the window. She wanted to get farther away, but she was too exhausted. Too much blood had left her body.

Alexis allowed her eyes to close and tears welled up inside. There was a great deal of uncertainty over whether or not she would ever open them again, but she didn't care. All of the pain and fear had disappeared. She just wanted to sleep. So, without much resistance, Alexis closed her eyes, and slept.

Officer Ricardo Torres was the first to arrive on scene. What he witnessed was unlike anything he'd ever seen in his fourteen years on the force. An unconscious woman lay sprawled across the front lawn of a two story property. The grass was like

Christmas; a kaleidoscope of reds and greens. Her skin was ice and her pulse was faint. But outside was the bearable portion of what he discovered, inside was far worse.

Within minutes, paramedics and three other police cruisers arrived. With backup on site, Ricardo took the initiative to enter the building. The bloody body of a middle aged man was the first thing Officer Torres noticed upon entering the home. The smell was horrible and the sight was worse. This house was the first of many things for him. The first time he had seen a half-eaten cat. The first time he had seen a child's room transformed into a makeshift cell. The first time he thought maybe this line of work wasn't for him.

Alexis Tomani lost everything after that night. She lost her ability to walk. She lost the ability to lift her right arm higher than her chest. And, she lost her job.

By the time the police and paramedics had arrived, Adam had disappeared. Once she had recovered, Alexis gave the detective her description of the boy, but to this day, they have yet to find him. The likelihood that Adam is still out there, possibly continuing to kill while wearing that deranged smile like a badge of honor was small, but it was still enough to keep Alexis up at night. She slept with a gun by her side. Every creak that her apartment made became him, the blond haired boy ready to pounce on his prey, ready to rip her throat out the same way he did to his father. As time went on, Alexis continued losing sleep and lost her grip on reality.

Currently, Alexis is an inpatient at the Cross Hill Grove Psychiatric Hospital. For ninety minutes a day, she is granted access to mingle with the other patients in the common area where she can watch television, play board games, or read magazines. The rest of the time she is barricaded within a padded cell and is listed within the vicinity as a "Danger to both herself and to others." But, Alexis partakes in none of those activities. Instead, she sits on the couch, props her knees up tightly against her chest, and sways back and forth repeating the same word over and over again.

"Smile. Smile. Smile."

The Widower

Welcome to Somerset, Indiana. The year is 1953. A year in which Queen Elizabeth II was crowned the new queen of England and baby boomers were popping out faster than reruns of the Milton Berle show.

Mild squalls swept numerous gold and orange leaves amidst a densely populated forest. It was a cool autumn day. The sky was cyan blue and cloudless. And beneath it all resided a fifty-two year old man named Henry Climer; a veteran author and newly turned alcoholic due to the recent death of his wife, Carol. For over a month, Henry has been plagued with the curse known as writer's block. Whenever he picks up a pen or sits in front of the typewriter, he spends hours staring at the empty pages.

Hoping to find some motivation, Henry decided to take an impromptu trip up to the family cabin. He figured that garnishing his daily routine with the positive memories attached to the cabin would be just the thing to alleviate him of his writer's block and recent night terrors. On a nightly basis, his mind loves to remind him of how he failed to save Carol's life on that humid, summer night.

Now, With the last few weeks of Henry's life having been consumed by rage, nightmares, booze, and failed writing attempts, he clambers up the five rotted wooden steps of the cabin's front porch. He limps forward, opens the front door, and enters the residence located on the outskirts of nowhere.

It is here that our story begins.

The aroma of the cabin was all too familiar as Henry closed the door behind him. It smelled of his deceased wife's favorite perfume, *Moonlight Mist* by Gourielli. His sunken, ebony eyes shifted around as he surveyed the wooden interior; his right hand holding a suitcase filled with clothes and his writings (or lack thereof), and his left holding something much mightier...A twelve pack of Budweiser.

Releasing an aged sigh, Henry stepped towards the dining room table and placed his suitcase and beer on its surface. It had been fourteen years since Henry had been to the cabin on his own, but the guilt that burdened him over his wife's death had to be cleansed. It was driving him mad. And, if there was one, this would be the solution to all of his problems.

Night after night, Henry would snap awake drenched in his own sticky perspiration. His mind loved playing this sick, twisted game where it punished him with the visions and sounds of his wife screaming and burning whilst pinned beneath their car. The car that *he* crashed.

The couple had been on their way home from a party that a friend of theirs was hosting. It was an evening filled with drinking, laughing, and reconnecting with people whom they had not seen in years. Both Henry and his wife had their fair share of drinks, but unsurprising to Carol, Henry's fair share was nearly twice as much as everyone else. Henry had never been an angry drunk, but always a controlling one.

"Give me the keys Henry. I'm driving us home tonight."

"Nonsense! I'm fine, don't worry about it. Just get in the car." His speech was comparable to that of a toddler with a speech impediment. He slurred his words and had trouble annunciating his 'r's. Carol tried fighting the idea, but Henry had never been one to take 'no' for an answer, especially once he got to drinking. So, it was he who slid into the driver's seat and chauffeured them down the dark, winding roads.

"Have I told you how beautiful you look tonight?" Henry redirected his focus from the road to his wife. He leaned across the center console and attempted to kiss her on the neck. Carol leaned away noticing that Henry's grip on the steering wheel was veering to the right.

"Honey, please. You need to focus on the road." Henry pouted and turned his head forward. The night was rushing at the car with supersonic speed. Or, at least to Henry, it felt like it.

The neverending darkness weighed down on Henry's eyes. The longer he drove, the heavier they became. For a split second, the vehicle swerved across the yellow line and into the oncoming lane, but Henry caught himself and recovered. It felt like he was driving through a kaleidoscope of colors. Again, the car began to drift, this time in the opposite direction.

"Sweetheart, I know that you want to drive, but I think you should pull over and let me finish the trip home. You're beginning to swerve and it's scaring me."

"It's only fifteen more minutes. We'll be home in no time. Stop worrying, would ya?" Carol tapped her fingers against her knees. It was a nervous tick of hers. That, along with biting her lip which tasted like chemicals from the cherry red lipstick smeared across it.

Henry rubbed his hand roughly down his face hoping that it would help him focus. He knew that he should switch positions with Carol, but an alcohol fueled voice in the back of his head urged him to continue on as he was.

Suddenly, a huge blur of brown and white bolted into the middle of the road. It froze with fear. The deer's big, round eyes reflected the beams of the car's headlights. Henry turned the steering wheel hard to the right causing Carol's head to smash against the passenger door window. Shards of glass were sent flying as the window shattered. Henry then turned the steering wheel hard to the left in an attempt to regain control. The tires lost traction and the vehicle began to spin out. Henry spun the wheel back and forth but ultimately couldn't prevent the car from flipping over and rolling one, two, three times. The couple were left trapped inside, and upside down.

An echo sifted through the air as Henry popped the tab to his first of many beers for the day.

It was 10:30 in the morning, which as of recently was a late start for Henry.

The heavy black typewriter sat in the middle of the dining room table, right where he had left it. It was the place where Henry had written over a dozen best selling novels in what now felt like a previous life. Layers of dust covered the circular keys which hadn't been touched in nearly a year.

Henry took a hesitant seat at the table. He stared at the typewriter, and the typewriter stared back. The two were having a mental pissing match. Which was stronger? The will of a man or the patience of a machine?

Henry's legs shook uncontrollably as he struggled to find the words meant to fill the paper. He lifted the lukewarm can of Budweiser up to his lips and took a sip. Tepid, yet still refreshing. There was a constant drip coming from the faucet in the connected kitchen which, in Henry's mind, sounded like a herd of elephants. The frustrated drunk released a groan as he slid the chair out from under him and walked over to the kitchen sink to examine the faucet. Henry turned both of the knobs as hard as he could in opposite directions to ensure that they were turned off. Still, the water continued to drip.

"The hell is this?" Henry questioned aloud. Again, another empty groan. He walked back to the table, picked up his beer, and drank the entirety of what remained. Prior to throwing out the empty can,

Henry was already equipped with a full one from the fridge; this one a little bit cooler than the last.

Once more, Henry found himself seated in front of the antique typewriter, waiting for the words to pour into his mind. And still, the inside of his skull remained empty. Across the room and above the fireplace was the trophy head of a white-tailed deer Henry had shot and killed while out hunting a few years back. Two hundred twenty-five pounds, his largest kill to date. For a long time it had been Henry's most prized possession, an achievement that would follow him to the grave. But in the ominous silence of the house, Henry could feel the deer's eyes follow his every move. They were black pits capable of reflecting the hollow man that he had become. They could also reflect the headlights of a speeding, oncoming car...

Time slowly passed by. Seconds turned to minutes which evolved into hours. Still, the page that laid within the mouth of the typewriter remained as blank as when he had placed it there.

The sweltering sun that had been illuminating the cabin's interior was now leisurely falling behind the hills that sat out in the distant skyline. Henry stumbled over to the fridge and grabbed the last Budweiser off of the top shelf. With a swipe of his index finger, he cracked open the can and swallowed half of it in a few gulps.

"This isn't gonna get the job done." Henry found himself once again staring deep into the eyes of the deer head mounted on the wall. He raised the cold aluminum can to his lips and chugged the rest of the alcohol. "Carol!" the man bellowed out as he threw the empty can across the room. "Are you here with me?" A few slices of wind slapped against the outside of the window. "Please, just answer me! Give me anything, I don't care what it is! Just don't leave me alone. I'm a mess, Carol."

Bewitched by a drunken rage, Henry took hold of the typewriter and threw it to the floor while emancipating a murderous cry; his mind consumed by a poisonous cloud of alcohol. He then sent the blank pieces of paper that laid on the table soaring through the air with an off-balance swipe of his hand. The case of beers that he consumed in less than three hours came back to haunt him as he lost his balance. There was a loud bang as he hit the ground.

The crackling of the fireplace filled the living room as Henry laid on the floor surrounded by a sea of white paper. He raised his hands to his face and rubbed them across his cheeks and chin. He hadn't shaved in weeks. A monochrome bush lived on the lower half of his face.

"What am I becoming?" the man whimpered. A tear slid down his face until losing itself within the forest that was Henry's beard.

"What am I without you, if not just a drunken fool?" Another tear slid down his face as he halfheartedly gazed at the crumpled beer can he had earlier thrown to the other side of the room.

Using the couch as a crutch, Henry pulled himself to his feet. It took a minute before he could completely balance himself. The room was spinning and the walls were pulsing. With a few wobbly steps, Henry worked his way over to the empty can, leaned over to pick it up, and raised it to his lips, only to feel a few bitter drops fall onto his tongue. He allowed the can to fall from his hand and back onto the floor in disappointment.

With his vision blurred and perception altered, Henry stammered over to the table, grabbed his car keys, and fumbled out the front door. His intention was to drive into town, go to the store, and purchase more beer. Although alcohol had not assisted him in his writings since the death of his wife, he figured that it was better to attempt as a drunken fool than a sober one. Carol had always said the thing that made him an amazing author was his ability to embrace the obstacles of his own life and then turn them into stories for his characters. The decision to go out and get more alcohol was Henry embracing his obstacles to the fullest.

Henry stabbed the key into the ignition after a few missed attempts and turned the key to the right. The revving of the car's engine felt like ice picks chipping away at his head. Through the windshield he stared at the cabin, noticing that he had left all of the lights on inside. For a split second he contemplated going back in and turning them off, but laughed off the idea as he put the car into reverse.

The car slid backward down the dirt path, most of which was hidden beneath layers of crunchy, dead leaves. Then, out of nowhere came a loud thud. Henry's body whipped forward into the steering wheel. Dazed for a moment, he again started to laugh upon realizing that he had forgotten to turn on his car lights.

Henry opened the car door and stepped out to see that he had backed into a tree. The back of the car was badly damaged and his left tail light was fractured.

"Fine!" the drunk screamed into the surrounding woods. "Guess I'm done for the night. Are you happy?!" The only response came from a sweet serenade conducted by a choir of crickets, chirping their familiar songs into the cool, night air.

The front door slammed open. Henry nearly fell through the doorway but caught himself before taking another tumble onto the wooden floor. The scattered papers and upended typewriter silently welcomed him back home from their places on the floor.

"What are you looking at?" Henry asked, staring deep into the trophy's lifeless eyes. He let out a deep sigh before looking back down at the typewriter on the floor. It was time that he came to terms with the fact that this was going to be another day where no work would be getting done. "Tomorrow." he mumbled to himself lightly. "I'll make you proud of me tomorrow."

Henry wobbled over to the wall and flipped the light switch. A forbidding darkness was cast across the first floor.

After two minutes of struggling up the stairs, Henry finally made it to his room. He collapsed onto the bed and could feel the world spinning around him, even with his eyes closed. With the bottom of his left shoe, he kicked off his right, and with the heel of his right shoe, removed his left. The lower half of his legs dangled over the edge of the bed.

"Henry…" A woman's voice whispered his name. Henry smiled. He was too exhausted to open his eyes. "Henry…" the voice whispered again. A pair of hands rubbed along the sides of his neck, and then made their way down to the ball of his shoulders. The touch was comforting.

"Carol," Henry moaned. He wanted to open his eyes, but the alcohol had numbed him. It was too much of a chore to try and move anything. The stroking and whispering continued.

Before long, Henry was fast asleep.

Henry's eyes shot open. A sharp pain ran through Henry's side as he found himself trapped within his car. He looked to his side and could see that his wife was unconscious. Blood spilled from her neck. It had been carved by shards of the glass window.

"Carol!" Henry yelled, struggling to unfasten his seat belt. "Carol, honey, open your eyes!" He reached over and shook her limp body. Her eyes remained closed. A panicked frenzy took hold of him after noticing that the front end of the car was covered in dancing flames. An auburn radiance illuminated the scene.

Henry tightly clasped his hands around the seat belt. Finally, he was able to release it. His body dropped out of the driver's seat and slammed against the roof. He kicked at the window until his leg went bursting through the glass. A flock of birds flew off into the night, scared away by the sound.

Pieces of his flesh were ripped open as he crawled out of the window. Henry fell out of the vehicle and onto the road. The sizzling of the tiny inferno consuming the four door Austin A30 Sedan sung behind him. He rose to his feet, still feeling the effects from the evening's festivities.

"Carol!" Henry yelled while shambling to the opposite side of the car. He reached inside attempting to release her from her constraint. Carol's eyes gently opened. Her hand flung directly toward her neck. Blood poured down her arm as she tried to speak, but she couldn't; her voice had been stolen from her.

The longer that Henry struggled, the more the car was taken over by fire. Sweat fell from his face as the heat became unbearable. "Come on, damn it!" he yelled, shaking the seat belt back and forth violently in frustration. The flames burst through the windshield and smacked Henry in the face, forcing him out of the car. He tried and tried again but the heat from the flames was too much to endure.

So there he was, on his hands and knees left to watch his bloodied wife be burned alive before his very eyes.

Runny streaks of black mascara ran down Carol's wrinkled face as she stared into her husband's soul, gagging on her own blood as she strived to scream for help. Henry laid motionless as he listened to the gurglings forced from his wife's throat as she maniacally tossed her head in directions that a human's neck should never go. Threads of brown hair burned off of Carol's scalp and fell out of the car window before landing on the pavement and smoldering into nothingness. All the while, tears poured down Henry's face; Carol's skin poured down hers.

As Henry wailed for help down the empty road, Carol's head slumped to the side. The stillness of the night hushed over them.

The timber cabin was noiseless. The full moon hovered high in the sky above the part-time home. An unnatural, chilled breeze traveled through the air and across Henry's body, awakening him from his short lived slumber. The hairs on the back of his neck stood on end. Goosebumps covered his arms.

Henry looked over at the window and could see that the bright, twinkling stars still kissed the black night. Forcing himself up, still feeling off balance from all of the drinking that he had done, he maneuvered his way out of the room and across the hall to the bathroom. He flushed the toilet after urinating and wobbled in a daze back over to the bedroom. Somewhere in his mind Henry expected Carol to be lying on the other side of the bed, staring back at him. Back and forth he tossed; a cold spot taking the place of where there once was a warm body.

He closed his eyes. *Tick. Tick. Tick. Tick tick tick.* The mysterious noise coming from somewhere in the house caused Henry to sit up. There was a baffled look across his face hidden behind the darkness. His broken heart began to speed up.

"Not another one of those damned raccoons." It wasn't rare for a raccoon or squirrel to sneak into the cabin through the fireplace. In the past it had happened on multiple occasions. Showing obvious signs of annoyance, Henry got up from the bed and turned on the bedroom light. He didn't feel like tending to the problem, but the paper that he brought with him was all that he had. If it all got ripped apart he would have to travel back into town to get more. And currently, after what had happened this evening, his car was in no condition to be driven.

Henry grabbed his hunting rifle from out of the gun closet and made for the living room.

The stairs creaked beneath his every step. Based on the incessant ticking and rustling, the furry culprit had no intention of stopping. As Henry reached the bottom of the stairs, he lifted the butt of the gun up to his shoulder and flipped the light switch on. He expected to witness some form of animal scurrying across the floor, but there was nothing. No animal, and even more peculiar, no more sounds.

Henry looked down at the ground. All of the papers were right where they had been when he went up to bed. Not one sheet had been ripped, stepped on, or crumpled. He was also astonished to see that there were no traces of an animal entering through the fireplace either.

The wind howled relentlessly. Henry could faintly see his car still backed into the broad tree trunk.

Henry laid his rifle on the couch and wondered whether or not he was imagining the noises. For the first time since his wife's death, he contemplated whether or not he was drinking too much. He turned around and headed back toward the light switch. On his way over, Henry bent down and lifted the pages from off of the ground. As he picked up the last of the papers, he noticed that the typewriter was gone.

"It was right here." Henry said aloud to himself. He looked around the room and then there it was, sitting on the table face up as if he had never thrown it to the ground earlier. Henry steadily stepped in the direction of the typewriter, awestruck by how it could have found its way back onto the table. The paper that he had shoved into the mouth of the 1946 Smith Corona Sterling typewriter was still there, only now Henry could see that there were words that had been typed. As it had been only a few minutes prior, Henry could feel his heartbeat quickening, to the point that pain strung up and down his rib cage like a classic guitar.

With a tender tug of the paper, Henry pulled it from the typewriter and stared down at the words. Without his glasses perched high onto the bridge of his nose, the print on the paper was too small for him to read. He surveyed the room until noticing his glasses propped up nicely on the kitchen counter. The widower hurried over to the counter. He tucked his glasses behind his ears and allowed the lens to bring form to the letters.

HENRY,

I NEED FOR YOU TO BE NEAR ME AGAIN. I KNOW THAT YOU NEED ME TO BE THERE WITH YOU TOO. WHY DID YOU HAVE TO LET ME DIEEE, HENRY? I WAS SO SCARED THE NIGHT OF THE CRASH. DO YOU KNOW HOW PAINFUL IT IS TO HAVE A CAR PINNING YOU TO THE EARTH WHILE YOUR BONES ARE BEING CRUSHED TO DUST?

YOU LET ME DIEE, DIEEE.

WILL YOU COME BE WITH ME ONCE AGAIN, MY LOVE? I DIEEED, BUT I KNOW THAT YOU DID NOT KILL ME. WHY DIDN'T YOU SAVE ME?

I'M DEA...SaVeD.

I KNOW THAT IT'S NOT YOUR FAULT. YOU WILL SEE ME AGAIN MY LOVE.

-C. C.

Henry dropped to his knees and began to sob hysterically. Tears fell from his face and onto the letter. "Carol? You are here, aren't you?" A sprinkle of laughs were mixed into his crying.

He took the letter up to his room and laid it on the end table beside the bed. For the first time in over a month, Henry slept with a smile on his face. The next morning came faster than it had ever come before. No sooner did Henry close his eyes, the sweltering sun was beating against his face through the window pane. The first thing that shot into his mind when he woke was the letter that presumably had been written to him from his deceased spouse. Henry immediately looked onto the end table to make sure that it was real and not another one of his nightmares.

The letter was still there.

Henry grabbed for the letter so that he could read it again. Something about it felt inauspicious. Regardless, it was better than nothing. It was the glue that would help put his heart back together.

Henry was unable to release the letter from his grip. All morning he kept it close; the sheerness of the paper may as well have been Carol's skin. Around nine o'clock, he picked up the phone and dialed 0 for the operator. The lady on the opposite end of the receiver was pleasant and had a perky attitude. She expressed that she was more than happy to connect him with a local mechanic who could come up and take a look at his car.

There were three short lived rings before a burly sounding man picked up the line.

"Hello? Joe's Auto Shop, how may I help you?"

"Hi, my name is Henry Climer and -"

"Henry Climer? The author?" the man asked, his voice stricken with excitement.

"Yes, that's correct," Henry answered with a chuckle in his voice, humbled by the fact that he was speaking with a fan of his work. He had been so lost in his own grievances that he'd completely forgotten the fact that there were tens of thousands of readers across the country who loved his work.

"Well I'll be. I'm a huge fan! When are you gonna come out with another book? It's been a mighty long time since I've read anything new from you." Henry wanted to answer the man by telling him that he had no idea when a new book was coming out. That his wife had died and the only impressive thing that he could accomplish these days was finishing a case of beer in what would be considered record time in most places. But, he didn't.

"Well," Henry began, "you'll be happy to know that I'm actually working on something new as we speak. I've had a little bit of a busy schedule as of late, but I think that I've finally gotten the time to focus on a new book." The more he spoke, the more excitement he could feel coming from the man on the other end of the phone. Henry glanced down at the letter received from Carol.

"Well you don't know how glad I am to hear that news. And from your mouth directly! But anyways, don't let me hold you up. How can I help you Mr. Climer?"

"That's the funny thing. You see, I accidentally backed my car into a tree last night. I'm up here in the woods north of Somerset and I completely missed the tree as I was backing up. I don't know how." Henry lied through his teeth as easily as a snake slithered through grass. He wasn't about to reveal to a fan that he crashed because he was piss drunk before trying to operate his vehicle. "It gets pitch dark out here in the woods late at night. Guess I should've known better than to try and drive."

"Definitely a big risk you were taking there Mr. Climer, trying to drive out of there at nighttime." The mechanic sucked his teeth and started tapping a pencil against the brim of his hat as he looked over the day's schedule. "Listen here Mr. Climer, since I'm such a big fan, I'll head on up to your place personally and see what I can do. Just give me an address and I'll be there as soon as I get a free minute." Henry provided the man with his address and ended the conversation.

For the first time that morning, Henry relinquished possession of Carol's letter and placed it onto the dining room table; but not before reading it over one more time. The words sent chills down his spine and a swarm of butterflies into his belly.

Three hours passed before Joe the Mechanic found his way up to the cabin.

"Here she is." Henry said, walking Joe over to the car. The mechanic released a high-pitched whistle.

"Oh boy." Joe said, shaking his head.

"Oh boy? What do you mean, oh boy That doesn't sound too good. You're going to be able to fix it right?"

"Yeah I can fix her. Might not be cheap though."

"Money's not an issue." Henry assured the mechanic. The two bickered for a while before Joe got to work. He had brought a myriad of tools with him in his truck. While he worked, Henry stayed outside and watched. By the time the mechanic was done, the sun was beginning to set. Henry paid the man, and he was off on his way; a hero who rode in a white truck rather than on the back of a white horse.

"Remember," Joe said as he rolled down the driver side window, "I'll be looking forward to that next novel."

"And I'm excited to finish it." The window was wound back up, and Joe drove down the dirt path before disappearing behind the trees. A few minutes later, Henry climbed into his car and followed down the same road. A new determination to write had come over him after reading Carol's letter, but still he figured he would write better with some alcoholic influence.

The bell above the convenient store rang as Henry pushed open the door. Like clockwork, he headed directly to the back freezer to where the alcohol was. He picked up a 12-pack of his favorite beer and closed the freezer door. The thought of cracking open a cold one and pressing his fingers against the typewriter's keys made him salivate. He then took a few paces toward the front counter before turning around, walking back to the chilled freezer door, and grabbing another 12 pack of Budweiser. The need for more beer in the future was inevitable, so Henry took the chance to be proactive and save himself another needless drive into town.

"Preparing for the storm that's coming this way, Mr. Climer?" asked the thick bearded, rotund cashier.

"Just not going to be getting out much. I'm working on my newest book and I want as little distraction as possible. Figured I'd stock up a little." answered Henry.

"Very well," the cashier simply replied while bagging the cases of beer. Henry paid the man and before long was pulling up to the cabin in the woods.

The night was much more tranquil than the previous. No blustering wind pounding against the cabin. The band of crickets had dissipated into the midst of the dusky wood. And an enormous alloy-silver moon was blotted out by the dimly lit clouds; each one bloated with millions of raindrops ready to pour across the earth.

Henry opened the front door of the cabin and flipped on the light. The perfumed fragrance that had originally hung in the air inside of the cabin ceased to exist, but instead was replaced by the fetid scent of rotting. Sprawled across the floor were three mutilated rabbits, each with their necks slit from ear to floppy ear. One of the rabbits hadn't been completely killed and Henry stood in the doorway paralyzed with shock as it wiggled disturbingly around the ground, suffering as it fought for the little bit of life that it had left . A trail of blood traveled from each of the rabbits, up the leg of the dining room table, and onto the letter that had been typed by who Henry could only assume was the spirit of Carol. Specific words had been highlighted in blood.

HENRY,

I WANT YOU TO BE NEAR ME AGAIN. I KNOW THAT YOU NEED ME TO BE THERE WITH YOU. WHY DID YOU HAVE TO LET ME DIEEE HENRY? I WAS SO SCARED THE NIGHT OF THE CRASH. DO YOU KNOW HOW

PAINFUL IT IS TO HAVE A CAR PINNING YOU TO THE EARTH WHILE YOUR BONES ARE CRUSHED TO DUST? WILL YOU COME BE WITH ME ONCE AGAIN, MY LOVE? WILL YOU LET YOUR BONES BE CRUSHED TOO?

HOLd MeEE.

I KNOW THAT YOU DID NOT KILL ME, BUT I WISH THAT YOU WOULD HAVE SaVeD ME. NOW I AM DEAD, SaVeD, dead...DEEEEAAD. I KNOW THAT IT'S NOT YOUR FAULT THOUGH AND BELIEVE ME WHEN I SAY THAT YOU WILL SEE ME AGAIN MY LOVE.

-C. C.

"You...need to die. I will...kill you. It's your fault my love?" Henry read the highlighted words out loud. He dropped the letter onto the floor and fell as his knees buckled beneath him. The brown rabbit that had been suffering within a pool of it's own gelatinous blood died as the paper elegantly touched the ground. Henry shot up from his adolescent position from which he had fallen, and ran to escape out of the front door.

It slammed shut before he could reach it.

The swollen clouds erupted, and a tirade of the sky's teardrops could be heard viciously pounding against the roof of the cabin. Henry grabbed at the doorknob and twisted as hard as his arms would allow, but it wouldn't budge. He lifted his head to a position where his eyes now locked onto an anomaly staring back at him from the opposite side of the door. It was a sight that he had wanted to see for so long, but one that now possessed him with the deepest, most hellacious fear that he had ever experienced.

It was Carol.

Her decayed, earwax green skin hung loosely from her bones. What Henry remembered as being bright, scarlet blood that poured from her neck the night of the crash was now a dull, cranberry color that stained her white blouse. With a faint flick of her wrist, the grotesque corpse rapped on the front door six times.

"Henry dear," Carol whispered through the door in a seductive tone. "I want to be near you again. Don't you miss me?" She coughed, spewing specks of blood from out of her mouth and against the window of the door. Carol lifted her bony index finger and rubbed the droplets in circles against the glass, obscuring Henry's vision of her.

"Carol, please," Henry mouthed as he started to cry. "Please, don't do this." As if not seeing him, Carol knocked on the door six more times; but these knocks were harder, hostile even. A lump formed in the back of Henry's throat. Thunder struck in the distance. Strikes of lightning momentarily lit up the sky.

"Henry!" Carol yelled. "Please, I'm so cold. Let me in. My neck is hurting. You'll save me this time, won't you? I think that I need to lie down."

"Just go away, Carol!" Henry yelled. "You're dead! You're dead." Over and over Henry repeated himself as he slammed his head against his forearm which was propped against the door.

Tick. Tick. Tick. Tick tick. Tick. Ding!

Henry raised his head and turned around. He was horrified to see the typewriter typing without anybody there to press on the keys. The disturbed author darted over to the typewriter while his undead wife continued hysterically banging on the door, wailing in tongues like a demon sent from the infernos of Hell.

"Let me in! Let me in now, Henry!" Carol followed her demands with a series of sentences spoken in a language he had never heard before. Then, she was back to English. "I'm so cold, and you need to warm me up. Just let me cook you dinner, the way that I used to. I can save you," she whispered, her face pressed hard against the front door. Chains of blood slid down the glass as more and more was being ejected from the deep gash in her neck.

Henry tore the paper from the typewriter and the keys continued clicking away. He adjusted his glasses with his shaking hands and wiped the tears from his eyes before looking down and reading the paper.

DIEEE WITH ME. DIEEE WITH ME. DIEEE WITH ME. DIEEE WITH ME. DIEEE WITH ME. DIEEE WITH ME. DIEEE WITH ME. DIEEE WITH ME. DIEEE WITH ME.

-C.C.

"I'm sorry!" Henry screamed as Carol continued pounding on it.

"Let me take care of you. Henry, it's me. Don't you love me anymore? Don't you recognize me?"

Henry fell to his knees and covered his head with his arms. The constant banging, the roar of the thunder, and the ticking of the typewriter were enough to drive him mad. Henry screamed at the top of his lungs hoping to drown out the rest of the noise with his own. As he hollered, a short vignette played in his mind. It starred his hunting rifle and the inside of his mouth. He was willing to do anything to make the noise stop.

"I'm so sorry." he whimpered. Henry stood up and turned around to grab his rifle off of the couch. "I have to send you back to where you came from." He picked it up and swung around, his gun gripped firmly in his hands, the butt pressed against his chest. The door remained stained with blood, but Carol was gone. The tapping of the typewriter keys stopped.

Henry ran over to the telephone. He lifted it off of the receiver and dialed 911, but the phone was unresponsive.

"Hello? Hello?! Anybody, please!" There was no answer. He ran up the stairs to the bedroom and started throwing all of the clothes that he had brought back into his suitcase. The rain was coming down harder now. The booms of thunder smashed frequently. As quickly as he could, Henry grabbed the last piece of clothing, threw it into the suitcase, and zipped it up. He spun around and standing in the doorway staring back at him was Carol; she had a lemon colored grin smeared across her rotted face. Her white blouse was soaked with blood. The few remaining strands of her brunette hair drenched from the downpour.

"Where are you going, my love?" Carol tilted her head to the side. More blood seeped out of her neck, dripping onto her already red stained clothes.

"I can't stay here with you, Carol." Henry said, his voice trembling. "You're dead."

"That's not something you say to somebody that you love! If I was dead, how could I be standing here?" Henry shook his head.

"I don't know."

"What did you say? I couldn't hear you. Speak up when you talk to me!" Carol slammed her head into the door with a force so intense that it left behind an indentation in the shape of her skull. "I'm sorry honey," she said with a laugh, "I didn't mean to scare you. Come. I hate when I lose my temper like that. Let's just go downstairs and I'll make you some dinner. How does that sound?"

Henry dropped his suitcase on the bed and reluctantly followed her downstairs. Perhaps he could convince her to let him leave. Or if only he could get his hands back on the rifle that he was stupid enough to not keep with him. He was prepared to use either fight or flight in order to survive.

"Sit." Carol pulled out a chair at the dining room table. Henry eyed the front door, but was too nervous to make a run for it. As instructed, he sat at the table. Carol walked over to the dead rabbits that laid motionless across the floor and picked all three of them up by the ears. She placed them on the kitchen counter and lined them up one next to the other.

"What are you doing?"

"Making dinner." Carol responded. "Don't worry, it will be ready soon."

Carol pulled out a sharp knife and began to dice the rabbits into large, chunky blocks. Henry could feel the inside of his stomach beginning to churn, and knew that if he watched her do it any longer he would vomit. She finished butchering the poor animals and licked the blood from off of her fingers. Lines of blood were smeared across her face.

"Mmm-mmm. So good." Carol walked over to her husband and bent over him. "You haven't even given me a kiss since you've seen me." She leaned over and flashed her golden-brown teeth before closing in on Henry to kiss him on the lips. Henry stood up with a sudden burst of energy and pushed Carol away. She lost her balance and fell back into the wall.

As fast as he could Henry ran over to the door and attempted to escape, but the door was still locked. He pulled and twisted the knob, but the door never budged. Then, with a hard swing, Carol bashed Henry across the back of his head with the edge of the typewriter.

He was unconscious before his body hit the ground.

Disoriented, Henry opened his eyes and could feel his brain pounding against his skull. He tried to move, but he couldn't. His arms and legs were tied around the chair that he was sitting on at the dining room table.

"You're awake!" Carol screamed as she brought over a plate and placed it in front of him. "I couldn't let you leave before dinner was ready. Now, how rude would that be? Tonight is the beginning of us being together forever. But, we can discuss that a little later. Eat up!" Henry looked down at the plate and wretched at the smell of the uncooked pieces of rabbit. Images of the dainty animal squirming in it's own blood flashed before his eyes.

"Carol, you can't be serious. Just let me go, please." Carol shook her head.

"You know that I can't do that. I've been watching how sad you've been without me, so now I'll never leave you again. Here, open wide." She took a fork and stabbed it into a piece of rabbit liver that had been marinating in a puddle of blood. Henry refused to open his mouth as the meat was raised close to his face. "Well we can't have you not eating dear. Going hungry will kill you, and then we can't be together. I found a way back, but there's no guaranteeing the same for you once you've died."

The sharp edge of a butcher knife had been stabbed into a wooden cutting board keeping it erect. It was the same knife that Carol had used to cut up the varmint. She yanked the blade from out of the wood and danced back over to Henry. "Will you eat?"

"I can't eat that." Henry replied. Carol's face grew twisted with frustration as she raised the knife high above her head with both hands before thrusting the edge of the blade into Henry's foot. A monstrous cry of pain echoed through the cabin. With his mouth still open, Carol took the fork and shoved the piece of bloody rabbit meat inside.

Gagging ensued as the tough piece of meat rolled around his tongue.

"Swallow it! Swallow it up!" Carol grabbed Henry's jaw tightly forcing it up and down until he swallowed the meat. The gagging became uncontrollable to the point that the meat was vomited back up. "Is my cooking really that bad?" Henry didn't reply. He was too afraid of further upsetting the zombified nightmare that was once the woman he loved. The flaring of pain within his head and foot were like nothing Henry had felt before.

"Eat more!" Carol stabbed the fork into another piece of rabbit and floated the meat towards Henry's mouth.

"Please, Carol," Henry sobbed. "Please, stop it. If you love me then stop this!"

Carol laughed.

"You've grown to be one silly old man." she responded. "I'm doing this *because* I love you. You know that. Don't play dumb with me." The second piece of meat was forced into Henry's mouth. Again, he swallowed, but this time he was able to keep it down. "How much of that night do you remember? The night of the accident?" Carol forced the fork into another piece of meat, this time feeding it to herself.

"Everything." Henry responded. "I remember everything!" Tears and mucus were caked amidst his peppered beard. "A deer ran out in front of the car and I tried to save us. Then the car flipped. I remember it felt like time had stopped. I blacked out and remember waking up and seeing you in the seat next to me. There was so much blood and you weren't breathing."

"I want to relive that moment with you. It's the final moment that we were able to spend together. The romanticism behind it would be to die for." Henry raised his head and looked deep into Carol's black eyes. They were no different than those of the deer that hung on the wall behind him. It was a stare that had become all too familiar to him over the past few dozen hours.

"Come, come." Carol ripped the knife out of Henry's foot and placed it on the table. Henry projected another painful holler. Drops of blood slid off of the sharpened silver. The rope binding Henry's arms and legs was loosened.

Carol grabbed the car keys off of the kitchen counter and opened the front door with ease. "Let's go for a drive."

Henry stood up and winced every time he had to put pressure onto his left foot. Hobbling, he exited the cabin and trudged outside into the mud and rain. "I'll drive this time." Carol insisted. She swung the key ring playfully around her finger while marching toward the car. Meanwhile, Henry's mind was focused on how to escape. He needed to get away from her, but how could he? With the condition his foot was in he could barely walk.

Henry opened the passenger door and sat down. He grabbed for the seat belt and Carol slapped his hand down while giving him a firm stare.

"There will be no seat belts," Carol said, pointing at the polyester material. Afraid of getting stabbed again, Henry listened without argument. He hoped that she would just drive into town like everything was normal. Somebody would have to notice that something was wrong. Then, he could escape with his life barely intact. That is, if he could go long enough without angering or provoking her further.

Carol put the key into the ignition and awoke the sleeping engine. While whistling an off-pitch melody, she pulled out into the narrow dirt lane. Besides the steady pitter-patter of rain that slapped against the outside of the car, there was only silence. After a few minutes, the car came to a stop.

"What are we doing?" Henry asked, as politely as he could bring himself to do.

"What we're doing is going to be together forever! That way you will never be sad again. Our bones will be crushed to dust and will become one with the earth." Carol shoved her foot onto the gas pedal and sent the car flying forward. The forward momentum sent Henry flying back in his seat.

"Carol, stop! You need to slow down!" Henry pleaded, but his pleas were left unanswered. "The road ends Carol, you'll take us right over a cliff. Stop! You'll kill us if you keep driving at this speed!" Carol rolled down the window, released the steering wheel, and spread her arms out like a bird prepared to take flight. She looked over at Henry and smiled that sinister, crooked smile that he had grown to despise through the nights hours. At that moment, a flash of lightning illuminated the car. He could see her blood stained teeth and the gash across her neck that she received on that horrible day not so long ago. Seconds later, the car was sent flying over a seventy foot cliff, and into a large body of water.

The car sank deep into the icy water of the river and remained there for the next thirty-six years until it was discovered by a local scuba diver in June of 1989. Upon recovering the car, only one body was found inside. Forensics research identified the person as one Henry Climer, a well known American author who mysteriously vanished almost four decades prior.

Many years before the discovery of Henry's body was the discovery of his woodland cabin. It had been found trashed and littered with empty beer cans weeks after Henry's disappearance. A family of raccoons had moved in, feasting off of the raw meat that was left sitting out. Soon after, The cabin was demolished as a result of all the blood that had soaked into and warped the wooden floorboards. No efforts of scrubbing and bleaching could remove the stains and smell of rotting flesh that lived inside.

However, the remains of Carol Climer, the wife that returned from the dead with an unnatural desire to tend to the needs of her mentally defeated husband, were never found. No jewelry. No clothing.

Nothing.

Had she been real? Or were the events of that night simply figments of a psychotic drunk's imagination that lead to his untimely demise? The answer to these questions will forever linger in the farthest depths of madness, in a place where only the most unfortunate souls find themselves trapped.

May this be a friendly reminder to all...Be careful what you wish for.

Whistle By The Water

It was entering into the latter days of a
sweltering hot summer. A stroke of blood orange
spilled across the evening sky to the east while dark
gray clouds rolled in from the west. A pair of
brothers frolicked through a field of corn in a game
of hide-and-seek. Beads of sweat dripped from both
boy's foreheads and roosted atop their bronze
eyebrows. Thick globs of mud stuck to the bottom
of their worn brown boots making their calf muscles
burn beneath their matching blue jean corduroys.
They had been at it for hours. Chasing each other
through the labyrinth of weeds and maize, jumping
out at each other hoping to elicit a frightened
reaction whenever one could sneak up behind the
other without them knowing.

The fields smelled of ripened corn, soil,
grass, and pesticide. A concoction of sickening
sulfur, peppermint, and earth. It was an odor that
one had to learn to love. And for the two boys, it
was a smell that they had been living with for their
entire lives. A smell that brought comfort to those

who resided there but would cause your average city slicker to pinch his nostrils between his fingers.

Growing up on a farm in rural Indiana during the mid-1980s was an amazing experience for the Perkins family. One that they wouldn't trade for a million dollars. There was peace and quiet. Crops were growing well. The cows and chickens were producing an abundance of eggs and milk.

Theresa Perkins, the matriarch of the family was entering the second trimester of her pregnancy and was elated to have recently discovered that she was having a baby girl. Hunter Perkins, the patriarch, was out deep in a nearby wood with his hunting rifle clasped tightly within his calloused hands, searching for a doe or buck to shoot and return home with so that he could turn the meat into a salty pot of venison jerky. Just the thought was enough to make the man's mouth salivate.

Then, there were the two sons. The Perkins boys as they were known in the nearby town of Mongo. The eldest of the two boys was Jake. He was nine years old and had the energy of a kitten hooked on catnip. When he wasn't sleeping he was either running, jumping, playing, rolling, lifting, talking, and/or any other -*ing* verb that could come to mind. He had a full head of shaggy dirty blonde hair that was more often than not matted to his scalp with mud and sweat after a long day of play. His eyes were dark blue and constantly in motion. Jake's right lateral incisor was missing leaving an empty black rectangle between his front teeth when he smiled. His skin was a mix of peach and sun-kissed orange. His picture could be found next to the clinical diagnosis definition of Attention Deficit Hyperactive Disorder.

The younger brother was Theodore. He was seven years old and was everything that his older brother was not. A soft-spoken youth who enjoyed quietly playing with the farm animals and reading books. A pair of thick round glasses always dancing along the bridge of his nose. His hair was buzzed short and clean. The slightest bit of dirt beneath his fingernails was enough to make Theo sprint inside and hop into a cold shower. The only commonality between the two brothers was the sunburnt skin peeling from off of their shoulders.

"Got you!" Jake jumped forward, quickly turning around with his palms pressed against his chest, his heart beating rapidly. Theodore pushed his glasses up his nose with the tip of his index finger and smiled. It was the first time all day that he had gotten the best of his older brother. Jake was much more athletic than Theo and it was rare that the younger sibling ever won at anything. So when he did, there was a great sense of pride that came with the victory.

"You scared the crap out of me, Theo!" Jake scolded. Theodore laughed and shoved his hands into the pockets of his overalls.

"Good, I was trying to!" Jake gave his little brother a scolding scowl. It was embarrassing to lose to someone like Theo, but somewhere deep down Jake was proud of his little brother.

A flash of white split through the approaching clouds, soon after followed by the crashing roar of rolling thunder. The wind was gaining momentum; a storm was on the horizon.

"Looks like rain," Jake said out loud, more to himself than to Theo. Both boys looked up into the darkening sky.

"Yeah," Theo agreed. "We should go home. Ma will be really mad if we get soaking wet." Jake nodded his head. The two boys turned around and began walking in the direction of their house. Another swift gust of wind sped past making the stalks of corn dance to a silent song.

"Help…" Jake and Theo stopped dead in their tracks and looked at each other. Another flash of lightning within the clouds gave birth to a barrage of thunderclaps, these much louder than the last. Theo cupped his hands over his ears in anticipation of another wave of booming thunder.

"Did you hear that?" Jake asked. Theo dropped his hands and nodded his head causing his glasses to slip down to the edge of his nose. The two boys listened intently.

"Help me...Please." It was a young girl's voice, faint and distressed. The sound rode effortlessly atop the winds of the impending storm.

"It sounded like it came from over by the lake. We should go check it out."

"But we're going to get in trouble," Theo whined, reminding his older sibling of the wrath that their mother was capable of with nothing more than a single look. "The rain is getting closer."

"Yeah, but it sounds like someone needs help. What if they're drowning?" Theo dropped his head. He hated making his parents mad. It scared him whenever his mother or father raised their voices at him. Jake on the other hand had grown used to breaking the rules. Most anything that came out of his parent's mouths were in one ear and out the other. "Just go back without me. Tell ma I'll be home soon." Jake turned his back to Theo and barely took a step before a tug on his wrist prevented him from moving.

"What if I get lost? It's starting to get dark." Jake yanked his wrist from out of Theo's grasp; a pink ring the size of tiny fingers glowed against his skin.

"Either come with me or go!" Jake yelled in frustration. Theo's eyes dropped to his mud covered shoes. The smell of the air was changing. There was a mustiness to it now.

"Please, help me. Hurry!" It was the girl's voice again, not quite as loud as before. Mixed within the words was an unusual whistling undertone.

"I'm going, so make your choice quick." Jake darted off through the corn. Almost immediately, Theo decided to tag along behind him. Leaves from the stalks slapped against the boys tanned skin as they raced through the field. Theo struggled to keep up with his older brother. His legs were much shorter and he wasn't as athletic. It didn't take long for him to fall behind. His throat burned and his lungs were spent. Theo followed the sound of crunching footsteps for as long as he could, but suddenly, he was alone.

"Jake!" Theo cried out. His heart was racing within his chest and tears were starting to well up in his eyes. "Jake, where are you?" Theo turned in a complete circle. Panic was settling in as he realized that every direction looked exactly the same. Corn, corn, and more corn. The thick stalks towered over him, dancing back and forth to the melody of the storm. He hated how they creepily swayed on their own.

Theo cupped his hands over his mouth and repeatedly cried out for his brother, but there was no response. The sky was now a bleak gray; tiny water droplets tapped against the boy's shoulder. *Great, Theo thought to himself. Now I'm lost, and I'm going to be in trouble for being wet when I get home...If I get home.*

That last thought scared him.

Theo thought about what it would be like to die out in the corn field. He wondered if it would be painful when the creepy crawlies ate away at his eyes and slithered up his nose and down his throat to live in his tummy. "JAAAAKE!" He yelled as loud as his lungs would allow. His legs started to move on their own and all of a sudden he was running again. *Forward. I'll just go forward.* "JAAAAKE!" he yelled once more.

"Hey! Can you hear me?" It was Jake's voice, and not too far away! "Little girl, are you okay? If you hear me, say something so that I can find you." Theo ran toward the sound of his brother's voice until finally he emerged from the maze of corn where he appeared on the edge of an oblong shaped lake. Jake was standing out in the water, his lower half completely submerged. The water had an unappealing olive green tint.

"Did you find her?" Theo asked. Jake shook his head, continuing to survey the lake. The rain was falling harder now. The tiny aquatic daggers that fell from the sky had evolved into liquid spears. The drops were longer, heavier, and sometimes even painful as they crashed into the boys' skin.

"Over there!" Jake yelled, pointing off to his right. Twenty meters away were a stream of air bubbles rising from the depths to the water's surface. The rain was pounding against the lake creating millions of ripples across the water.

"Where?" Theo asked. The younger sibling moved closer to the water but his brother was already submerged from the neck down as he pumped his arms, left, then right, then left again, swimming toward what he assumed to be a drowning child. Too afraid to go in, Theo stayed on land. His eyes widened as he watched Jake dive into the lake and disappear.

Another bolt of lightning cut through the sky; a crash of thunder followed shortly after. Theo waited and waited for what felt like an eternity for his brother to reemerge. He counted slowly in his head but lost his count when a loud wave of thunder startled him. The clothes Theo wore stuck to his skin like glue. His eyes burned from the torrential rain.

"Jake, are you okay?!" Theo's words were muffled by the storm. The bubbles that had been rising to the water's surface had stopped. At least a minute had passed since Jake had gone under, maybe more, Theo wasn't completely sure. He had never been good at estimating time.

His heart was pounding inside his chest; a strange ringing noise flooded his ears. Theo had almost given up hope until Jake's head burst through the water, gasping for breath.

Theo wanted to scream and cheer as he watched his older brother make his way back to land, but he noticed that Jake was alone. His eyes drooped and his skin was wrinkled from the water.

"Did you find her?" Theo asked as Jake walked past him.

"No," was his only response the rest of the way home.

The front door flew open as the two boys marched into the house. Their clothes dripped water onto the hardwood floor leaving behind a trail of tiny puddles. It didn't take long for their mother to come waltzing into the foyer from around the corner, her face dressed with a devilish scowl.

"Where have you two been?" Theresa scolded. "Both of you are soaked and you're dripping water all over my floors! Get to your room and out of those clothes, NOW!" The volume of his mother's voice caused Theo to jump, but Jake's expression never changed. His eyes still drooped, his posture riddled with exhaustion. Theo lowered his head and briskly walked past his mother. Jake followed behind.

"Told you we'd get in trouble." Theo said in frustration while stripping off his clothes. He took his soiled corduroys and shirt and threw them into a corner of the room. A squishy *plop* sounded as they hit the floor. "Jake? Are you okay?"

The elder brother had his right arm outstretched in front of him and was slowly wiggling each finger one at a time. The index, then the middle, followed by the ring, the pinky, and lastly the thumb before starting the cycle over again. His head was cocked at an awkward angle and his eyes were glazed over with a hazy film. The bedroom door flung open and Jake's arm immediately fell to his side.

"Seriously, Jake?" Theresa questioned. "I'm not playing these games with you. Get your wet clothes off so that I can get them ready to hang out on the clothesline. And Theo, pick your clothes up off the floor and hand them to me, that's not where they belong." Theo dashed over to the corner and collected his clothes. "Thank you. Now go take a shower. Jake, you better be ready to get in by the time Theo is finished."

While the water from the showerhead rained over him, Theo couldn't understand the reasoning behind taking a shower when he had just finished being wet from outside. He then thought about the girl's voice that hummed through the cornfield begging for somebody to help her. *I hope that she's okay,* he thought.

The towel was rough against Theo's skin as he dried off. Pieces of peeling flesh stuck to the fabric and fell to the floor. He stuck his legs into his Batman and Robin comic book themed undies and stepped out of the bathroom and headed for the bedroom. As Theo pushed open the door, he was met with a naked Jake kneeling in the middle of the room. His head was bent toward the ceiling; eyes rolled into the back of his head with only the whites showing. Within his hands was the wet T-shirt he had been wearing. Droplets of water fell from out of the shirt and down the boy's throat as he squeezed and twisted the cotton. An eerie croaking echoed from out of Jake's mouth.

Jake dropped the shirt onto the floor. His eyes rolled back into the front of his head. Then, like a bat out of Hell, he took off past Theo and out of the bedroom running on all fours. Jake raced down the hallway and into the bathroom where he slammed the door shut and locked it. Theo was left behind in the room quivering in fear. *What's wrong with my brother?* The young boy wondered.

Theo put on a shirt and a pair of shorts as quickly as he could. He wanted to be out of the bedroom by the time that Jake returned. The boy knew that something was wrong with his older brother and after taking some time to think, came to realize that Jake had been acting strangely ever since resurfacing from out of the lake. He was used to Jake being bossy and demanding, but he had barely said a word since entering the water.

The creaking of the wooden floor beneath his feet sent shivers down Theo's spine. With every sound of splitting wood beneath him, Theo expected Jake to come running out of the bathroom. The thought of seeing his brother with his eyes flipped inside of his skull, crawling around like some human arachnid was enough to have his tiny heart beating like a drum inside of his chest.

Tiptoeing past the bathroom door, Theo could hear two things: running water from the shower, and whistling. It was a tuneless melody. Theo had never heard Jake whistle before, yet he was switching between high and low pitches like someone who did it for a living. As fast as he could, Theo scampered down the steps and into the kitchen where he wrapped his arms tightly around his mother's waist.

"My goodness!" Theresa exclaimed as she pried her child's arms from off of her. "What's wrong?" Theo stared up at his mother with tears in his eyes.

"Something's wrong with Jake." Theresa scrunched her face in confusion.

"What do you mean? I just saw him. He *is* taking a shower isn't he?"

"Yes, I think so. But, he's...Different." Theo responded to his mother after a slight pause. The boy didn't know the words to describe what he had seen. He was certain that there were some grown-up words that would do his strange encounter with Jake justice, but he either couldn't think of them, or did not yet know them.

"I'm sure he's fine, Theodore. He's probably just trying to scare you. You know how Jake is. Now, can you start setting the table? Dinner will be ready soon."

"Yes ma'am." There was resistance in his response. Theo dropped his head and went out into the dining room. Four plates and a collection of silverware sat in the center of the dining room table. Before Theo was able to set even half the table, the front door swung open and in came his father. Hunter's dirty blonde hair was stuck to his forehead; a sticky mixture of rain and sweat. His clothes were drenched, covered in grass and earth. However, the man was smart enough to leave his dirty boots outside, lest he face the wrath of his wife for muddying her floors.

"I was starting to get worried." Theresa stepped out of the kitchen and provided her husband with a flurry of pecks on the lips. "Did you get anything?"

"Got a buck." Hunter answered. "Have it out in the barn. I'll get to it later. Damn things are heavy. It's the reason I'm getting back so late. Got caught out in the storm and all that."

"I see. Well, why don't you get dried off and out of those clothes. Dinner will be ready in about five minutes. Theo's setting the table as we speak."

"Sounds good to me." Hunter replied as he started up the stairs. "Smells good too!" The sound of his father's voice provided Theo with a sense of security. Whatever Jake was up to, Theo knew that his father would put a stop to it.

Dinner was roast beef with mashed potatoes and roasted carrots as sides. The family of four sat around the dining room table, silverware clinking against their plates as they silently ate their dinner. The rain had come to a stop leaving behind a blanket of mist to hover over the property. The moon cut through the night sky like an ivory scythe.

"Mommy," Jake said, breaking the silence. "Come to the lake with me."

"It's late sweetheart, not tonight anymore. Maybe tomorrow."

"Come to the lake with me mommy, please? It won't take long. We can be quick." Theo stared at his brother. There was life in Jake's smile, but death in his eyes. "It will be quick." Jake reiterated one more time. One of Jake's eyes quickly shifted toward Theo while the other stayed locked on their mother. It was only for a split second, but that was plenty long enough for Theo to notice.

"Just go with him hun," Hunter said before piling a forkful of food into his mouth. "The rain seems to have stopped for the evening. It'll do you good to get out a little."

"Don't go, mommy!" Theo blurted out. "Just stay home. It's late."

"Shut your mouth!"

"Jake!" Both parents scolded in unison. "That's not how you speak to your brother. We'll finish eating, and then we can go. Speak to your brother like that again though and the deal's off. Understood?" Jake never answered his mother. Instead, he smiled at his little brother with a devilish grin.

That's not my brother. Theo thought to himself. But how could he make his parent's realize it too?

"Theo, you can help me in the barn while your mother and brother head to the lake." Theo wanted to object, but knew better than to disobey his father. Through observing his brother, he knew that most disputes with father ended with a rear end being introduced to the wooden paddle.

"Yes sir," the boy answered humbly.

There was an empty pit left behind in Theo's stomach as he watched his mother and brother walk hand-in-hand into the darkness toward the lake. He was scared for her, but what could he do?

"Come Theo, you can help me with the buck." Theo sighed as he followed behind his father to the barn. He wasn't like his brother. He didn't like dirt and he especially didn't like blood. It smelled like old pennies.

The heavy barn doors creaked open as the father and son stepped inside. Hunter held an oil lamp in his hand that burned bright, casting twisted shadows that danced across the walls. The lamp was placed on a workbench revealing the carcass of the buck; it's tongue hanging out the side of its mouth, a bloody bullet hole a few inches below the neck. Theo winced upon seeing the dead animal.

"There should be a hunting knife over on the table in the corner. Go and grab it for me, will ya?" Theo nodded his head and was more than happy to turn his head away from the dead creature. He moved slowly through the dark barn with his hands outstretched before him. Crickets chirped loudly along the fringes of the barn, hidden away in the black of the night.

It wasn't long before Theo bumped into the table and found what he was searching for. The knife felt heavy in his tiny hands, nearly a sword to a child his size. The blade which had once been a bright silver was bloodstained giving it a copper undertone.

"Thank you, son." Hunter said as Theo handed him the knife.

The squishy sound of steel piercing through flesh was enough to make a lump form in Theo's throat. Blood rushed over the knife, over Hunter's hands, and poured across the workbench and onto the ground. The laborious cutting gave birth to deep grunts from Theo's father. While he worked, his father appeared more beast than man.

"Dad?"

"What is it?" Hunter answered, pulling a thick sheet of flesh back revealing the animal's slimy pink innards.

"I don't think that Jake is himself, and I think that he wants to hurt mommy." Hunter laughed as he sliced away at more flesh. "I'm serious! He went into the lake earlier. We heard someone crying for help, and Jake went into the water to see if he could help them, and when he came out he seemed…Different. It's not him! I know it."

"Relax, Theodore. Nothing is wrong with Jake, and he isn't going to hurt your mother. You know that he likes to try and scare you. He's probably just pulling one of his pranks. That boy never learns to grow up."

"Well can we at least go check on them? Just to be sure?"

"No," Hunter replied. "I don't want this meat to spoil. They're fine." Theo wanted to panic. He wanted to kick and scream and throw a tantrum until his father was left with no choice but to listen. He was frustrated and didn't know what to do. Meanwhile, the crickets seemed to be growing louder, almost as if in response to something. *They're warning each other*, Theo thought. *They know something is wrong too.*

"There you are." The voice belonged to Theo's mother. Theresa and Jake stood in the doorway to the barn, the dark of the night revealing only their silhouettes. Hunter dropped his knife, wiped the blood off of his hands on a nearby rag, and picked up the oil lamp.

"Why are you both soaking wet?" Hunter questioned. "It's not raining anymore." Theresa and Jake's clothes were dripping onto the ground, their hair sticking to their prunish skin. And that scary smile that sent electric vibrations along Theo's spine…They both wore it now. Mother and son.

"Come with us to the lake." Theresa instructed. "It will be quick."

"Promise you'll come." Jake interjected.

"No," Theo mouthed quietly, aware that whatever had gotten hold of his brother earlier had now gotten his mother as well. Theresa and Jake stepped forward entering into the light cast off by the lamp. Their skin hung off their bones like cheap Halloween costumes. Their teeth were jagged and their eyes were a faded yellow where before they were white. Patches of Theresa's hair were ripped out revealing pale sections of skin across her skull.

"Honey, what's happened to you?" Hunter's eyes darted back and forth between his wife and son. His voice squeaked as he asked the question. There was a vulnerability in his voice, something that was foreign to Theo.

"Let us show you something. It's just out in the water. It will be so quick." The mother and son continued to slowly move forward, their features growing more horrific the closer they got. A trifecta of bloody scratches reached from Theresa's left cheek down to her throat. Jake's upper lip had been busted open in the middle giving it a cleft palate look.

Hunter dropped down on one knee and patted his hand across the ground beneath the workbench, feeling around for the rifle he had used to score a kill earlier in the day with. He refused to take his eyes off of his wife and eldest son which were nearing ever closer with each passing moment. After a few seconds, the palm of Hunter's hand came in contact with the butt of the rifle.

"Stop moving!" Hunter yelled, standing up with the rifle propped up awkwardly in his left hand, the oil lamp still dangling from his right. Theresa and Jake obeyed the order. They couldn't have been more than twenty feet away. Theo, meanwhile, was standing off to the right of his father, frozen in fear.

"Honey, please." Theresa pleaded, her arms opening for Hunter to step forward into her embrace. "The water has made me whole. Come with us, it doesn't take long."

Theresa took a subtle step forward but was met with the bang of a firing rifle. The bullet whizzed past her shoulder and through the wooden barn. Theo screamed, falling backward onto his bony rear. Jake positioned himself on all fours before rushing toward his father and jumping onto his chest. Another shot echoed through the barn and out into the night, but once again, was successful in only chipping away at more of the wooden structure surrounding them.

Theo watched on in horror as his brother beat down on their fathers face with his fists; an eerie gold illuminating the scene from the flame inside the lamp which was now laying horizontally across the ground. Hunter tried fighting off his son but was overpowered by the boy's otherworldly strength. The two tussled on the ground for what felt like an eternity. Theresa cheered her son on with guttural croaks and squeaky whistles that she fluidly altered between. On and on they fought with one another until a familiar sound sent shivers down Theo's spine; it was the sound of steel piercing flesh.

Hunter roared in pain as Theresa ripped the hunting knife out of his shoulder before plunging it back into his chest over and over again. The piercing sound exploded in Theo's ears with each plunge.

"Mommy, stop it!" Theo yelled, translucent streams pouring from his eyes. "Please, stop hurting daddy!" A burst of adrenaline rushed through the boy as he got to his feet and ran at his mother before hearing a loud *whack* ring through the air. The sound processed before the pain. It took a few moments before Theo realized that he was back on the ground and his vision was blurred. Jake stood over his younger sibling, the palm of his hand beet red from whipping it across his brother's face. Shards of glass littered the ground from the shattered lens of Theo's spectacles which had been sent flying into the dark unknown.

Again. And again. And again. Theresa drove the blade into her husband's chest. He had stopped moving more than a dozen seconds prior, yet the steel and blood continued to soar. Theo crawled along the floor searching for his glasses, the sound of the stabbing knife piercing his ears.

"Bring them to the water." Theo couldn't see, but he knew his mother's voice. Jake grabbed his brother by the collar of his shirt and pulled him off the ground with Herculean strength. Theresa withdrew herself from over her husband's body which had the same amount of life left in it as the buck that laid across the workbench; it's skin flipped open like a pair of pink, wet wings.

Theresa bent over and picked the oil lamp off of the ground. She swung the lamp around while whistling a tuneless melody and pirouetting through the barn; an orange glow leaping from wall to wall. Then, with a flick of her wrist, she sent the lamp flying into the barn wall causing an eruption of flames to begin eating away at the wood and straw that covered the ground.

Theo could feel the heat from the flames as Jake yanked him back by his shirt. A pair of cold, clammy fingers wrapped around Theo's neck. He couldn't help but sob as the distorted image of his older brother looked nothing like what he remembered. The crackling fire consuming the barn was spreading rapidly. Everything in the barn that had been hidden away in darkness seconds earlier was now revealed in the reds, yellows, and oranges of the flames.

"Bring him to the water. Quickly now! Our family's been trapped beneath the surface for long enough."

"Yes, father." Jake replied.

"What do you mean, father?" Theo managed to say between breaths. "Our father is being dragged across the ground right now! Jake, please stop this. You're scaring me." Jake had no response for his younger sibling. He simply led his brother out of the burning barn with his hand around the back of his neck. Theresa dragged Hunter's body by his legs out of the barn as well.

A transparent silver mist covered the ground while another rose into the sky from off of the burning barn. The sun had set hours ago and the temperature had plummeted into the mid-forties. The euphoric scent of honey and green plants helped ease Theo's mind as he marched past the cornfield and toward the still water. It was hard to believe that it was only a few hours ago that he and his brother were chasing each other through the tall, leafy stalks.

The water was silent, yet alive. A trail of blood from Hunter's body being dragged across God's creation led all the way back to the barn. Theo started crying hysterically as Jake pushed the heel of his foot into the back of his knee causing him to drop down into the water which came up a few inches above his waist. It felt ice cold.

"We'll be back for him." Theresa said as she pulled the dead body out into the water. "Don't let him move. His skin will feel nice."

"I won't, father." Jake replied. Theresa pulled the body into the water until they were out far enough to submerge. Theo could barely see without his glasses. His eyes were nearly swollen shut from crying. He could hear the water ripple as his mother and father disappeared beneath the lake's surface. The smell of smoke lingered in the air; the sound of insects rode atop the water.

"Let me go, Jake." Theo begged. "Please, Jake, I don't want to go in the water. I'm so scared. Please, don't make me go in. I don't want to go in there!" Theo's words were barely that as he struggled to speak through the crying. Tears fell down his face mixing with sticky snot and slobber.

"He's ready." Jake announced. Theo dissected his brother's response before realizing that the words weren't spoken to him, but to the two figures standing out in the water. The shapes of the bodies looked familiar. Theresa and Hunter. *Mother and father.*

"This skin can't be permanent, but it will do until we can lure in some others." The voice belonged to Hunter. "We are only a few of many. We have lived beneath the water for long enough, and we will use these bodies to blend in until there are more of us on the surface then there are of you. Now, come child. Allow us to switch places. Succumb to the revolution and be a vessel that will help bring an end to humanity. For *we* are the future of this planet."

Theo never had an opportunity to speak. The creature living in Jake's skin forced Theo into the lake; a mouthful of muddy water rushed down the boy's trachea. Theo coughed which opened up the opportunity for more water to go flooding into his mouth and into his lungs. At first there were only two arms holding Theo beneath the surface, then came three, four, five, and six as he was pulled out toward the center of the lake.

A scaly, yellow eyed, green-skinned creature floated around Theo until his body stopped moving. A supernatural tranquility fell over the property. The maize stood still as statues. The barn blazed bright in the night. The singing crickets had all gone mute. And out of the water came four bodies. A mother, a father, and their two sons.

The family followed the bloody trail all the way back to the farmhouse with their skin hanging off their bones like wet laundry hangs off a clothesline. Together, they whistled, each performing their own tune. The crickets didn't dare join in.

Upon entering the home, they closed the door, locked it, and drew the blinds to all the windows. Then, for the rest of the night, the creatures scurried along the walls and ceilings on all fours croaking and hissing and whistling in the dark. And at the break of dawn, they would find more vessels, and lure them into the water with a cry for help and a simple whistle.

Sanatorium of Souls

"Sony ZV-1. Panasonic GH5 Mark II. Olympus OM-D Mark III." Mateo slowly walked down one of Best Buy's electronic aisles, reading off the names of different cameras to himself. "Sony A6400. Eight-hundred eighty-three dollars. Yikes."

It was Mateo's fourth lap around the electronics department circuit and by this point, all of the names and prices were starting to meld together. Each camera had become nothing more than a random assortment of letters and numbers jumbled into one. Mateo didn't have the slightest clue what the difference was between a Sony ZV-1 and a Sony A6400 other than one of them cost one-thousand dollars and the other a little less than nine hundred. A similarity though was that either option would take a pretty chunk out of his wallet.

This is an investment, he kept telling himself. *The better the quality of the camera, the more people that will want to watch your videos, which means the more money you will make. This is an investment.*

Mateo lifted the Sony A6400 as far as the cord attached to the back of the camera would allow and rotated it around in his hand. It felt light and comfortable as he held it. Below the price were the words **REASONS TO BUY** and below that were three bullet points:

- Superb autofocus
- Bright viewfinder
- Great video features

Mateo set the model back down and glanced over the row of cameras that neighbored the Sony A6400. "Decision, decisions," he muttered to himself whilst tapping his foot rhythmically against the store's blue carpet. Each of the cameras was black. Each of them had a touch screen and each was capable of recording video in 4k. Before walking into the store, Mateo figured that choosing his newest vlog camera would be as easy as comparing apples and oranges but he was now realizing that it was more like comparing peaches and nectarines without getting a chance to taste them.

"Can I help you with anything?" The voice came as a surprise to Mateo as he nearly jumped out of his skin. He had been so enthralled in the cameras before him that he nearly forgot that he wasn't the only person inside of the store. When turning around, Mateo was greeted by a curly-haired boy in his late teens with a pencil-thin mustache and a patch of scraggly hairs at the base of his chin. The blue polo-wearing employee couldn't have been much younger than himself.

"Yeah, actually that would be great." Mateo's voice shook as he was still composing himself after the sudden shock from the employee. "So, I'm a Youtuber, and I'm looking for a really good vlog camera. Something lightweight, but with great picture quality and good battery life." The Best Buy employee nodded his head and walked up beside Mateo. Pinned to the right side of his chest was a nametag that read **KAYDEN**.

"Going off of everything that you just told me, you're standing next to some pretty good options. I saw you looking at this Sony model right here and I can say without a doubt that this is a solid option for vlogging. When you picked it up, did you like the weight?"

Mateo couldn't remember. He was looking for something lightweight but had been so overwhelmed by all of the other bullet points that he completely forgot to take notice of how it felt while he was holding it. He lifted the Sony A6400 once again and this time focused solely on how it felt in his hands.

"I do like it," Mateo confirmed. "It feels good."

"The battery life is probably going to last ninety to about one-hundred twenty minutes give or take. Also," using his hand, Kayden captured Mateo's attention and lured it back down to the **REASONS TO BUY** listings, "it captures video in 4k which is what it sounds like you're looking for." Mateo nodded his head. "Are you thinking of getting it or do you want to look at some other options?" Mateo looked down at the camera for a few seconds, deep in thought before answering.

"I'll go with this one. I like it."

"Great!" Kayden responded. "If you'll just follow me this way I'll grab a model for you out of the back and ring you up over at the front register."

"Awesome, thanks." Mateo followed behind the lanky teen up to the front counter before watching him disappear into a back room. The shuffling and moving of cardboard boxes echoed from within. Meanwhile, a mother and a young child, no older than eight, were arguing in the distance about why she wasn't going to buy the boy a pair of three-hundred dollar sunglasses that connected to Bluetooth and played music as you wore them. The whines and cries of the boy were ear piercing and Mateo wanted nothing more than for the kid to come back with his camera so that he could get out of the store and make it back home.

He had a live stream to prepare for.

"Alright, finally got it. Sorry about the wait." Kayden apologized as he set the box down onto the counter and scanned the barcode with the handheld scanner. A series of black numbers that were preceded with a dollar sign appeared on the pin pad. Even though Mateo was making some pretty decent money off of Youtube, it didn't nullify the sting of seeing a number greater than one thousand appear before having to insert his debit card into the always hungry card reader.

"If you have a chip in your card you can go ahead and insert it," Kayden instructed. Mateo did as he was told and stared down at the **DO NOT REMOVE CARD** warning that appeared after doing so. "So what's the name?"

"The name?" Mateo questioned.

"Sorry, of your Youtube channel. You said that you were a Youtuber."

"Oh, right. Tales of the Dead. I do a bunch of paranormal stuff and the channel just hit one million subs yesterday."

"Wow, seriously? That's insane! Congrats man, I'm going to have to check you out. Oh and you can enter your card pin whenever you're ready." Mateo looked down and the card reader was staring back at him. Those four underscore lines patiently waiting to be filled in so that they could rip the money away from him.

"Actually to celebrate the milestone, I'm doing a live stream on my channel tonight with a buddy of mine. We're going to be spending the night at the abandoned Wakefall Sanatorium so if you're into scary stuff and you have the time, stop by in the chat." The words **PLEASE REMOVE CARD** appeared on the card reader. Mateo pulled out his Wells Fargo debit card and tucked it back into the front pocket of his black leather Alpine Swiss wallet.

"Most definitely!" Kayden confirmed. "Alright, you're all set. Take it easy and be safe out there tonight."

"Thanks. And no, worries. Everything will be just fine." Mateo grabbed the bagged camera from off of the counter and exited through the automatic sliding doors of Best Buy's front entrance. There was an early autumn breeze that brushed against him as he stepped outside and walked toward the parking lot. The sun was still at a high point in the sky, but would be gone after giving birth to the moon and its stars in a few hours. Then, the night that he had been planning for in anticipation of one million subscribers for the past week could finally come to fruition.

As Mateo stepped through the front door of his apartment he was immediately rushed and greeted by his black labrador Yennefer, named after the sorceress from *The Witcher* book series. "Hey, baby girl!" Mateo greeted as he leaned down allowing the dog to enthusiastically slobber all over his face. "Did you miss me?" His question was answered by another series of sloppy, wet dog kisses. "Ohhhh, I missed you too!" Mateo scratched between Yennefer's ears for a few seconds until the dog felt that the greeting had lasted long enough and walked away.

It was hard for Mateo to think of a much better feeling than opening a brand new piece of electronics. He carried the bag with the camera to his room, his stomach filled with the butterflies fluttering around in the pit of your stomach on Christmas morning feeling. Within seconds, the plastic was ripped off, the tabs of the box strategically opened, and the camera removed and placed on the desk. Mateo pulled the black charging cable from the box and immediately plugged the thin end into the camera and the blocky end into the wall outlet. The camera needed to have as much of a charge as possible.

While waiting to play around with his new toy, Mateo left his room and entered the kitchen. The excitement of the night to come left no part of Mateo interested in cooking a lavish meal for himself, so instead, he settled for the quicker option of Totino's pizza rolls. He dumped somewhere between ten to fifteen rolls onto a baking pan and preheated the oven to four twenty-five. His mind wandered and reminisced on the six-year journey that it took for him to reach the incredible milestone that was one million subscribers on Youtube. The hours of filming and editing had all been worth it.

Beep Beep Beep.

The oven was ready. Mateo opened the oven door, slid the baking tray onto the top rack, closed the door, and set the oven timer for thirteen minutes. Outside the sun was falling deeper and deeper beneath the horizon. The blue sky from the west mixed with the glowing orange sun from the east and in the middle created a rippling streak of pinkish purple. Inside, the apartment filled with the smell of melted cheese and pepperoni. Mateo's stomach growled with hunger.

It wasn't until Mateo returned to his room with the plateful of pizza rolls that he noticed he had three missed calls from his best friend Fomo.

His real name was Joshua but everybody in their friend group had been calling him Fomo since the tenth grade. The nickname came as a result of the story *The Raven* by Edgar Allan Poe. In English class, there was an entire marking period dedicated to the works of Edgar Allan Poe and Joshua had become obsessed with saying "Forever More" at the end of his sentences, just like the raven in Poe's story. Most people found it annoying, especially since it went on for months after the focus on Poe literature had come to an end. But, Mateo and some of Joshua's other friends found it hilarious and in turn came up with the nickname Fomo. The first two letters in *forever* combined with the first two letters in *more* and voila, Fomo was born!

The phone went through two series of rings before Fomo's voice came through on the other end.

"Yo, bro! Are you ready for tonight?"

"How couldn't I be? Are you?" Mateo replied.

"Most definitely. That's why I was calling. I didn't know what time you wanted me to come over before we head over to Wakefall."

"I posted on Twitter and Instagram that I'd be going live at nine, so if you want to be here by eight that gives us some time to get over there and make sure this new camera and everything is set up and working. I still have it charging so I haven't messed with any of the features or anything. Plus I still have to attach the mic to it."

"Sounds like you better get on that. Anyway, you said that you want me to be in charge of your phone and the live stream, right?" Mateo nodded his head with the phone pressed against his ear, a gesture made even though Fomo was unable to know it happened on the other end of the line.

"Yeah. I just got back not too long ago from Best Buy. I'm going to be filming with the camera because I'll probably take the footage, edit it, and then upload it as a video on the channel. Meanwhile, we'll be live on Youtube with my phone for those that want to experience everything with us. So you'll have the phone and I'll have the camera."

"Okay, I got you. Well, I'll give you some time to get acquainted with your new camera and I'll be over in a little bit."

"Sounds good bro." Mateo pulled the phone away from his ear and touched the red circle to end the call. As he put down one piece of technology he picked up another. Mateo removed the charging cable from the camera and pushed the button to power on the device. The quality of the camera's picture through the small screen was much better than the camera Mateo had been using to film his videos. He also had a Sigma 16mm lens that he would attach to the front for even better quality. The thought of what his content would look like in comparison to his old videos made the young man giddy.

As if done by a flick of a switch, day turned to night.

There was a knock at the door which caused Yennefer to break out into a frenzy. "Relax Yen, it's just Fomo." The black lab barked and barked until Mateo opened the front door and she was able to see the person who stood on the other side. When the dog saw who it was, the barks turned to whines as she hopped against Fomo's legs.

"Yennefer, get down!" Mateo scolded.

"It's cool." Fomo redirected his attention from Mateo to the dog that was pounding against his thighs with her front paws. "Hey there, Yennefer. Aren't you such a good girl?" Fomo knelt and embraced the dog as she showered his face with sticky saliva. Then, in typical fashion, Yennefer quickly grew old of the greeting game and waltzed off to be alone somewhere in the back half of the apartment.

"This is it. Are you ready?" Fomo questioned before grabbing a sheet of paper towel and wiping the slobber off of his face. "The big one million subscribers live stream!"

"It still feels so crazy to hear it. But yeah, let me grab the camera, spare batteries, and flashlights quickly and then I should be good to go." Mateo did a slow jog back to his bedroom to grab the backpack that he had filled with accessories (and a few snacks) and the camera. Lying next to the backpack across his bed was Yennefer with her head perched above her front paws.

"Hold down the fort for me girl. I'll be back in the morning." Mateo grabbed the camera and slung the right strap of the backpack across his shoulder. He leaned down and kissed the dog on the head. As he turned away, Yennefer began to whimper. "It's okay Yen, I'll see you bright and early in the morning. Don't you worry." Mateo turned off the bedroom light and left down the hall. Even in the darkness, the dog continued to cry.

Before leaving, Mateo did a rundown of his mental checklist. The same one that he always did before leaving the apartment for a decent amount of time. The list included:

Making sure that Yennefer has food and water.

Making sure that all of the lights were off.

Making sure that he had his keys.

Making sure that the door was locked.

"Who's driving?" Fomo asked as the pair exited the apartment building.

"You can if you want. I need to jump on social media quickly and let everyone know that we're heading over to Wakefall and that the live stream is still good to go." Fomo pulled on the

Adidas lanyard hanging from his pocket that had the keys to his 2014 Chevy Malibu and a Los Angeles Lakers keychain attached. With two successive button presses on the key fob, the car doors unlocked and the two friends began the last ride of their lives.

Mateo was scrolling through Twitter reading the comments on his latest post which read: **Heading over to the abandoned Wakefall Sanatorium now with the boy Fomo! Livestream in 45!!! Make sure to come thru!** Most of the comments were positive and consisted of fans confirming their excitement for the stream or saying how they should be careful while inside. But of course, there were the internet trolls and the people who made it their livelihood to stir up drama online. There was one comment in particular that stood out to Mateo.

"Hey, listen to this comment, probably the funniest one yet. It says 'All of your videos are fake as shit. You two are pussies and won't make it twenty minutes inside.'" The two laughed.

"What's his name?" Mateo turned the phone so that the screen was facing Fomo who quickly took his eyes off of the road to read the Twitter handle BadDaddy-Milkman02. "Wow?" Fomo questioned in between chuckles. "And how many followers does he have?" Mateo made a zero with his hand.

"You may also like to know that he does surprisingly have a profile picture to go along with his zero followers though and it's a cartoon cow being milked with a gigantic grin on its face."

"Jesus. At least he took enough time to have the picture fit the name." A feminine British voice from Google Maps maps spoke and instructed Fomo that he was to make a left turn in five-hundred feet and that the destination would then be on the vehicle's right in eight-tenths of a mile. Mateo locked his phone screen and shoved it into his front right pocket. He then leaned over the center console and reached into the back seat to grab his backpack.

Both Mateo and Fomo's hearts were racing inside of their chests as the colossal Sanatorium came into view, but for different reasons. Mateo was filled with excitement and intrigue, almost unable to contain his anticipation to explore the abandoned building while his followers watched along with him for the first time live. Meanwhile, Fomo didn't want to admit it, but he was afraid. He had never joined Mateo on his paranormal escapades before. He was a believer in the paranormal and was well aware of the stories that surrounded the abandoned mental hospital. It was believed that spirits of the abused haunted the rotting decrepit hallways of Wakefall and that the dead were waiting for the living to come in so that they could experiment on visitors the way that the medical staff used to experiment on them. Of course, he knew that these were nothing more than old wives tales, but it didn't stop them from being terrifying.

Fomo pulled the car over into the grass and turned the key to shut off the ignition. The interior light came on. Mateo unzipped the middle pocket of his backpack and removed two black LED flashlights. He handed one of the flashlights to Fomo before zipping up the pocket and then unzipping the larger pocket above it. A crumpling sound came from within as Mateo rummaged through the contents inside.

"Fruit snacks?" Mateo asked as he held out a small blue bag of gummies to his friend.

"No, I'm good," Fomo responded. His stomach was in knots. The last thing that he needed was to provide his insides with fuel that could later be spewed back up.

"Suit yourself." Mateo ripped the pouch of gummies open and began shoveling the treats into his mouth. It wasn't long before the fruit snacks had been devoured and the duo exited the car.

A spectral silence filled the air. Wakefall Sanatorium was a massive ten-storied structure with shattered windows for eyes and decaying wood for bones. The vines crawling up the bricks were veins spreading an invisible life force across its earthy skin. Graffiti covered the walls both inside and out, a majority of it dedicated to satanism and the occult. Surrounding the building was a tall, chain link fence put into place to prevent people from doing the exact thing that Mateo and Fomo were preparing for...entering. A gust of wind swept by sending a group of brown leaves skittering across the ground and with them came the sour stench of death.

"What is that smell?" Fomo questioned while pinching his nose. "It's horrible."

"Probably dog shit or something. Come on, let's get over the fence." It took some smart maneuvering but Mateo and Fomo found a way to get themselves, the backpack, and the camera over the fence all in one piece. Mateo took his phone out of his pocket to check the time. 8:48.

"So how are we getting in? The front door is boarded up." The white beam from the flashlight illuminated the words **Free Hugs Inside** that were spray-painted in red on the wooden boards that covered the front entrance. An electrifying chill ran up and down Fomo's spine.

"Let's look for a window to climb through. Just be careful that it doesn't have any loose glass lying across the sill." Much of the Sanatorium's white paint had peeled off giving exposure to the original red brick. There was a high-pitched whistling coming from the wind that raced through cracks in the exterior. "Over here, this looks like it might be a good option."

An eight-foot-high window with the glass broken out and a white bed sheet acting as a curtain was the suggested option. Fomo shined the flashlight on the sheet making it appear nearly transparent. The base of the wooden window frame had been spray painted a light blue making it stand out from the other windows whose paint had all but faded or chipped away due to weather exposure.

"I'm going to put the camera down and climb in first. Once I'm in, you can hand the camera up to me and I'll help you up. Do your best to keep the light on the window so that I can see."

"Alright, no problem." Mateo gently placed the camera onto the ground and surveyed the windowsill for glass. After careful observation, he jumped up and grabbed the window. It was a struggle, but Mateo managed to hoist himself over the lip of the window and into the sanatorium. He looked around but without a flashlight the only thing that he could see was darkness.

"Did you get in okay?" Fomo yelled from outside. Mateo brought himself to his feet and pushed past the bed sheet so that he was facing outside.

"A couple of scrapes and scratches, but nothing serious. Want to come and hand me the camera? Then, as soon as you're inside we can get the live stream set up."

"Yeah, give me one second." Fomo lowered the flashlight. As he started walking toward the window he noticed out of the corner of his eye a shadow swiftly move from the left side of the building to the right behind the bed sheet that Mateo was standing in front of. He lifted the flashlight back up and shined it into the building.

"Bro, my eyes!" Mateo shouted as the LED light shined in his face. "What's wrong?"

"I swear I just saw somebody walking behind you."

"Chill, that's not funny."

"I'm not kidding!" Mateo grabbed the sheet and moved it off to the side to get a better view of the room while Fomo shined the light through the window. His eyes traveled from right to left taking in everything that he could see with the small amount of light that made it inside. The walls were crumbling. A headless doll sat propped up against the wall on the far side of the room, but there was no sign of another person nearby.

"There's nobody here. You probably just saw my shadow being cast off of the sheet by the way that you were holding the flashlight. Come on, get in here! This place is absolutely insane!" Fomo made his way up to the window and lifted the camera so that Mateo could hoist it inside. Then as his friend had done, Fomo climbed through the window, flinging his left leg first, then his right leg over the windowsill. He hopped down onto the floor which created a loud *thud* that echoed through the barren halls.

"Are we sure this is a good idea?" Fomo asked, his light shining onto a huge hand-drawn pentagram in the center of the floor. A dark, dried liquid covered much of the pentagram's center. Tiny animal bones were littered about the room.

"We're here now, aren't we? Might as well just get on with it." Mateo opened up the Youtube app on his phone and went into the settings that allowed him to set up the live stream. It was three minutes past nine. The words **YOU ARE NOW LIVE** appeared at the top of the phone screen. Before Mateo could even hand the phone off to Fomo, a flurry of comments began pouring into the chat. The posts were scrolling too fast for Mateo to read.

"Here you go, we're live baby!" Mateo handed Fomo his phone. With the flashlight pointed at Mateo in one hand and the phone pointed at him in the other, the night had officially begun.

"What's up, everybody? I see the comments already pouring into the chat so thank you so much for taking time out of your night to stop by the stream and support me and the channel. I have my buddy Fomo here with me, he's going to be in charge of holding the phone during the live stream and as you can see, we're here! The inside of the notorious Wakefall Sanatorium." Fomo did a slow pan around the room so that the viewers could soak in the atmosphere.

"How many people are watching right now?" Fomo looked down at the phone.

"Currently about thirteen thousand."

"Wow, okay. No pressure then." Mateo stuck his hand into his back left pocket and pulled out a folded piece of lined notebook paper. "So the goal guys is for us to spend the entire night in the building. I don't know if the live stream will last that long because I can only stream as long as my phone has battery life but I'll try to stream for as long as possible. As you can see, I also have this brand new Sony A6400 camera that I'm holding so this experience will also be going onto my channel as an edited down version that will also include anything that may not make it into the live stream. Make sure you keep your eyes peeled for that."

"For those of you that are familiar with my channel or have been around for a while, you know that anytime I go into one of these abandoned buildings I first like to give you a quick rundown of its history just so we're all aware of what the place is all about." Mateo held out the folded notebook paper so that Fomo could catch it on screen before laying down his camera and unfolding it. There were several historical facts about the Wakefall Sanatorium bullet-pointed down the left margin.

"First off, this is the Wakefall Sanatorium also known as the Wakefall Asylum for the Feeble-Minded and Mentally unwell. It was originally built in 1892 and at first housed only patients with long-term illnesses, most of them suffering from tuberculosis. It wasn't until 1923 that the hospital was revamped and turned into a mental institute until its doors were permanently closed sixty-three years later in 1986. During its time as a mental institution, Wakefall was known for its controversial practices including inhumane experimentation on patients as well as disturbing procedures carried out specifically on women and people of color. Like most mental asylums across the United States in the twentieth century, Wakefall was understaffed and overpopulated. The building was originally constructed to house around -"

A loud bang shot off on the floor above them. Mateo and Fomo silently stared at each other and listened. Nearly half a minute went by with nothing but silence. Most of the chat looked something like *WTFFFFFFFFFFFF!!!!!!* In the upper corner of the room, a spider spun its sticky web.

"I feel like someone's here, man. I'm just having a really bad feeling." The only thing moving faster than Fomo's eyes was his heart.

"It was probably just the wind knocking something over. I'm sure it's fine." Fomo released a breathy sigh and focused the phone and flashlight back onto his friend. Mateo picked back up from where he left off.

"Wakefall was built to house approximately seventeen-hundred patients but realistically was home to about twenty-five hundred, many of them being minors under the age of eighteen. Local newspapers reported the institute to be filthy and filled with abuse including kicking, punching, slapping, and biting. There were even instances of staff arranging situations for the patients to abuse one another. Sadly, during the sixty-three-year operation, nearly nine thousand patients died inside the walls. Many of the deaths were results of malnutrition, abuse, or neglect. The building is now known to be a hotspot for squatters, vandals, and devil worshippers. I would say that the last part is pretty spot on."

Mateo motioned for Fomo to point the phone down at the floor where the large pentagram was drawn. Many people in the chat implored for the boys to be safe. Mateo folded the paper back up and returned it to his pocket. He lifted the camera off of the ground and turned it on. There was a short chime as the device came to life.

Behind a veil of darkness down a corridor the length of half a football field, a group of rats scurried between rooms. Rays of moonlight filtered in through a pair of broken windows bathing a broken wheelchair and remnants of narcotics in its ashen glow. Chilled radiators that had once been silver were covered in amber rust. Meanwhile, a thin gown lay strewn across a metal-framed bed stained in dirt and bodily waste. Together they formed just a tiny fraction of the horrors that were Wakefall.

Mateo and Fomo had officially begun their tour of the building. Just like the outside, many of the walls were covered top to bottom in colorful graffiti with even more colorful language. Not only was there evidence of satanic cult activity, but gang activity as well. Wakefall had become a home for evil both in terms of its activities and its guests.

Still, on the first floor, the two entered into a room that was approximately halfway down a long central hallway on the left-hand side. The walls of the room were covered with drawings of inverted crosses, more pentagrams, and the words **IT WAS MORE FUN IN HELL** spray-painted in red. Pushed against the back wall was a twin mattress littered with stains.

"Do you think someone stays here?" Mateo asked, documenting every inch of the room with his camera. Fomo shrugged his shoulders.

"I've got no idea, but I really hope not. I want nothing to do with anybody hanging out in a place like this." Fomo looked down at the phone and read some of the comments scrolling through the chat. "The Real Wayne Brady says that he would hang out in this place. If that's true bro, you're weird. This place is scary as hell."

"Wayne Brady's in the chat?" Mateo questioned.

"Apparently so," Fomo replied with sarcasm. Mateo gave an approving thumbs up with the hand that carried the flashlight. They exited the room and continued exploring the first floor. After a while, the rooms started to blend. Each one practically a replica of the one that came before it, plus or minus some graffiti or furniture. It wasn't until they reached the end of the hallway that they had to make their first actual decision on where to go next for the night. Two sets of stairs were in front of them. One set went up to the second floor, while the other set descended into the basement.

"Which set do you want to take?" Mateo asked.

"I'm not going downstairs."

"What do you mean?"

"I mean, what I said. I'm not going down there bro. I've got to draw the line somewhere."

"What if we just quickly go down there? Five minutes max."

"I'm not going downstairs," Fomo repeated.

"How about we let the chat decide." Fomo wanted to respond by telling Mateo how stupid of an idea that was, but he never got the chance. "Hey chat, what do you guys want to see? Do you want us to go upstairs or downstairs? Type what you think in the comments." Mateo walked over beside Fomo and the two stared down at the phone as a frenzy of comments came flooding in from many of the now twenty-three thousand people watching.

Downstairs
Downstairs
Downstairs
Downstairs
Downstairs

"I think the people have spoken, my friend." Mateo gave Fomo a friendly pat on the shoulder and walked over to the top step.

"Y'all are some assholes." Fomo directed his words directly into the phone's camera. The response he received was primarily of funny crying emojis as well as people telling him that he needed to grow a pair. Easy for them to say from the safety of their own homes.

Nineteen steps were separating the first floor from the basement. Fomo counted. There was a cold air that lived in the basement that was not present on the floor above. The concrete walls were a prison for things that both could and could not be seen. Overhead inside of a series of pipes came the *tap*

tap tapping sound of rodents traveling back and forth. A wheelchair sat out of place in the middle of the corridor; one of the wheels was missing causing it to lean at an angle. On the seat was a tattered piece of paper with sloppy writing scribbled across rows of faded blue lines.

"Something's written on here. A decent amount actually." Mateo lifted the paper and held it in front of him. "Can you shine the light on this while I read it?" Fomo agreed with hesitance. His body was covered in goosebumps.

"This country is fucked!" Mateo stopped reading and shot a surprised glare toward Fomo. He continued. "Eleven years of my life that I dedicated to this country with my hand over my heart and a smile across my face, yet here I am with no food, no money, and nobody giving a shit! I did multiple tours in Afghanistan. I "Yes, sir'd" and saluted some of the most arrogant pricks I've ever had the displeasure of meeting in my life without a single complaint. Not to mention I've been shot at multiple times all for Uncle Sam to give me a pat on the back upon returning home and provide me with a 'Thanks for your service'. Well fuck that. I was better off living in that desert hell with a rifle as my pillow than I am here in the good ol' U S of A.

"But it's fine. I'll stay here though...at least for now. It's not the cleanest, but there are mattresses still in the building. Anything beats a park bench or a damp underpass. This settles my shelter problem. Now, what can I do for food?"

Mateo set the paper back down onto the seat of the wheelchair.

"Is somebody living here?" Fomo asked.

"It sounds like it. Seems like it was written by a homeless military vet. Sad stuff." From down the hall echoed a muffled sounding laugh. It was quiet and was gone as fast as it came. It sounded like it would have come from either a female child or a frail older woman. Mateo and Fomo looked at each other to confirm that they had both heard the same thing. Both boys shined their lights down into the suffocating darkness, but there was nothing. A few cockroaches darted across the walls slipping through cracks in the foundation to avoid the light, but nothing more.

"You're crazy if you think I'm going down there. I don't know what that was, but it's not for me."

"Fine, I'll walk down there on my own. I guess just stay here and entertain the chat. I'll take the camera with me so that they can see if I find anything interesting when I upload the edited video. I'll be back in two minutes."

"Joshua." Fomo lifted his head.

"Since when do you call me that?" Mateo turned and expressed a look of confusion.

"Call you what?"

"You just said my name. You said Joshua, but you haven't called me that in like ten years." Mateo faced his friend with a blank stare.

"I think you're hearing stuff. I promise I didn't say anything at all. You probably just heard a sound coming from the pipes that maybe sounded like your name. There's lots of creepy noises coming from this place, ya know?" Fomo shook his head but didn't know what else to say. Mateo had his moments where he could be a prankster, but there was an honest sincerity in his voice. It was true, there had been a bunch of noises that neither guy could explain, but this one had sounded so audibly clear. Fomo knew what he had heard, and it was definitely his name.

Mateo turned toward the darkness and slowly began to make his way down the hall. For a while, Fomo could see his friend and the flashlight moving deeper into the possible neverending blackness. Then at some point, he was just gone.

It had been a few minutes since Mateo had last seen the cylindrical beam from Fomo's flashlight. He knew that he had mentioned returning in two minutes but the curiosity of exploration continued to pull him deeper until the darkness swallowed him whole.

"Is anyone here?" Mateo's voice bounced between the walls. All of a sudden, the narrow corridor widened into a large room built in the shape of a semicircle. Mateo had traveled as far as he could. If he and Fomo did truly hear the voice of another person, there's nowhere else that they could have gone.

Along the walls were rows of square lockers, each with a single handle located on the left side. Scattered around the room was a handful of gurneys. Mateo looked around in disbelief. "I think that this is a morgue," he said aloud as he scanned the room with his flashlight and camera. "Should I open one of the lockers?" For most, talking to themselves would feel awkward, but Mateo had mastered the art of showmanship and knew how to entertain his audience.

Mateo walked over to the far side of the room. He ran his index finger across the handle of one of the lockers and was taken aback by how cold it felt against his skin. A cloud of dust flew off of the handle and hovered in the air causing him to sneeze. After gathering himself, he wrapped his fingers around the handle of one of the lockers, pulled down, and then pulled.

It was heavier than he expected. Mateo pulled with all of his strength and the door swung open with a whiny creak. "Let me show you what's inside," Mateo said to his future audience. He lowered the light and camera before having the chance to look inside with his own two eyes. A tiny sound came from within. As Mateo bent down to get a look for himself, a swarm of hissing cockroaches came storming out. Some fell onto the floor and split off into various directions while others climbed the walls and escaped toward the ceiling.

Mateo nearly dropped his camera from shock and disgust. He backpedaled until bumping his lower back into one of the vacant gurneys. Then, something soft and squeaking ran across his foot. By the time Mateo lowered his flashlight, the creature had already vanished into the darkness. The unwelcomed sensation of things crawling across his body made him itchy.

Suddenly, from out of the corridor where Fomo stayed behind, came a murderous scream. Mateo turned his shoulders with a snap of his waist and started to run back in the direction of his friend. "I hope that wasn't Fomo screaming like that," Mateo said aloud, more to himself than to the camera. It wasn't long before he encountered a bouncing light moving quickly toward him.

"Mateo, is that you?" The voice was a familiar one.

"Yeah! Are you okay? Why did you scream like that?" The young men were now standing face to face; their flashlights casting a series of dancing shadows along the walls.

"I thought that was you that screamed. That's why I came running. I was standing back in the same place that I was when you left talking to the viewers." A look of bewilderment fell across both of their faces.

"Okay, that's scary as hell. The hairs on my arm are standing on end. Did you all hear the scream in the chat?" Mateo asked, turning his focus onto the phone. While waiting for the replies to come through, he noticed that the battery life was at sixty-four percent. Then, a flurry of the word *yes* took over the screen.

"I want to get out of this basement."

"I'm right there with you." Mateo never mentioned the morgue to Fomo and Fomo never asked. Their focus was strictly on getting down the hallway as fast as possible and back up the stairs. When they arrived and saw the tiniest rays of moonlight peaking into the first floor, it felt as though a huge weight had been lifted off of their shoulders.

Thirty-six was the number this time. It was the number of steps separating the basement and the second floor. Fomo would have been more than happy to stop counting at the number nineteen, walk down the hallway, jump out of the window, and drive as far away from Wakefall as possible. But Mateo had other plans. He climbed the first set of stairs, rounded the corner, and continued climbing until arriving on the second floor.

Exploration continued as the two entered, observed, and then moved on from room to room. Inside of an area with a placard outside identifying it as Room 207 was a porcelain doll with black hair and ivory skin hanging from a noose. The doll's eyes had been gouged out and the word WHORE was written across the dress in red lipstick. Graffitied along the wall to the left upon entering the room was **WE WATCHED. WE CRIED. WE KILLED. WE LAUGHED.**

It wasn't until Mateo and Fomo reached the end of the hallway that they found anything else of interest.

"This must be the medical wing," Mateo announced. They entered into a room with three exam tables lined up next to each other spaced only a foot or two apart. A detailed mannequin of the human torso with exposed plastic organs was laid on its back on the middle table. Sticking out from between the intestines was a piece of paper that had been rolled into a tube. Mateo pulled the piece of paper out and eyeballed the message.

"Is it written by the same guy?"

"Seems like it." Mateo went on to read the message left behind. "The most humiliating thing is having somebody look at you as if you're not another human being. That's what life is like when you spend nearly every waking second posted up on some random corner begging strangers for a little bit of spare change. I couldn't even begin to say how many days I've had to do just that. It all just blends together after a while. The sun comes up and the sun goes down. Probably the only real constant in my life.

"Yesterday, I asked a young couple wearing nice clothes if they had a spare dollar or two for food. Instead of giving me money, they gave me this journal and a pen. 'You can use this notebook as a way to talk to God. When you get right with the Holy Lord above, everything else in your life will fall into place.' So now I'm writing in that very journal as a way to waste away the day.

"Not sure if God's listening to what I've got to say or not, but if you are...I'm still hungry."

"I can't lie, my heart goes out to the guy. He went from serving our country to begging for money. Hopefully, God answered his call." Fomo nodded his head in agreement. Mateo re-rolled the piece of notebook paper and placed it back where he found it. Upon pulling his hand away, both of the flashlights began to flicker on and off.

"Come on!" Mateo yelled as he bashed the bottom of the flashlight against the heel of his hand. Fomo tried the approach of flicking the on-off switch up and down. "I just put brand new batteries in these flashlights this morning. There's no way both of them are dying."

"And at the very same time," Fomo added intuitively. All of a sudden, the flickering stopped. Both flashlights were working fine as if there had never been a problem at all. "Things are happening in this place that aren't normal. I don't know if you need more evidence of that, but I'm pretty convinced." Mateo nodded his head.

The sound of yet another door slamming down the hall with thunderous force startled both boys. Coming from the floor above was a succession of methodic footsteps, the floorboards creaking beneath the weight of each stride. Mateo pushed his index finger against his lips as a sign for Fomo to remain silent and then pointed up toward the ceiling.

Creak. Creak. Creak. Creak.

The footsteps weakened as they traveled farther away. "We're not alone here," Fomo whispered. Mateo motioned with his hand for Fomo to come over to him. He could feel his heartbeat pulsing in both his wrist and neck.

"Okay, guys listen," Mateo directed toward his Youtube audience. "I don't think we're alone in this building. I also don't think that it's the best idea for us to stay here for the rest of the night. Our priority has to be our safety. So, we're going to get out of here." There was a part of Mateo that wanted to believe that the sounds were nothing more than the creaking of deteriorating floorboards or the scampering of rats. But then again, he was well aware of the phrase *curiosity killed the cat*, and he hated cats.

The distance between the medical room and the stairs felt longer than before. A few hundred feet suddenly felt like miles. The sound of footsteps could still be heard coming from the floor above. They were faster now, nearly mimicking the pace of the boy's stride for stride. Louder. Harsher.

Descending the stairs was like journeying from one ring of Hell to the next. It was a brisk forty-eight degree Fahrenheit outside, but that didn't prevent a layer of sweat from building atop Fomo's brow. He wiped away the perspiration with the back of his hand as they stepped onto the first floor.

"What is that?" Mateo raised a single eyebrow in confusion.

"What do you mean?"

"There, don't you see it?" Fomo questioned, pointing toward a room down the hall on the right side. "It looks like something's glowing from inside that room. That wasn't there when we first got here." Mateo looked again. Fomo was right. A tiny golden hue flickered from down the corridor. Then, a storm of whispers came from down the hall in the direction of the light. A tall figure dressed in a black robe walked from the room with the light in it to the room that was across the hall. In his hand, he held a burning candle made up of red wax. Both Mateo and Fomo pressed their flashlights against their legs so as to not alert the other intruder.

Then the chanting began. Were there two voices? Three? Four? The young men couldn't tell. Mateo pulled Fomo by the sleeve of his shirt and signaled for them to head back upstairs. Fomo shook his head and made a motion that was meant to mean *Let's make a run for it!* He wanted to leave but they both knew that there was no getting past the others unnoticed. They had too much equipment and it would take a couple of minutes to get both of them and the stuff safely out of the window.

Fomo pointed the phone in the direction of the chanting. It made sense to document everything going on. The chanting grew louder. Cartoonish shadows played games of tag along the walls. Something rotten plagued the air.

The comments in the chat were coming in so fast that Fomo couldn't keep up with what everyone was saying. On the bottom of the phone, it said that over fifty thousand people were watching, and then the screen went black. Just a few moments later, both flashlights shut off. Mateo quietly flicked the power switch up and down but the device was dead.

"Let's go up the stairs a little," Mateo whispered. "Inside of my backpack are spare batteries. Grab them so we can switch these out." Fomo nodded his head in agreement. Tiptoeing and holding their breath, the two made their way up the stairs far enough that they now stood halfway between the first and second floors. Fomo slowly unzipped the backpack and rummaged around until finding the batteries. He handed a pair of C batteries to Mateo before pulling two more out and clumsily dropping one onto the floor. The battery clunked as it hit the ground, and then clunked a few more times as it rolled down step after step.

The chanting stopped.

"Who's there?" The voice was deep and guttural. "Why not come play with us?" Fomo held his hand over his mouth as the two listened to the sound of multiple thick-soled boots walking in their direction. "Come on out!" the voice boomed. The footsteps were getting closer. One of the cultists pulled the end of a metal pipe along the floor. It sounded like dragging nails on a chalkboard.

"We have to move," Mateo whispered. The two started making their way up the stairs, attempting to make as little noise as possible. No matter how hard they tried, the floorboards creaked beneath each step.

"Is this a battery?" one of the robed figures said at the base of the stairs. "It looks brand new. Is this what we heard? Come on out!" The yell bounced off of the walls amplifying the volume of the scream creating the illusion that they were closer to Mateo and Fomo than they actually were.

Startled, the two began to sprint up the stairs. Their presence was no longer a mystery.

"We're coming for you!" one of the cultists yelled as a storm of footsteps came stomping up the stairs behind the two friends. Mateo and Fomo reached the third floor but decided to skip past it and flee higher into the building. The footsteps that they had been hearing above them still lingered in the back of their minds. Not only were there people below them, but there was somebody up above as well. The only question was where?

The footsteps were growing louder. Nearer. The two raced past the fourth floor as well and even the fifth. It wasn't until the sixth floor that Fomo decided to race forward and dart into one of the many rooms. Mateo continued racing upward. He climbed another two flights before realizing that his friend was no longer with him. The sounds of shoes pounding against the stairs had blended into one within the darkness, and even louder had been the beating of his heart ringing within his ears. Mateo rushed forward and slithered into the fourth room on the right side of the hall.

Two floors below, Fomo hid behind the door of the room. He tucked Mateo's phone into his pocket and used his free hand to shield his nose and mouth. In the other hand, he wielded the small flashlight like it was a mighty sword, prepared to bash it across the skull of the first person who dared to enter. He closed his eyes. *Slow your breathing. You're too loud.* His palms were sweating. His knees were buckling. And his mind was riddled with delusions.

"Joshua." Fomo's eyes shot open. He scanned the room for the source of the voice, but he was the only one there. He could still hear the cultists talking amongst each other, but they sounded like they were on the floor below him. This voice sounded like it was whispering directly into his mind.

Fomo inched his way along the wall until his shoulder was pressed up against the corner of the room. He then slid down until he was sitting on the ground.

"Joshua." the voice whispered again. "Let us in."

"Let us in." There was more than one now. Fomo couldn't tell which direction they were coming from. A storm of screams and cackles came soaring up the stairs as the horrible sound of the metal pipe banging against the wall continued. Tears slid down the sides of Fomo's nose as he swallowed a lump of phlegm that had been lodged in the ball of his throat. He tucked his head into his knees and continued to cry as the voices both in and out of the room continued to grow more deafening.

"Let us in."

"Let us in." Continued the whispers that ate away at the man's mind.

"Come on out! We only want to play!" Fomo took his hands and wrapped his fingers around his neck. He squeezed, digging his nails into the top of his spine, deep enough to draw blood. The voices were inside of him now. They lived in his brain. What started out as whispers were now screaming demands.

"LET US IN!" The voices commanded. Sometimes it would be in English, other times in Spanish. Then other voices joined in. Italian voices. Gaelic voices. Latin voices. All jumbled up into one incomprehensible language. Fomo pounded his forehead into the crown of his knee. The first time he did it he blackened his left eye. The second time he broke the bridge of his nose. The third time he disoriented his vision, and the fourth time he achieved what he wanted by knocking himself unconscious.

Silence.

Meanwhile, Mateo fiddled around with the camera on the eighth floor. He pushed every button that the device had to offer but for some reason it wouldn't turn back on. Even in a time such as this, his obsession with views and money remained his main focus. Irritated, Mateo shoved the camera into the largest pocket of his backpack. He then brushed his hands against the front pockets of his jeans in search of his phone.

"Shiiiit." Mateo's plan was to text Fomo and figure out where he was. At least that *was* the plan until he remembered that Fomo still had his phone. The voices from the cultists could be heard, but they were still fairly far away; far enough away that Mateo could hear them talking but not make out what was being said.

Across the room was a large rectangular window that overlooked the grounds of the asylum. Mateo walked over and peered outside. He could see the car sitting in the same place that they had left it; it's glossy finish glowing in the moonlight. The trees were waving in the wind, taunting the fact that he was stuck inside and they weren't. Mateo wondered if this was how the patients of Wakefall felt while they were stuck inside of the asylum. Isolated and in constant fear of the next interaction that they had with another human being.

Mateo stepped away. He scoured the room for something he could use as a weapon. Anything would do, but there was nothing. With the timidness of a field mouse, Mateo poked his head out of the room before cautiously making his way into the room next door. Again there was nothing. He checked across the hall, then in the room next to that. Still nothing to use as a weapon, but there was another note sitting on top of a chair. Mateo stepped toward the window and used the tiny bit of celestial light that entered as his lantern. The handwriting on the paper was familiar to him now. He read the note silently to himself.

"They" prey on the weak minded. And when I say "They", I'm talking about the invisible entities that wander these crumbling halls. I call them entities because there's reluctance to refer to them with a definitive title. Ghosts? Spirits? I don't know what they are, but I've seen and heard what the people cloaked in black constantly try to conjure up. Listened to the curses that they place upon this building. And if my recent experiences are to act as validation, I would say they've been successful. So maybe I should call Them by what they truly are...

Demons.

I can feel them poking at my mind as I write this. They are looking to satiate their hunger. "Let us in." They beg me. "Let us in." And the more afraid I become, the weaker I am to their haunting solicitations. Let them in?

I ponder. I ponder. I ponder. Okay.

Let them in.

Loud banging from below shook the floor beneath Mateo's feet. The sudden sounds startled him. He dropped the paper onto the floor and moved toward the door. Blood curdling screams filled the halls. His heart sank as he could hear the metal pipe bludgeoning flesh. Quietly, Mateo listened to the yelling and the smacking until the building grew eerily silent.

He couldn't move. The silence was deafening. Mateo wanted to cry out for his friend and see if he was alright, but he knew better. His hands were clenched around the door frame. A black spider crawled down the doorway and across Mateo's knuckles, but he didn't notice. His mind was somewhere else.

Suddenly, there was a sound that snapped Mateo out of the trance. It was metal being scraped along the walls and it was getting closer. He slapped the fuzzy arachnid away and immediately wanted to vomit. A surge of stomach bile launched upward. Mateo's esophagus burned as he managed to swallow the acidic fluid.

A single set of footsteps ascended the stairs until they reached the eighth floor. Down the hall they came. Each menacing step accompanied by the tune of screeching metal. Mateo backed into the room knowing that he was trapped. He had nothing to defend himself but the flashlight in his hand.

The person was right outside of the room now. Mateo held the flashlight out, fully prepared to fight for his life. A dark silhouette appeared within the doorway. All of a sudden, a beam of white sprayed from out of the flashlight, bathing the figure in a scintillating glow.

"Fomo?" Mateo nearly choked on the name. He looked ahead at his friend who stood in the doorway. Blood dripped from off of the pipe. Fomo's hands, face, and clothes were drenched in crimson as well. "Are you okay? What happened down there?" With each question, Mateo moved a little closer. Fomo never responded. His eyes had become black portals to an empty, soulless vessel. "Hey man, answer me! What the hell happened down -"

Before Mateo could finish his sentence, the edge of the pipe came crashing against the corner of his skull. His eyes rolled into the back of his head and his body collapsed onto the floor.

Ezra sat in front of the family computer furiously clicking away. Floating around the dining room were half a dozen helium balloons with the generic message: **Happy Birthday** written across them. On the dining room table was a barely eaten piece of chocolate cake that sat in a pool of melted vanilla ice cream. It belonged to the frizzy haired boy who earlier in the day had celebrated his ninth birthday with his friends and family.

Ezra had requested the third helping of dessert, and fully intended on eating every last bite, but that was before his night had been ruined.

"I don't understand! Why isn't it working!" Ezra yelled as he clicked the refresh button at the top of the page a few more times. The boy's mother walked into the room and stood behind her son. He was sitting in an office chair that his father used while working remotely from home. It was Ezra's favorite chair because he could use it to spin in circles until his stomach got all tied up in knots and his head began to feel all funny.

"What's wrong, sweetheart?" Ezra's response came more as a grunt than an intelligible response.

"The stupid thing isn't working! I've been waiting for this all day and now nothing wants to work. This is the worst birthday ever!"

"Calm down, Ezra. I'm sure it will fix itself any second now. You just have to have a little bit of patience." The boy crossed his arms against his chest and dressed his face in a sour scowl. He wanted to punch the stupid computer right in its stupid computer face. "Are you done with your cake and ice cream?"

"Yes." Ezra grumpily responded, his arms still crossed like a pretzel. His mother picked up the plate and carried it off into the kitchen. The boy could hear his mother scraping the remains of the dessert into the trash and then washing the plate off in the sink.

Ezra stared at the red play button icon at the top left corner of the screen. He clicked the refresh button one more time and to his surprise, the livestream was back up! "Mom! Mom! It's back on! It's working!" Ezra was joyfully bouncing up and down in his seat.

"See, what did I tell you? Have a little bit of patience and it will fix itself." Ezra's mother leaned down and kissed her birthday boy on the cheek. His soft skin felt warm against her lips. "I'm heading upstairs to finish folding and putting away the rest of the laundry. Do you need me to get you anything else before I go up?" Ezra shook his head.

Watching Tales of the Dead videos on Youtube had become the boy's latest obsession. Seeing his favorite Youtuber live felt like a dream come true. He had even stolen his father's credit card earlier so that he could use it to donate a few dollars in support.

"Nope."

"Alright sweetie. Enjoy your video." Ezra pulled the chair up as close as it could go to the computer table. He placed his gaming headphones over his ears and turned the volume of the video up to the max.

"Wait, mom! Can you turn out the light? There's a glare and it makes it hard to see."

"Of course." Ezra's mother flipped the lightswitch leaving the computer screen as the only source of light in the room. She continued up the stairs happy to leave her child behind to be entertained by somebody else for the rest of the evening. It had been a long day and the party had left her exhausted. The rest of her night consisted of a large glass or two of merlot (filled nearly to the brim) and watching a few more episodes of a new thriller series that a friend recommended she watch on Netflix.

Ezra listened carefully to what sounded like heavy wheezing coming through his headphones. The picture was pitch black, but it definitely said that the video was live at the bottom. He hovered the mouse over top of the full screen icon and clicked. The black video engulfed the twenty-seven inch computer monitor. Still, there was nothing, yet the breathing was getting heavier. Then, another sound came alive all of a sudden. It was the sound of something being dragged, but Ezra couldn't figure out what it could possibly be.

The dragging sound was ear piercingly loud now. It was right beside the camera. A light appeared and it became apparent that the camera was laying on the floor. A metal pipe was slammed down right in front of the camera sending a loud clanging noise through Ezra's headphones. It caused the boy to nearly jump out of his skin. He laughed the scare off and continued intently watching.

The camera was lifted off of the ground. The person carrying it remained behind the lens and out of focus. The movements were slow and methodical. Out of the room and down the hallway they went; the cameraman and Ezra on what felt like their own private journey. They didn't travel far before turning and entering into another room. In the center was a gurney with a body laying on it. The camera moved closer until it became apparent that the person laying on the gurney was Mateo. His eyes were closed and most of his face was a bloody mess.

Ezra sat back in confusion. *Maybe they're doing a skit* he thought. Something about the video playing on screen caused the boy's stomach to feel a bit nauseous, but he knew that it was all just entertainment. A big grin pushed Ezra's cheeks up against his eyes. He was fully prepared for whatever Tales of the Dead had planned for him.

The camera panned to the left. Beside the gurney was a cart with a tray that was filled with surgical instruments. A bloody hand reached forward into frame and grabbed a scalpel. The focus zoomed in on the scalpel until the instrument was nothing but a blur. The camera then zoomed back out changing it's focus from the blade to the body.

The cameraman moved closer, his bloody hand that held the scalpel still in view. Ezra couldn't help but feel like he was watching the real life version of a first person shooter video game.

With lightning fast speed, the hand sprung forward sending the sharp blade into Mateo's jugular. His eyes shot open and filled with fear as he frantically grabbed at his throat. Strange croaking noises escaped from Mateo's throat. A waterfall of blood ran freely from his neck. Then again and again and again the scalpel punctured through his skin. He clawed at his neck in an attempt to contain the blood, but by the seventh stabbing he was dead. Mateo's hands fell to the side of the gurney. Blood could be heard dripping onto the cold floor.

The focus stayed on Mateo's lifeless body for an uncomfortably long time. His eyes stared lifelessly into the camera, the corners of his mouth still frozen in horror.

Ezra's body felt funny. His head hurt and he wanted to be sick. He was waiting for his favorite youtuber to jump up and announce that he was okay, but he never did. A lump formed in the birthday boy's throat. His eyes began to water.

Mateo was dead.

The camera awkwardly danced around the room to the tune of the wheezing videographer. The walls had been covered in cobwebs and in time the spiders would weave their webs around Mateo as well. His corpse would become a part of Wakefall.

Ezra didn't want to watch any longer but he couldn't bring himself to move. He wanted to cry out for his mother but his throat felt as dry as the Sahara.

The camera stopped swinging back and forth and turned its focus on the person recording. Fomo wore the face of the dead. His skin was pale and his eyes were ghastly. The ball in his throat bounced in between each raspy breath. A wooly hand fell out of the darkness and grabbed Fomo by the hair. His neck snapped back exposing the ridges in his throat. Another hand holding a shard of glass came into view and ended the young man's life with a vicious horizontal slice. A fountain of blood sprayed into the air and onto the lens of the camera.

Fomo's hair was released and his body collapsed to the ground. The camera smacked against the floor and landed upside down. Ezra watched on as Fomo's legs twitched on screen. A slender man with a grizzly beard and green camouflage hat exited the room. The video continued streaming to the sound of silence.

It took a few minutes for Ezra to build up the courage to close out of Youtube. He removed his headphones and gently placed them on the computer table. With a press of a button, the monitor shut off. The nine year old constantly replayed the scene in his mind. All he could think about was the blood and the looks in their eyes.

Like a zombie, Ezra limped upstairs, passed his parents room, and climbed into bed. Even beneath the blankets he felt cold.

For months, he was haunted by night terrors. Purple bags formed beneath his eyes. What was once a lively and energetic child was now a shell of a human who no longer talked. And it's all because on his ninth birthday, Ezra witnessed a tale of the dead so disturbing that he could never tell another living soul.

Rumspringa

Bright red, liquid mercury smashed against the bubble shaped tops of thermometers as the temperature on the day was close to a record high for the state of Pennsylvania. A sweltering one hundred three degrees Fahrenheit scorched the inhabitants of the state. Realistically, it felt closer to one hundred nine degrees with the added humidity.

What you are about to read takes place in the present day. The person who unfortunately and unexpectedly experiences it is sixteen year old Jerry Sikes; a teen who's never been popular in school, and has had zero luck when it comes to the opposite sex. However, within the past month, this young man has found himself falling head over heels in love with a girl, a girl who in this particular circumstance belongs to the Amish community.

In the melting pot that is Lancaster Pennsylvania, the Amish normally tend to keep to themselves. No significant contact with the outside world. No use of modern technology. No partying.

That is unless it's during rumspringa.

Rumspringa is roughly a two-year period where Amish teenagers get the opportunity to venture out into society and discover for themselves whether or not they wish to stay or leave the conservative customs of the Amish community. It is during this particular rumspringa that Jerry had the opportunity of meeting Sally Miller; a polite, soft spoken, golden-haired Amish girl who's in the process of figuring out who she wants to be for the rest of her life. But, this is no ordinary rumspringa. Unfortunately, Jerry is unaware of the terrifying events that are soon to take place, for Sally's rumspringa is one that takes place not only in the rural heartland of Lancaster Pennsylvania, but somewhere in a twisted void located between light and shadow...

"You're absolutely ridiculous!" Jerry proclaimed out of the side of his mouth. It was directed toward his best friend Michael Ferguson. "Do you honestly realize how stupid you sound right now?" Jerry shoved an orange spoonful of mango and kiwi flavored frozen yogurt into his mouth. The chilled yogurt melting against his tongue sent his taste buds into a frenzy.

It was mid-evening. The sun was beginning to set in the far distance creating a beautiful smearing of red and orange in the background. Sweat poured from the boy's foreheads as they laughed and joked about Jerry's unusual, yet personally satisfying new love interest.

"Dude," Michael began before piling another pink spoonful of frozen yogurt into his mouth. As opposed to Jerry's, Michael's flavorful blend of choice was strawberry and banana. "She's Amish." Michael snapped both of his wrists forward and let loose a whipping sound as he pretended to guide an invisible horse and buggy. Jerry let out a sarcastic chuckle before snapping back with a retort of his own.

"For a guy who's never had a girlfriend in his life, you're real quick to judge." Michael pushed his glasses higher up onto his nose and looked away from Jerry. "What? All of a sudden you've got nothing to say?" Jerry placed his frozen yogurt onto the small green table they sat at outside of the frozen yogurt shop which was appropriately labeled FROZONE.

"I've had plenty of girlfriends in my life. It's just that none of them have been worth mentioning." Michael rocked anxiously back and forth in his chair. The boy could hardly keep a straight face as his lie had a strange tickling effect on him. "Besides, we're talking about you, not me. Come on man, you know that I'm just playing around. I'm happy that you've finally found someone who's interested in someone as weird and ugly as you." Michael laughed as Jerry wiped the sweat from his brow, a smirk smeared deviously across his face. "I don't even understand how you two could have possibly met."

"That's because you don't listen." Jerry replied. "I've told you three times already, we met at the fair. She was with a couple friends and I was with Justin and Luke."

"Oh yeah yeah yeah!" Michael interrupted. "You were standing outside of the bathroom or something while Luke was taking a crap and she came up to you and it was love at first sight. She was immediately attracted to your pimples and you just couldn't get enough of her little head covering." Michael's retelling mocked Jerry's shrill, yet puberty stricken voice. The two boys had been best friends since their early years in elementary school but sometimes Jerry wondered exactly why that was.

"So much for being supportive. You know, out of all our friends, I expected you to be the most supportive of the fact that I found a nice girl who actually likes me for me." Jerry scraped the bottom of the styrofoam cup to get the last little bit of frozen yogurt onto his yellow plastic spoon. The two teenagers joked around for a while longer talking about sports, girls, video games and whatever else popped into their minds. Within the hour, the sun had dropped low behind the horizon ensuing in the dim bulbs of the street lights to turn on. A gentle breeze rode through the air and felt good against the boy's sticky skin which at this point had been stained with dirt and sweat.

"So when do you plan on seeing her again?" Michael asked as the two were making their journey home.

"Tomorrow actually. She wants to meet over at Long's Park around two and hang out for a little."

"I thought that they weren't allowed to interact with normal people or something whacky like that." Michael's joke left him on the receiving end of a stern glare from Jerry. "Oh come on, you know what I mean. People that aren't Amish, I guess? I don't know how it works. This might come as a shock to you but, I have zero Amish friends." Their childish banter continued as the boys walked down the sidewalk. The street lights created what looked like poorly centered spotlights in an under budget screenplay.

"It's rumspringa."

"Excuse you?" Michael responded.

"Rumspringa stupid." Michael gave Jerry a puzzled look. "I don't know man, it's kind of hard to explain. Honestly I don't really understand it much myself." Jerry shrugged his shoulders displaying a huge lack of confidence in himself. His hands dug deep into his shorts pockets and his eyes surveyed the ground. The two were silent for a while before Jerry spoke up again. "I googled it the other day."

"Googled what?"

"Rumspringa! Have we not been having this conversation all day?" Michael threw his hands up apologetically. "I wasn't sure what it was so I looked it up. Basically it allows Amish teenagers between certain ages to go out and associate with people outside of the Amish community. Then, it's during this time that they can choose whether or not they want to be baptised in the Amish church or leave the community. The scary part was if they choose to leave, the Amish practically disown them and treat them as if they don't exist."

"Who would choose to stay Amish? No TV. No internet. No video games! Just a bunch of churning butter, washing clothes, and petting horses. You have to be so stupid not to leave. Tell her that she needs to come to the dark side." Michael said in his best (which was not very good) Darth Vader voice.

"You would be surprised. According to Google, a large majority of the Amish choose to stay within the church and in their own community." Michael snickered and shook his head.

"That's because they don't get to experience the real fun stuff! All they do is go bowling and hang out with creeps like you! Churning butter...Or hanging out with you? After weighing my options, all of a sudden now I want to become Amish too." Jerry raised his fist into the air and aimed it towards Michael's face. "Hey I'm kidding, I'm kidding!

Relax." Jerry unclenched his fist and gave Michael an unsuspecting shove that caused him to trip out onto the side of the road. As Michael looked up he could see bright white headlights quickly closing in on him. Overtaken with shock, the boy closed his eyes and could hear the squeal of the rubber tires burning against the road as the car swerved around his body.

"Stay the hell out of the road! Stupid kid!" screamed an older man who was driving the rusty turquoise truck that had almost just ran Michael into the ground. The boy raised to his feet and gave Jerry a stern look.

"Seriously? I could have just died!" Michael scolded, brushing off his t-shirt. Jerry apologized and assured his friend that there was quite some distance between him and the oncoming truck. It took some time, but Michael decided to forgive him and the boys continued homeward.

The sun had completely faded into the distance giving birth to a full moon and a star studded night. "So, any idea what you're going to do with Sally once you get to the park?" Jerry scratched his head furiously, hard enough that he had to fix the now crooked placement of his glasses back onto the bridge of his nose.

"Nope." the boy answered. "It's hard to communicate with her since they can't use technology of any kind, so I'm honestly not even sure if she'll even show up. But, if she does, I'm guessing we'll just walk around and talk. Maybe feed some ducks over by the pond."

"God you're so booooooring! Where's the hot steamy action?" Michael whined. "All she's gonna be thinking about is getting home and hanging clothes out to dry which would probably be a lot more fun than what you have planned."

"Did you like it out in the middle of the street almost getting hit by cars? Because I can make that happen again if that's what you want." Michael lifted his hands out in front of his body as if to surrender all whilst still mocking Jerry.

"You can't kill me just yet." Michael protested. "At least not before I get to hear all about how you screw up this date tomorrow. After that, you can push me into as many streets as you want. As a matter of fact, I'll probably want to throw myself into the street after hearing about how badly this goes." Michael gave Jerry a pat on the back and turned down the street that he lived on. "Text me after your date tomorrow so I can hear all about it sweetheart!" Jerry lifted both hands into the air, each representing the same obscene gesture as the other before continuing to walk until he himself arrived home ten minutes later.

The next day Jerry woke up at eleven, had his hair and teeth brushed and his best looking outfit (in his own opinion) on by twelve, and left for the park at one leaving plenty of time to get there ensuring that he wouldn't be late. He arrived at the park at one forty and sat down on a bench that overlooked a pond crowded with ducks. His stomach churned. An uneasiness lingered the closer that the time ticked towards two. Patiently, Jerry waited on the bench afraid to skulk around the park and miss Sally's arrival.

Within twenty minutes, Jerry had checked Instagram seven times, played three games of Candy Crush, had once again Googled rumspringa in an attempt to educate himself more, and had taken four selfies and uploaded them to Instagram receiving only two likes on each picture from his Grandma who he believed should not be on social media at her not so ripe age of seventy one, and from Michael who left a comment on each picture, both of them subtly calling him a homosexual.

Jerry stared down at his phone. He grew increasingly worried once the white numbers displayed across his home screen read ten minutes after two. The boy stared out over the pond and watched as two ducks chased and flew after each other soaring elegantly across the murky green water. A part of him felt jealous of the relationship those two ducks had and he felt foolish for actually believing that there was a girl who seriously showed some sort of interest in him. Again, Jerry looked back down at his phone which now read two sixteen.

Releasing a sigh of defeat, and feeling a small part of his mind bend and heartbreak, Jerry shuffled towards the pond and pulled a tiny ziploc bag of bread crumbs out of his pocket. He had planned on feeding the ducks with Sally, but figured there was no use in wasting the food if she didn't come. So, he decided to feed the ducks by himself. He placed his hand into the baggie and pulled out half a handful. The tiny cubes expanded as they landed on and absorbed the water. Jerry watched as an army of ducks came swooping down from every direction. Once they realized that it was he who provided the treats, they waddled over and honked in anticipation of more.

"You're starting without me?" a soft voice said from behind him. Jerry spun around attempting to hide the widespread smirk that was strewn across his babyish face. Sally's hair was a thin, wavy golden just like he remembered it. Most of it was hidden beneath her black prayer covering that sat on the top of her head. Per usual, Sally was clothed in a conservative, light purple dress that fell to right above her white sock covered ankles.

"Um, no!" Jerry blurted out as he struggled to make eye contact with the girl. "The ducks just seemed hungry so I figured why not give them a snack sized portion while I wait."

"I see." Sally held her palm out, waiting for Jerry to dump some of the bread crumbs that he had into her hand. The two teens sat on the bench in front of the pond at the park talking and laughing for hours. It was a beautiful day with the sun hovering above far away in the sky, beaming thin rays of light down onto the earth. The longer that they talked, the more Jerry could feel himself developing feelings for the girl. She was smart, funny, strong willed, and most importantly, interested in him! Everything about her seemed too good to be true.

"Wow, I can't believe that it's five thirty already." Jerry said, looking down at his phone. "What time is your father coming to get you?"

"I think that he's coming around six."

"That's going to be here before we know it." Jerry released a moan, wishing in his head that he could live in this moment forever. It was as though in these last few hours, nothing else in his life mattered. The boy didn't have a worry in the world. "Do you think that this will happen again?" Jerry squeaked out as he stared down at his shoes, embarrassed at the fact that he had to ask such a question. He was new to the dating world and he hoped that her conservative lifestyle had left her as clueless to the circumstance as he was.

"I would like it to." Sally answered. Jerry lifted his head up with a newly found strength of confidence and again found himself unable to hide that childish smile that would on occasion possess the bottom half of his face. "How about Saturday?" He made a sucking noise with his teeth and made a facial expression that made it appear as if he was in deep thought.

"I think I could make that work. I might have to switch around some of my daily activities like watching T.V. and doing nothing. But I guess I can push doing nothing back until Sunday if I really have to." Sally laughed and a strand of her golden hair fell onto the front of her face and clung to her nose.

"Oh no! Please, don't let me interfere with your busy schedule. I wouldn't want to complicate things for you." Jerry stared out over the pond and watched the ducks gracefully glide over the water even more beautifully than they had done so just a few hours prior. The rippling water and breaths of wind were serene.

"Saturday is perfect." For a while, the two sat in silence and watched the green and brown ducks wade effortlessly across the murky pond water. Jerry looked down at his phone again and the time now read five fifty-seven. "Only a few more minutes." Jerry spoke quietly. Sally looked down at Jerry's phone and gave him a puzzled look.

"Why do you have big headed turtles with eyes on your phone?" she innocently asked. Jerry immediately felt a wave of embarrassment flood over him. *Why wouldn't you change your wallpaper before coming out here?* He questioned himself. *You're so dumb!*

"They're teenage mutant ninja turtles! They're awesome! They like, fight crime and eat pizza and stuff." Jerry attempted to play the ninja turtles up as best he could without coming across as a lunatic. But even he thought it all sounded extremely far-fetched the longer he went on explaining. So for a girl who has had no exposure to television and cartoons, she must think that he's lost his marbles.

"That's kind of weird." the girl said with a giggle. "Can you take pictures on your phone?" Jerry smiled and nodded.

"Yeah of course! See." He turned the camera on and handed his phone over to the girl. "Take a picture of whatever you want." Sally swung the phone around observing the world through the rectangular screen.

"What about us?" Sally questioned in a high spirited shrill. Jerry asked for the phone back and changed the camera setting so that they could see themselves while taking the picture. He handed his phone back to the conservative girl and explained how to take the photograph. She stretched her arm out in front of them and snapped a couple of photos with a gentle press of her thumb against the screen.

It was hard to make out, but Jerry was sure that he saw a tattoo on the girl's forearm of what looked like the head of a goat as her sleeve rode up her arm just a tiny bit. He didn't get a clear look at it, but his level of intrigue was high. The chances of seeing a unicorn gallop through the park were greater than seeing an Amish teenager with a tattoo. Then again, Google did inform him that rumspringa was the time for Amish youth to 'let loose'; so maybe that was the case here.

After four pictures, Sally was content.

"Now you can put that picture on your phone instead of those weird turtles." Jerry reminded Sally that the turtles were awesome and that they were ninjas, not just any normal turtles.

"I didn't know that you had a tattoo." Jerry said with a smile. Sally tensed up and pulled down on the cuff of her sleeve. It was apparent that his question immediately sent an uncomfortable shock through her entire being. He was reluctant to ask the following question, but figured he would anyway. "Do you think I could see it?"

Sally pinched the bottom of her sleeve again and pulled it down towards her hand. It was subtle, but she moved her body a few inches away from Jerry on the bench. What had been an evening filled with talking and laughter now seemed troubled by an awkward silence between the two shy teens. Jerry couldn't help but to be curious as to what he had seen. Maybe it was an oblong shaped bruise that she had somehow come to have and his eyes had deceived him? He had only seen the dark coloring on her skin for a split second. Then again, she was Amish, so how weird would it be for her to get a tattoo of a goat if she did decide to be wildly spontaneous one day and get one? *Goats are hip in the Amish community, right?* Amidst the wrestling match taking place between his thoughts, Jerry came to the conclusion that he too would probably get some type of farm animal as a tattoo if he were Amish. It just seemed right.

In the near distance, Jerry could hear the echoes of trotting hooves nearing closer and closer. Sally turned her head and watched as a thick bearded man along with a young boy approached them in a horse and buggy. Both the man and the boy were wearing dark-colored suits with solid-colored shirts, black shoes, and straw broad-brimmed hats. The older man's face looked heavily labored. Strings of gray stood out in the deep hairy forest that formed into his beard and deep wrinkle lines caused his cloudy eyes to appear sunken into his skull. The young boy who looked to be no older than the age of seven had dirty blonde hair which was neatly cut; bangs in the front, parted in the middle, and slicked over the side to cover his ears. Jerry stared at the boy who stared back at him with his bright blue eyes. Despite glowing in the sun, they gave off a dark, lifeless energy.

"There's my father! And over there beside him is Isaac." Sally stood up and began to walk in the direction of the buggy. Jerry stood as well but hesitated to move towards the horse drawn locomotive. The two riders inside gave off an unsettling feeling. "Come say hello," she insisted, waving for Jerry to walk over with her.

"Oh, of course!" Jerry said, pretending to be dumbfounded. On the outside, Jerry performed the part of the excited boy meeting the parent for the first time perfectly. But internally, he was overridden with anxiety and had absolutely no desire to meet Sally's father. With a tight pull of the reins, Sally's father brought the large brown horse to a halt. He sat high up in the buggy like a king looking out across his lands on a mobile throne.

"Father," Sally said in a tone that provided more emotion than her body showed. "This is Jerry." The girl's father looked down on the boy and gave off a heavy snarl before looking back at his daughter and speaking in a heavily accented Pennsylvania Dutch. Jerry had no choice but to sit back and watch the father and daughter speak to each other in the foreign dialect. He could feel his face getting hot as he awkwardly watched the two converse about him in a tongue that he couldn't understand.

"Jerry, is it?" the thick bearded man asked the boy with an intense glare. Jerry felt his entire being tense up. He wished at that moment that he had a shell like the teenage mutant ninja turtles in which he could hide in.

"Yes, sir."

"My daughter seems fond of you for whatever reason, which as a father pleases me." Jerry felt his lips uncontrollably twist into an embarrassing smile that he attempted to hide before either Sally or her father saw for themselves. "Then again, what kind of a father would I be if I did not see these qualities that she is so fond of for myself? For this reason, I extend the hand of generosity from myself and my family to you, and if you were to accept, it would be a pleasure for us to have you over as our guest for dinner this coming Saturday." Jerry felt a nervousness and a heavy anxiety that he had never experienced before. Sally's father spoke with such intellect that Jerry narrowly understood what was being said to him even though the words being spoken were in English. He felt a way for Sally that no other girl had ever made him feel before, and for this reason he knew that there was only one way to answer.

"Yes please, or um...Thank you! I mean, that would be great." Jerry fumbled through his words like a developing infant. "It would be an honor sir to get to know you and your family more."

The hazy grey spheres that were the conservative man's eyes glared with a concentrated ferocity. Sally's father turned to his daughter and the quiet child Isaac. He gave a slight nod to his children before a few more accented words were exchanged between him and Sally. The way that they spoke and motioned toward him made Jerry feel like he was an object being bid for at an auction. The main question being - was he worth the price?

"Very well!" The elderly man blurted out. "Would you have a problem with meeting us here at the park on Saturday at five o'clock?" Jerry nodded his head in approval. "Great, we can pick you up here. Until then," Sally's father tipped his hat forward like the cowboys would do in those old western movies. With a gentle stroke of his bulky ashen beard, he adjusted his body in preparation to depart. "You are indeed a kind boy with an exceptionally pure heart. We expect nothing less from our guests."

With a fierce whip of the reins, Jerry watched as Sally, her father, and the quietly ominous Isaac were trotted out of the park. Walking gingerly in the direction of the park's exit, he couldn't believe how quickly his relaxed plans of hanging out with Sally turned into a formal dining with her entire family. Their newborn relationship felt like it was moving at lightspeed.

"Are you a freaking idiot? Like, seriously? You're really going to go over there?!" Mike shouted through the phone into Jerry's ear as he lay sprawled across his bed. It was dressed in an Xbox themed comforter and sheet set.

"Why wouldn't I?" Jerry asked his panicked best friend.

"Dude, they're like...Amish or whatever!" Jerry gave off a friendly chuckle but could tell that Michael was completely serious. "Listen to me, and for the love of God just do it for once. You're gonna go over there and they will have you folding laundry, fetching well water, and cleaning up horse crap like it's freaking seventeen eighty-two! It's gonna suck, big time!"

"First off, I am not going to be cleaning up horse crap. Secondly, this is why you have never had a girlfriend! It's because you're so ridiculously close minded. And no girl finds closed minded guys sexy."

"Wow, you had to go directly for my feelings, didn't you?" Both boys laughed as Jerry reached over across his bed and grabbed a small, spongy ball. He began throwing it up in the air and catching it repeatedly, all while continuing to lay on his back across the bed. "Besides, when did you find out what girls think is sexy? One Amish girl and all of a sudden you're a lady guru? *Pfffffft.* And just to make things clear, I have never had a girlfriend out of the fear that they would try to change me. I'm awesome as is! So, as the ladies start to mature they will come to realize what it is they've been missing out on."

"What does that even mean?" Jerry questioned as he tossed the ball clumsily into the air.

"Listen young padawan," Michael began in his cheesiest Yoda impression, "there are only twenty-four hours in one day. Video games I must play. Healthy it is."

"I see your point master." Jerry responded. Michael gave him an approving grunt from the other side of the phone. "Unfortunately, the dark side has a hold on me."

"Disappointed, I am." Michael answered, still in his terrible Yoda impersonation. "Well, while you're over in the corn fields eating dumplings, corn, and loving on Jesus by candlelight, know that I'll be home playing Call of Duty having the time of my life! There are nine year old kids out in the virtual world that need to feel my wrath! When you think about it, I'm doing the work of Jesus by blessing these noobs online with my amazing skills."

"Really, you had to bring Jesus into this? Because if that was your attempt to make me feel guilty, it didn't work. Besides, I like dumplings.

And hey, I'll even go as far as to say Jesus isn't even too bad himself."

"God, you're a loser." Michael scoffed into the phone. "Well, I have to go down and set the table for dinner before my mom starts flipping out, you know how that goes." Jerry shook his head up and down on the other side of the phone as if Michael was able to see his mannerisms. "I'll talk to you later." Jerry held the phone up in front of him and clicked on the red button that disconnected the call.

In less than twenty-four hours, Jerry would find himself traveling with a family that he did not know, to a place that he did not understand. The more he thought about what Michael had said to him on the phone, the more nervous he became. Eventually, brushing the thoughts out of his mind, Jerry stood up from the bed and walked over to his closet. He needed to decide on what he was going to wear to his first, and what would be his last Amish dinner.

Jerry gazed into the overcast sky as he sat on the same park bench that he and Sally had sat on not too long ago. The boy looked down at his phone. The time read seven minutes after five. *Were they not coming?* he wondered. *Was this his opportunity to leave and say that he thought that they forgot about the dinner?* Hundreds of thoughts rushed through Jerry's mind as he rubbed his hands up and down the creased thighs of his khaki slacks. Tiny droplets of silent rain fell into the pond forming a parade of circular ripples to shoot across its surface.

Jerry stood up from the bench and took another quick look at his phone which was now showing eleven minutes after five. Holding his hands out in front of him, Jerry let out a sigh and turned towards the entrance of the park. There was no need for him to wait out in the rain.

"Jerry!" All of a sudden, he heard his name shouted from a distance. Jerry turned around and could see a larger buggy than Sally's father had driven in their previous encounter riding up from about fifty yards away; the sound of clopping hooves soon followed. This buggy was led by two large, sooty brown horses instead of only one.

"Hop on in son." the bearded man said, bringing the steeds to a halt beside the wet teen. Getting into the buggy was more difficult than Jerry had imagined it would be. He found himself clumsily bumping into Sally, her father, and Isaac who still at this point had not said a single word. "Careful now. Come on, in with ye." The buggy was crowded. Jerry couldn't help but wonder why it was necessary for them to bring Isaac along for the ride knowing how small of a space there was. But, he didn't dare to ask.

The rain was coming down hard now. The sky was ominously dark for a midsummer day that hadn't yet reached six o'clock. Gray clouds blotted out the thin rays of sun that occasionally found a way to seep through and pierce the soaked ground. Riding with the family had been an uncomfortably quiet experience. Jerry wanted to speak up, but was afraid that the lack of voices may be due to cultural reasons. So, he decided to keep his mouth shut unless spoken to.

The strange buggy-fellows traveled far into the rural depths of Lancaster County. Rows of buildings and shops had been replaced with fields of corn. Jerry constantly slapped at his skin, fending off the bloodsucking mosquitos that craved for the nectar within his veins. With a swift jolt of his right hand, Sally's father redirected the horses to the left where they traveled far down a chalky, dirt pathway. In the near distance, Jerry could see a two storied white house connected to a red-roofed barn.

"Here we are." The Amish father's heavy voice startled Jerry after breaking what seemed like an endless silence.

Jerry stepped out of the buggy into an environment that felt like a completely separate world from the one that he was used to. Peering through the dark blue shuttered windows of the house from afar, Jerry noticed the uncanny darkness that swam around in the home's bowels. High pitched songs hummed through the air from tiny birds that fluttered around a rundown silo. Hanging menacingly above the stalks of corn that surrounded the property were unpleasant looking scarecrows bloated with straw. An odor that resembled that of iron owned the air.

"Come!" Sally's father said as he adjusted the black hat that fit atop his head like a snug glove. "Let's get inside before we get drowned out by all of this rain." Sally ran ahead and motioned for Jerry to follow close behind.

The worn screen door slammed behind Isaac as he entered the house last, closing the heavy wooden door behind him. Chilling shadows that were cast out by the candles sporadically placed around the home frisked about the walls. Jerry could not help but notice the disturbing art that hung about the house as he mindlessly followed behind Sally. One was the image of small children, no older than five or six, slaughtering cattle with devilish smiles sprawled across their juvenile faces. Another of a dark, long haired woman walking solemnly into a wood crowded with mutated imp like creatures prodding her with bloody spears. A third being a detailed painting of a cannibalistic horse feasting upon the corpse of a decaying foal while being straddled by a young girl wearing a blood-soaked white gown. Jerry's nerves grew uneasy but he played the paintings off as misconceptions caused by the house's poor lighting.

Sally stopped inside of a room that was immediately to their right after climbing a flight of rickety wooden stairs. Jerry stepped into the room behind the blonde haired girl and watched as she closed the door behind them. He was not yet afraid, but could feel himself being overwhelmed with an alarming uneasiness. Sally walked over to a wooden nightstand, picked up a book of matches, struck a light with the flick of her wrist, and lit a small pine scented Yankee Candle.

"It's really dark in your house. I bet it gets kind of scary here sometimes." Jerry barely recognized the sound of his own voice after having not spoken in such a long time. Sally refused to acknowledge his question, but instead paced around the room quickly jerking her head back and forth in a bestial motion. Slowly, the girl began to spin around while humming a gentle tune quietly to herself. "Are you alright?" Jerry asked in a weary, pubescent voice that cracked mid-sentence.

Little by little, Jerry could feel his uneasiness metamorphosize into an unmanageable fear. Instinctively, the innocent youth that lived within Jerry forced him to tread back into the corner of the room. As his second step landed onto the wooden floor, a high pitched creak dragged through the room causing Sally to stop spinning and unnaturally contort her head back into place. The girl's movements became swift and robotic.

"Dinner isn't ready yet." Sally said as she cocked her head stiffly at an angle. As she whipped her head around, Jerry could hear the bones in her neck crack and pop.

"That's okay," Jerry whispered hoarsely. "I'm not really that hungry at the moment."

"I am." the girl shot back instantly. "How about a drink? Are you thirsty?"

"No, I'm okay. Really." Jerry insisted on creeping his way as far and as deep into the corner of the room as his body could fit.

"Let's play a game." Jerry didn't know how to answer. His mind flashed back to the moment when Michael tried bribing him into staying home and playing video games all evening. The things that he would have done to be home comfortably in his room. "Come on, sit." Sally said as she walked over to her bed, sat down, and patted in a spot for Jerry to perch beside her. Apprehensively, Jerry pulled himself from the gloomy corner and moved over to the bed. Sally eyeballed his every step as he tiptoed through the darkness of the room without saying a word. The drumming of the rain against the hard surface of the roof struck with the melody of a soulless hymn.

"What kind of game are we going to play?" Jerry muttered as he sat his rear down onto the unexpectedly hard bed. Sally smiled a toothless smile and made eye contact with him, not saying a word for an uncomfortably long period of time. Jerry looked away multiple times with the hope that she would remove her gaze from off of him but the Amish girl kept her focus. A clock *tick-tocked* in the background.

"A fun one of course." the blonde finally replied to a question that was asked thirty seconds prior. "And, by the time that we're done, dinner should be about ready. It's going to be delicious." Sally's eyebrows danced across her forehead as if they had a mind of their own. She physically looked like the same girl that he had quickly grown so fond of, but something was wrong. Something was missing. Something was different.

Sally stood up from her position on the bed and walked over into a corner of the room which was now sheltered completely by darkness. Jerry squinted and could make out the silhouette of the girl opening a dresser drawer and pulling something out of it before hearing the *clunk* of the drawer being slammed shut. His eyes widened as he focused intently on what Sally was gripping firmly in her hand. Streams of sweat began to run down the back of Jerry's neck, sliding fleetly across the bony rickets of his spine. His breathing became heavy and rapid. *Why was this happening?* Jerry wondered in a state of mental despair.

Sally placed the dagger that had been clutched against her palm on the nightstand beside the flickering candle. Jerry could clearly see what it was that she had fetched from the drawer. He had thought she had a knife, but now the candlelight confirmed his theory.

The dagger was stained brown in certain areas that provided Jerry with the knowledge that Sally had used it before. Sally pinched at the cuff of her blue shirt sleeve and began to roll it up. She then switched to the right sleeve and began to roll that one as well. The tattoo that she had been so hesitant to speak of the other day nearly glowed against her forearm as the light from the candle shined against it. Jerry had been accurate when he believed that he saw the head of a goat tattooed on her forearm, but it was the rest of the tattoo that really frightened him. Stemming out of the goat's forehead were two long, hellish horns that curved to the outside. Connected to the animalistic head was that of a nude, human female torso and legs that were crossed over one another clothed in baggy pants. Massive, dark wings sprouted out of the beast's back while it's left hand pointed down in a diagonal position while the right arm arched upwards in a ninety degree angle. With time now to focus on the image, it was clear that the so-called tattoo on Sally's forearm was carved into her flesh, not created through the puncturing of an ink filled needle.

Jerry couldn't take his focus away from the hideously carved baphomet that was etched into Sally's body. As quickly as she had put it down on the nightstand, Sally grabbed the dagger and clenched her hand around the brown leather hilt. "Let's make the goat smile." She placed the point of the blade against her arm and pressed down on her skin.

"What? No! Why would you harm yourself like this?" Jerry screamed at the girl who was already puncturing through the skin on her arm. Blood rushed to the surface like a geyser. Sally carved an unsteady line across the face of the baphomet creating a grimly staggered smile. She did so without wincing or making a sound.

"I think that my picture is complete now, don't you agree?" Jerry watched horrified as vital fluid poured from the girl's arm and splattered onto the dusty hardwood floor.

"I think that maybe I should get your dad," Jerry said in a panic attempting to get up from the bed, only to be met with the tip of the silver dagger being pointed towards his face.

"Dinner isn't ready yet." the girl repeated. Swallowing a pasty ball of saliva, Jerry returned to the bed where he felt as though he had far overstayed his welcome. He closed his eyes and pinched his skin hoping to awaken from what he prayed was nothing more than a terrible nightmare. The frightened teen pinched harder and harder but as he opened his eyes he was met with the sight of a shrunken sword being waved around in front of his face.

"I want you to lick this." Sally thrusted the bloody tip of the blade back into Jerry's face.

"No, I'm not licking it. What is wrong with you? Why are you doing this?" A tear fell from Jerry's eye as he pleaded with the Amish teenager.

"I'm doing this because I exist solely for the purpose of making Him happy." Jerry shot off a puzzled look.

"Him? Who is Him? Your father? What could I have possibly done to anger your father? I just got here!" Jerry tried to get up but found himself being pushed back down onto the bed. Sally licked the blood off of her arm, tossed it around in her mouth for a few seconds, blended it with spit and mucus, and formed a rusty red paste in which she spat onto the boy's face.

"Lick the dagger, Jerry." Sally spoke in a stern, yet catatonic voice. Helpless, afraid, and alone, Jerry found himself crying hysterically on the girl's bed with his tongue erected out of his mouth with repulsed anticipation. The wad of spit that was ejected onto Jerry's face slid slowly down his acne populated cheek. Sally placed her middle and index fingers into Jerry's mouth and forced the cold, wet steel onto the top of his tongue. The tiny flame on the end of the candle flickered wildly as Jerry violently gagged and coughed uncontrollably. Behind the copious downpour and thick clouds, the sun had disappeared completely; right along with Jerry's willpower and hope. Sally laughed maniacally as she watched Jerry gag and fight with his reflexes to not vomit all over the floor.

"Now, it's my turn," Sally whispered into the boy's ear. "Put your arm out." Jerry shook his head defiantly. "This is how it works Jerry. I have to taste your blood since you've tasted mine. It's part of the game. You wouldn't want to make Him angry would you? Because He doesn't like those who refuse to have a little fun from time to time." Sally moved her wrist around in a circular motion with the dagger hovering above Jerry's neck. "He has to be happy! This is His day and you will not screw this up for Him!"

For the first time, he had heard the girl raise her voice and it frightened him more than anything ever had before. Jerry shut his eyes as tight as he could and outstretched his arm. He could hear the girl say in an undertone "He will be extremely pleased with your decision. You're making the right choice." As Sally placed the edge of the blade onto Jerry's arm and began to put forth the slightest bit of pressure, she heard her name bellowed from downstairs.

"Sally! Sally! Come on down now, it's time for dinner." Jerry left his eyes closed until he heard an intense slam of the dagger on the nightstand beside the bed.

"Dinner's ready." Sally pulled Jerry to his feet and again motioned for him to follow her through the house. He was unaware of whether he should feel relieved that he was getting out of that room alone with her and away from that dagger, or if he was to feel even more terrified of what may come at dinner.

Sally and Jerry entered into a large dining room surrounded by what felt like a faux gallery of distasteful, malevolent paintings. In the center was a long, dark wood table with six massive timbered chairs surrounding the perimeter. On the table were four place settings; each with a spoon, knife, and fork. A golden candelabra with five lit burning candles ruled as the centerpiece. Beside it was a heavily stained gold chalice. Already seated was Isaac, the mute child who still showed no signs of speaking up. The seat across from Isaac was assigned to Jerry while Sally positioned herself to the right of her brother.

"Here we are! Here we are!" Sally's father exclaimed merrily as he walked into the dining room with a large steaming dish of pot pie.

Wrapped around his neck was a pink apron stained in both new and old food that had been spilled during preparations. Perspiration slid down the man's face, eventually disappearing into the wiley wisps of his unkempt beard. He then exited the room and a few moments later reentered with a dish of corn, beets, and buttered noodles.

Jerry looked over at Sally and watched her rub the blood from her arm and smear it across the table. Isaac lifelessly stared forward; his eyes glossed over, lips bent downward, hair suddenly disheveled. The father anxiously sat down next to Jerry and began plating food first for himself, and then for Isaac. While doing so, Sally's father hummed the same tune that she had while upstairs in the torture chamber she called a room.

Unsure of how to handle himself, Jerry made an attempt to grab a couple pieces of food amongst the barbaric frenzy that was taking place at the dinner table. Sally and her father were sloshing food across their plates, dripping and dropping corn and pot pie all over. Isaac's eyes remained cold and dark, locked onto whatever was set before him, which in this instance happened to be a worrisome city boy. And out of the corner of that city boy's eye, he noticed droplets of blood falling from Sally's arm and into the food on her plate.

"Don't be shy son, eat." the father ordered. Jerry continued fetching food until Sally grabbed the plate from under him. She started tossing a portion of everything onto the plate, creating one big, uneven food mountain.

"Here you go." Sally said in a pleasant tone. "I'm starving." The girl raised her fork, but before she could drive it into a piece of food, she found herself being scolded by her father.

"Where are your manners?" the man questioned. "You know that we bless all of our meals before eating. You know that!" The blonde teen scowled and dropped the fork angrily next to her plate. "Hands." the man demanded. Sally rolled her eyes and grabbed Isaac's hand who himself made no effort to move at all. She then reached across the table and grabbed her father's hand who then turned to Jerry. He held his grizzled hand out anticipating the boy to grip it as everyone else was doing. Jerry grabbed the man's hand and stared forward, finding himself lost within the eyes of Isaac.

"Are you just going to stare at him all day or are you going to grab his hand?" The bass behind the question caused Jerry to jump. Reaching across the table with great hesitance, Jerry pulled on the boy's arm until their hands locked together. Isaac remained stiff as stone.

"Thank you for this delicious meal," Sally's father began in prayer. "If it was not for you oh Lord, we would be nothing. Our crops would not grow. Our children would not thrive. And we would have no true purpose. But with you, all is possible Lord, which is why we dedicate this night to you and ask for your blessing. May you become mightier with each day as we feel more and more honored to do your bidding as it should be done here on Earth. Amen." Sally, her father, and Jerry all released hands. Isaac's arms fell limp onto the table and into his food. The man and his daughter went on to take their index finger, place it against their sternum, line it down to the middle of their stomachs and then slide their finger from left to right.

"Hail Satan." Sally said before ferociously shoving a forkful of food deep into her mouth.

"Hail Satan!" her father reiterated in a louder, more triumphant tone. Jerry lowered his eyes to his plate. The level of shock and panic channeling through his body had left him devoid of emotions. "Do you know just how lucky you are, Jerry?" the elderly man asked.

Jerry didn't respond. Instead, he sat in his chair like a lifeless vessel, mirroring the young boy slouching across from him. "To be a sacrifice for Satan himself is such an amazing honor! The biggest actually." Tiny parcels of food sprayed out of the man's mouth and across the table as he lectured. "You did good this Rumspringa. You've gone out and found possibly the best sacrifice this community has ever seen! Pure-hearted. Virgin...I'm assuming. Satan will undoubtedly bless our family for many years to come."

"It was almost too easy father. Go out to where those idiots in the world believe that God is their savior," Sally said with a mocking chuckle in her voice. "Find a teenage boy who is gentle and has a pure heart, bring him back here for the annual sacrifice, and please the only Lord that this world will one day show mercy to. That being of course our lord and savior, Satan."

Jerry could hear everything that was being said, but his mind was refusing to process the meaning behind the words. Sally's father let out a moan of approval while shoveling a helping of pot pie into his mouth.

"Sweetheart, what's the matter? Don't you like my cooking?" Jerry found himself returning to a reality that he so desperately wanted to flee from. He looked up anticipating Sally's mother to walk around the corner, but there was nobody. "Honey, please. I spent all evening preparing this meal for us. You know how important this night is for Him and the people of our community." A sickening feeling overcame the family's guest as he realized there was never going to be a motherly voice in response.

Sally's father was looking and speaking directly to his son...Isaac.

"Dad, would you just leave him alone? It's very good, I promise. Everything tonight has been absolutely perfect. He will be very pleased."

"You're probably right. It's just nice to hear it or have it shown every now and then. She is supposed to be the love of my life after all!" The man threw his spoon onto the plate. Pieces of corn were scattered over the table.

"What are you talking about?" Jerry questioned, finally regaining all of his wits. "That's your son! Right?" Jerry looked concerningly around the table. "And your brother."

"I guess sort of, but not really. My mother's soul is inside of Isaac so physically he's my brother, but spiritually he's my mother." Sally responded nonchalantly. "My mother died while she was giving birth to Isaac. She was removed from this earth to a much better place so that she could slave away for our Lord. Anytime that a woman dies during childbirth, Satan places the woman's soul into the body of her newborn child so that He may then do as He pleases with the rotting carcass that we bury in the ground. So ever since Isaac was born, he has acted as a wife to my father in more ways than one." Sally smiled as she looked for signs of approval from her father.

Jerry understood now why the boy was the way that he was. *What form of horrors has he been subjected to in his young life? What heinous acts were forced upon his gentle soul? It's like his mind's been completely shattered.*

The strike of a grandfather clock turning eight in another room rang through the home. "Damn, we're running late. Can you get the things from the other room, Sally?" The girl nodded her head and gracefully excused herself from the table.

The room was silent. Jerry rocked back and forth nervously in his chair. He wanted to run, wanted to hide, wanted to scream. Wanted to live. Out of an old anxious habit, he rubbed his hands against his thighs. A hard, solid object was tucked into his pocket. Suddenly, he remembered that he had his phone. There was an effort to be as inconspicuous as possible as he tucked a few fingers into his front right pocket and pulled on the device.

Tapping on the screen caused the phone to light up. Jerry stared down at the picture of himself and Sally smiling next to each other at the park. It was a moment that he cherished, yet it felt like ages ago. It was a different time with what felt like a completely different girl.

As cautiously as he could, Jerry placed the phone firmly atop his thigh. Trying not to be too obvious, he opened the messages app and clicked on Michael's name.

HELP! They're going to kill me! Call the police!!! He hit send, watching as the thin delivery bar traveled halfway across the screen and stopped.

He looked up and felt on edge as Isaac remained seated across from him, still with that icy stare. Jerry dropped his head back toward the phone. The bar was still stuck halfway across the screen.

Like something dead that had been given a second chance at life, the green bar slid the rest of the way across the screen. A small notification appeared beneath the text confirming that the message had been sent. Jerry waited quietly in anticipation for his phone to vibrate against his unsteady leg. He could hear the clinking and clanking of Sally rummaging through objects from a nearby room.

Bzzzz. Bzzzz. Bzzzz.

The phone vibrated. Jerry cautiously dropped his eyes to his phone so as to not give away what he was doing.

One New Message: Micheal. Beside Michael's name was also the poop emoji, the unicorn emoji, and the rainbow emoji. Jerry slid his thumb across the screen and tapped his passcode in to unlock the phone. 0520. His birthday.

The phone lit up against Jerry's leg and revealed the message that Michael had sent back to him.

LOL! Told you that you would hate it out there. They've got you working like a slave huh? Call me when you get home so I can hear about

how right I was. Also, I've been killing it online, just an FYI...

I'm so stupid! Jerry thought. *Why am I wasting my time trying to contact Michael when I should be contacting my mom?* With a swipe of his finger, Jerry proceeded to go into his contacts and find his mother's number. He clicked on her name and a blank text message opened.

Mom, please come and get me! I need help. Sally and her family are talking about sacrificing me to the devil. I'm so -

"Give it to me," A voice insisted from behind him. It belonged to Sally. Jerry let out a loose sigh and felt himself die a little bit inside. He raised his hand from beneath the table and handed the girl his phone. She read the message silently to herself and then slammed the phone down onto the floor as hard as she could, completely shattering the fragile screen. Sally forcefully gripped Jerry's wrist and slammed it down onto the arm of the chair. Then, she reached behind her and grabbed a thick wire which she used to tie Jerry's right wrist down onto the chair so that he couldn't move.

"What are you going to do to me?" Jerry cried. "Please, just let me go home! I won't say anything to anybody about tonight. Nobody needs to know about any of this! I just really want to go home. I...I promise!" The boy found himself bawling hysterically as Sally tied his other wrist down to the chair. Her father stood from the table grabbing hold of the dirty golden chalice.

"Go grab the ceremonial dagger from your room. It's time. Everyone will be waiting." Jerry squirmed wildly in his chair but was unable to release himself. In a panic, he released a string of murderous yells.

"Help me, please!" Jerry screamed at the child who sat across from him. "We can both get out of here, away from these people! Please! I know what they've done to you. We can make this right!" Through all of Jerry's desperate antics, Isaac remained unphased. Nothing that he said or did was enough to elicit a reaction from the tortured life hunkered in the seat opposite of him.

"Here," Sally handed her father the dagger. With an expression of deep thought, the mentally twisted man stepped towards Jerry and placed the blade of the dagger gently onto the teen's forearm.

"The goblet," he commanded. Sally raised the goblet high above her head.

"Satan, I hear you crying!" she screamed, continuing to hoist the chalice above her. "May the rivers formed from this boy's blood guide you into our lives. We live for you! We die for you! We kill for you! Hail our lord, Satan!" Sally's body began to convulse. Jerry watched aghast as her eyes rolled into the back of her head becoming oval eggshells with skinny red veins.

"Pay close attention boy, for the hand of Satan guides her soul." Jerry refused to observe the disturbing convulsions and turned his head away. Sally's father tightly clenched his rough hands around Jerry's jaw like a vice, forcing the boy to watch as Sally emulated what he couldn't decipher as either a real or fake possession. "Let's drink."

The Amish patriarch cut deeply into Jerry's arm and let out a humorous laugh as the boy yelped in pain. During this time, Sally's ritualistic possession came to an end. She walked over, allowing Jerry's blood that fell from his arm to drip into the goblet. He watched in terror as the Amish man and daughter licked their parched lips in anticipation of filling their mouths with his blood. As the cup filled, Sally rose it to her thin lips and swallowed; left behind was a pulpy, crimson mask that covered her mouth. The goblet was again dropped below the arm of the chair. Jerry was forced to watch as more of his blood lined the sides of the chalice. His eyes were getting heavy. His thoughts were becoming foggy.

Sally raised the chalice once more and pressed it against her father's lips. Blood seeped from the corners of his mouth and dripped down into his tangled, ashen beard. As Jerry's eyes lowered, he could make out the girl once again filling the cup. There was still one more who needed to have their thirst quenched.

Sally skipped around the table and poured the liquid down Isaac's throat. For the first time that evening, the child smiled. The tongue of a serpent slipped between his lips; pink and split down the middle. In a clockwise motion, Isaac licked the blood from off of his mouth, stood from out of his seat, and walked to an unknown part of the house that existed somewhere outside Jerry's field of vision.

"Our part is complete. Everything's ready." Sally's father gave the confirmation. Jerry's head whiplashed backward as a bag was wrapped around his face. He tossed his fragile body around madly in the wooden seat as his eyes focused upwards through the cellophane and locked onto the bright blue eyes of Isaac, staring back at him in judgement. It took seventeen seconds for Jerry to fall unconscious. His head fell lifelessly off to the side of his skeletal shoulders.

Jerry's eyes gently opened. He found himself staring up into the hazy night sky. Thousands of bright stars twinkled up high. Warm gusts of wind slapped the boy across his face. In an attempt to raise his hand against the soreness in his cheeks, Jerry quickly came to the realization that he was unable to move. Dread devoured his mind as the events of the evening came flooding over him.

Jerry tried to raise his head up using all of the power that he could muster into his neck, but the attempt was futile. He tried again and again but the restraint around his throat was too strong. However, he didn't need his eyes to know that not only was his head strapped down, but so were his arms and legs. Each of his limbs had been confined to a large, circular wooden structure with a pentagram painted on it.

"The boy awakes!" a familiar voice roared. Jerry's head darted to the right and he witnessed a crowd of Amish men, women, and children all holding torches staring back at him. Sally stood at the head of the crowd as her father walked out from within the sea of people, exposing himself in a crimson red robe lined with frilly gold trimming. "Let the ritual commence!" He raised his arms into the air and almost as if on cue, a crash of thunder shook the sky. The crowd behind him released an intense holler as they shook their torches savagely into the wind. Jerry floundered around wildly within his constraints, but had no success in freeing himself.

"Hail Satan!" a young girl no older than four years old screamed from out of the noisy crowd.

"Hail Satan!" another man echoed.

"I don't understand!" Jerry screamed at the crowd. "Stop, I beg you, please!" A couple of people chuckled and pointed as they whispered among themselves. Isaac, like his father, emerged from out of the crowd and stood next to the robed man. The boy grabbed his father's arm and began rubbing his cheek up and down against the soft, silky material. "I thought that you people worshipped Jesus!"

The crowd laughed dramatically as if Jerry had just told the funniest joke they had ever heard.

"Of course you think that we worship *Jesus*." Sally's father said mockingly while pulling his arm away from Isaac and walking slowly over to where Jerry was pinned against the annually used sacrificial altar. The smell of iron that Jerry identified when first arriving poured from off of the dried blood on the altar and into the air.

"Do you think that everybody out there," the man said sternly while pointing out across the miles of crops, "would allow us to live our lives normally if they knew that we were Satanists? If they knew that we worshipped what they don't understand. Do you think that they would seriously accept us living among them? Every other day there would be someone new judging and plotting against how to get rid of us. All of you people are unable to see who's power truly rules in this world!"

"Amos," An elder man with large, dark bags beneath his eyes interrupted. "The clock has struck three. Our Lord grows hungry for the boy's soul, and thirsty for his blood." Amos shook his head with excitement and pulled the recognizable dagger out from within his robe. He then relinquished the robe revealing a body scarred with dozens of occult and satanic symbols. Only a pair of snug, white underwear prevented him from being fully nude.

While twisting the dagger back and forth in his hand, Amos leaned down next to Jerry's head and whispered into his ear.

"In about three minutes," Amos muttered with slimy specs of spit projecting into the inner sections of Jerry's ear, "you too will join a large number of sacrifices that have also learned that this almighty Jesus everyone speaks so highly about...Is dead." Amos gripped the hilt of the dagger firmly within both hands and held it up high above Jerry's stomach. "Hail Satan!" he bellowed which was immediately met with an identical response from the rest of the cult of dark followers.

"No, don't do this!" Jerry yelled in a shrill voice compared to the deep, low pitched repetitions of the hail Satan chants.

The point of the blade plunged deep into the belly of the boy and blood gushed out onto his shirtless torso. Amos ripped the dagger from the flesh and again buried the edge of the blade into the city boy's gut. Jerry opened his mouth to scream, but no sound came out. Pellets of blood spewed out through his jagged teeth, down his narrow chin, and onto his pale, bony chest. The vexing chants prolonged, growing more and more ear-splitting, more and more accelerated. Jerry's head fell freely to the side as he felt what little bit of life remained in him being torn casually away. He belonged to the Reaper now.

The last image that Jerry ever saw, was that of the timid blonde haired Sally standing hand in hand with her physical brother, yet spiritual mother Isaac. He had the largest grin smeared across his face that the boy had ever seen.

The chants of the Amish community went on for hours until the first signs of light peeked from behind the rolling hills in the horizon. It was the job of the Amish youth to remove the sacrificed body from the altar, and to bury it far out amidst the crops where it would never be found. Meanwhile, the women would go on to spend the entirety of the day cooking large meals to be consumed by the community at the day's end as a feast to praise yet another successful sacrifice to their dark lord.

As noon arrived on the following day, Amos waved and greeted customers from the nearby city and suburbs who purchased fresh bushels of corn from his shanty little stand that stood off to the side of a dusty backwoods road. The sun shined bright from high in the sea blue sky, illuminating the sign perched atop the corn stand which read **Thank you, and may God bless!** As the aging, follower of evil filled his pockets with the wrinkled bills received from his customers, Amos watched in disdain as the people would then drive off down the road none the wiser about the fate of young Jerry Sikes.

For the rest of Amos' life and for generations to follow, the Amish community would carry on taking money from the ignorant outsiders; all the while feeding their bodies to the harvest, and their souls to the devil.

Open Your Eyes

It was the beautiful smell of lilacs and sunflowers that woke her. A floral sweetness hung in the air as a band of blue jays sang beneath the morning sun. Sarah slowly opened her eyes, and for a short time stared up at the white ceiling above her. The morning light sprayed against her chestnut skin and gave a glow to her dark hair. There was comfort in the sun's touch.

Sarah turned her head and took notice of the digital clock sitting on the end table beside the bed. Nine o'clock on the dot. She released a sigh before pulling off the covers and swinging her legs over the side of the bed. Her feet dangled above the floor. There was a small *thud* as she pushed herself off the bed and landed onto the chilled wood. She eyeballed some of the furniture that filled the room. A dark wooden wardrobe was pressed against the far wall while a mint green vanity sat tucked away in the corner; makeup and hairbrushes lay strewn across the top. A large oval mirror hung nailed into the wall above the bed's headboard.

Sarah flicked the light switch as she entered the master bathroom. A low hum came from the lights that sat above the mirror. She grabbed the tube of toothpaste and squeezed out a blue lump on her brush before running it under a cold stream of water. As Sarah brushed her teeth with a toothy grin across her face, she couldn't help but stare at herself in the mirror. Her eyes were lively. Her hair fell across her shoulders covering up cartoonish pictures of wands and owls and sorting hats that decorated her *Harry Potter* nightgown.

The humming stopped as Sarah shut off the light. She looked back at the clock on the end table. Nine o'clock. The numbers hadn't changed. Sarah thought for a moment but it was obvious that not just one, but many minutes had passed by since she had woken. She walked over and observed the clock. A black cord connected the back of the machine to an outlet in the wall. Peculiar as it was, she didn't allow it to weigh too heavily on her mind.

"You must be broken," Sarah whispered to the object. She stared down at the clock half expecting the numbers to change in response, but they never did. If it was up to the clock, it would be nine o'clock now, and forever.

The floor felt cold against the soles of Sarah's feet as she stepped out into the upstairs hallway. Hanging along the wall were pictures of her and her two sons: Rami and Roman. The pictures varied from professional photoshoots to selfies at local amusement parks. A small smile spread across Sarah's face as she absorbed the images. Being with her boys was euphoric. She couldn't imagine living in a world without them. They were her reason for getting out of bed each morning.

Rami and Roman's bedroom was on the opposite side of the hall as her own. Sarah quietly made her way to their bedroom door. She placed her hand on the doorknob and was suddenly overcome with a feeling of dread. The sensation came out of nowhere. It became hard for her to breathe. Her legs became gelatin. A tightness formed within her chest. These were feelings that Sarah knew all too well; she was having a panic attack.

Sarah closed her eyes and slowly began to count backward from ten. By five she had regained control over her legs, and by two she had control of her breathing.

Slowly Sarah turned the doorknob and peered inside.

Across a field of toys, legos, and portable game systems was a metal-framed bunk bed. On top slept Roman, the older of the two, and on the bottom slept Rami. Sarah strategically stepped around the carnage on the bedroom floor. She knelt down next to the bed and admired her youngest.

My sweet baby.

Sarah leaned in and kissed Rami on the forehead. "Good morning, baby. Wake up. Open your eyes." There was an innocence as Rami's eyes opened and filled with life. He took his tiny hands and rubbed them across his eyes. He took a deep breath and stared at his mother for a few seconds before speaking.

"Hi, mommy."

"Hi, baby." They smiled at each other. "Do you want some breakfast?" Rami nodded his head. "Okay. Let's wake your brother up." Sarah stood up and pulled over a tiny chair that she used to stand on in order to be tall enough to see over the top bunk. She placed her hand on Roman's shoulder and tenderly shook it. The boy turned away from his mother, less prepared to wake up than his younger sibling.

"Rise and shine," Sarah whispered to her son as she shook his shoulder once again. "I'm getting ready to make some breakfast. How do pancakes sound?" Roman was silent for a few seconds. His head was buried deep into the pillow.

"Kin ooh ake ken too?" Roman's muffled question escaped from beneath the pillow.

"Yes, I can make bacon too." Roman turned over and smiled. Sarah kissed him on the forehead just as she had done with Rami. She stepped down from the chair and traveled back across the bedroom. "Pancakes and bacon coming right up!"

Sarah poured the pancake batter onto the skillet. She did her best to pour the batter in perfect circles. As they sat in the skillet, the pancakes sizzled and bubbled. Over time, they turned from a milky white to a sandy brown. Meanwhile, six strips of bacon sizzled and popped in a layer of grease within a pan beside the skillet. She cooked the bacon long enough for them to become slightly crispy. When done, she set the pancakes and bacon each on their respective plates. Sarah opened the refrigerator and rummaged through the top shelf until she found what would be the finishing touch to the family's breakfast. Orange juice!

Laid out on the dining room table were three plates, each with a pancake slathered in butter and thick maple syrup with a side of two slices of bacon. Each place setting was accompanied by a glass of orange juice (minus the pulp). Sarah wiped away a line of sweat from her forehead. "Boys, come on down! Breakfast is ready!"

Both boys came stampeding into the dining room. "Thanks, mommy," Rami said before lifting his fork and cutting away at his pancake.

"Thank you!" said Roman. Sarah took a seat at the head of the table and watched as her two children scarfed down the food. She had a plate made up for herself but for some reason, she wanted nothing more than to soak in every second she could of her children. Her appetite came from her eyes, not her stomach, and the sight of her boys were more than enough to satiate her hunger. The way that they talked, ate, laughed, and smiled. Sarah wanted to absorb it all.

"Aren't you hungry, mommy?" Roman asked. "Your food's going to get cold."

"Yes, baby I know. Don't you worry, I'll eat it." Sarah lifted a piece of bacon and broke it in half before placing a piece into her mouth. Not too crunchy, yet not too rubbery. Just the way she liked it. She lifted the other half of the bacon before noticing the time displayed on the microwave in neon green.

Nine o'clock.

Sarah placed the piece of bacon back onto her plate and walked over to the microwave. She pressed the button that said **CLOCK** and the first digit on the left began to blink.

"Do either of you boys know what time it is?" Rami shrugged his shoulders and Roman shook his head. Sarah typed in 10:30 and hit the **CLOCK** button once more to finalize the time. The time of 9:00 appeared back on the microwave. Sarah tried changing the time on the microwave three more times, but somehow always ended up back at nine o'clock. She grew tired of messing with what must be a malfunctioning device and carried on with her morning. It did strike her as odd that both the clock on the microwave and on her bedside table were having the same issue, but figured that behind it all must be a logical explanation.

Sarah's mood was bright and the day even brighter. She and her two boys had finished up their breakfast and had gotten dressed to enjoy the outdoors on this beautiful day. The sky was a majestic blue with scattered cirrus clouds; thin and wispy like pieces of ivory cotton candy. Bumblebees rode the wind carrying pollen from flower to flower. A pair of nearby squirrels chased one another up, down, and around a beautiful Japanese cherry blossom tree while pink petals rained down around them. It was the kind of day that Sarah wished she could experience forever for the rest of her existence.

"Can you get me a new jacket, mommy?" Sarah looked down at her son with a puzzled expression.

"But it's the middle of summer. Don't you think that it's a little too hot for a jacket?" Rami shook his head.

"No, I like them."

"Can I have one too?" Roman asked, joining in the conversation. "A red one!"

"And I want a yellow one!" Rami announced.

"Alright, fine. Later today, we can go out and get you both a new jacket. Even though it's ninety degrees outside." The boys' faces lit up with joy. Sarah couldn't help but do anything that would make her sons as happy as possible.

The family of three took a short car ride to a nearby park which had a playground, a hiking trail, multiple pavilions with public grills for family picnics, a dog park, two basketball courts, a tennis court, and a stream filled with a myriad of tiny colorful fish. Eleanor Grace Park was the name of the destination and it was a location where Sarah and the boy's commonly spent their free time. Rami and Roman both had their thing about the park that they liked most. Roman enjoyed the tranquility that came with splashing around and watching fish swim back and forth in the shallow stream while Rami enjoyed releasing his energy on the swings, slides, and monkey bars. And of course, Sarah had her thing too. The smiles and laughter that came from watching her children enjoy the youth that she wished they could maintain for eternity.

After arriving, the first destination was the playground. Sarah sat on a nearby park bench as her boys sprinted toward the equipment. It was a joy to watch her kids race down the slide, across the monkey bars, and through the cylindrical tubes that connected one side of the equipment to the other.

"Mommy!" Rami called while hanging from one of the monkey bars. "Come watch me!"

"Okay baby," Sarah walked over to where Rami had called for her and watched her son skillfully swing his arms from one rung to the next. Upon reaching the end, Rami turned around and cherished his accomplishment with a wide smile. Sarah kissed her son on the forehead, the saltiness of his sweat tingling her taste buds; first touching her lips and then her tongue.

"I'm so proud of you! You're mommy's little monkey." Rami took a moment to do his best primate interpretation where he bounced from foot to foot while pretending to scratch beneath his armpits before running off and disappearing behind one of the slides. Meanwhile, Roman was playing with another boy whom he befriended that was around his own age. The two were pretending to be explorers that were in search of buried treasure. Bumpy rocks and broken pieces of plastic were transformed by their imaginations into bars of gold and exquisite jewels.

"Jackson! Jackson, come on now, it's time for us to head home." The mother of Roman's newly acquired friend had appeared nearly out of thin air. Sarah hadn't noticed the woman the entire time she had been at the park, but then again, she wasn't looking for her. The woman had thick, brown curly hair and bright red lipstick. Thin tan lines peaked out from beneath the straps of her yellow sundress.

"But mom I want to -" the middle aged mother shushed her son and motioned for him to come along. Jackson said his goodbyes to Roman and pouted all the way off of the playground. A thin blue banded watch was strapped around the mother's wrist. Light from the sun reflected off of the watch's face and into Sarah's eyes. At first the glare was an annoyance, but then it led to a question that Sarah had been wondering all day.

"Excuse me. Do you happen to know what time it is?" The brunette peered down at her wrist and took a few seconds to study her watch.

"Nine o'clock. Still only the beginning of such a gorgeous day!" she answered with a crocodile smile.

"Thanks," Sarah watched as the lady took her son's hand and marched away down the nearby asphalt walkway. Something about the woman's response felt almost robotic. There was a friendly smile behind her answer but the words themselves felt flat. They were the verbal replicant of a soda that had lost its carbonation. "Rami! Roman! Come on, we should go too."

Her two boys didn't put up a fight at all.

The second stop of the day was at the stream. Sarah had dipped her toes in for a short while but her mind was furiously racing, not allowing for her to enjoy the moment. Meanwhile, Rami and Roman were having a blast, splashing each other with water. Doing their best to catch fish and tadpoles between their hands. Leapfrogging from one stepping stone to the next. What earlier would have been a smile across Sarah's face while watching her boys was now a look of someone lost in their thoughts. Her eyes were glued onto her children, but she wasn't actually seeing them. As amazing as the day had been, Sarah couldn't get over the peculiarities of some of the events.

Not only was her mind on a journey of its own, but so were her emotions. Suddenly, Sarah was overcome with a deep sadness. She missed her children. They were mere meters in front of her, yet she felt as though they were gone; lost to her forever.

Why did this have to happen to them? They're supposed to be here with me! Playing. Laughing. Needing. Come back. Come back! COME BACK!

"Mommy?" Sarah snapped out of whatever it was that she was lost within. "Why are you crying?" Roman and Rami stood in front of the large rock that Sarah was sitting on. Everything beneath the two boys' shins were gone, hidden beneath the murky brown water.

Sarah patted the corners of her face with the palms of her hands. She wiped away a stream of tears from both eyes. The wetness transferred from her face to her hands came as a shock.

"I'm okay. I just -" Sarah couldn't finish her sentence. There was a fabricated excuse to be made, one that would allow her to falsely explain to her children why she was crying, but she couldn't think of anything. Instead, Sarah brushed it off completely. "Last stop of the day boys. Let's head over to the dog park and watch some doggies run around. And if we see one that we like, maybe we can get one of our own sometime soon." Rami and Roman erupted with a series of cheers. All of a sudden they had forgotten about the unexpected tears that had been rolling down their mothers face.

They had forgotten, but Sarah could not.

The dog park was nothing more than a spacious grassy field filled with families and their canine pets. Frisbees were flying through the air. Belly rubs and treats were being handed out faster than fireworks on the fourth of July. Booming barks and high pitched yips echoed beneath the sky.

Sarah placed a mint green blanket down on the grass for everyone to sit on. As she laid back, Sarah could feel the blades of grass jutting into her spine through the thin fabric. A warm breeze slid across her skin as she stared up at the sky, listening to her boys debate over which type of dog was best. Rami argued that little dogs were better.

"They're easier to pick up and hold. Then you can squeeze them and love them." Roman disagreed. If it was up to the elder brother, the family would get a big dog.

"Nope, big dogs are better because they can protect you. And you're still little so you could probably even ride a big dog." The latest part of the argument caused Rami to pause and think. *Maybe big dogs are better,* he thought to himself. Although, he would never say it out loud because that would justify that Roman was right and he was wrong.

As the two youths continued with their debate, Sarah continued with her thoughts. It was impossible to deny the brilliance of the day, but something seemed off. The clouds appeared to be in the same spots that they were when they had left the house. The sun which should be reaching the upper corner of the west side of the sky at this point was still sitting content, tucked over on the east side. Then again, maybe it was just the fuzziness of her thoughts afflicting her judgment.

"They're easier to pick up and hold. Then you can squeeze them and love them."

"Nope, big dogs are better because they can protect you. And you're still little so you could probably even ride a big dog."

Sarah sat up. "Why did you boys just repeat yourself?" Roman and Rami looked at their mother in confusion.

"What do you mean mommy? We didn't repeat ourselves. We were talking about the dogs." Rami's voice was sweet and young, almost feminine.

"But you both said the same thing, twice." Neither boy validated her accusation. The most that Sarah got was two sets of blank stares.

"We don't know what you mean." Roman said. Sarah pushed her hands against her eyes in an attempt to regain her thoughts. She could feel her mind slipping away from her. Why was she the only one noticing these abnormalities?

Everything went quiet as Sarah stared into the darkness provided by the backs of her eyelids. She lowered her hands and opened her eyes.

Suddenly, the sky flashed red three times; each flash paired with the blaring noise of a heavenly trumpet. The people came to a standstill. The dogs' bodies stiffened and they toppled over like dominoes. People who were sitting began to stand. Rami and Roman were no exception. Heads snapped backward as everyone's gaze locked on to the sky. Streams of saliva fell out of the corner of mouths and onto the collars of shirts.

Sarah looked around, stunned and in disbelief. She was the only one who still had control over her body. The only one whose body didn't hang limp like an abandoned marionette.

"Roman? Rami?" Sarah circled her sons. Their eyes had a glossy lifelessness to them. She placed her hands on their cheeks and was taken aback by the lack of heat in their skin. They weren't cold but they weren't hot either. It was as if they were made of something waxy rather than of flesh and bone.

Sarah called their names another handful of times. It was an effort that would go unrewarded. The only response she received, if you want to classify it as so, was more spit falling from the creases of their lips. With the bottom of her shirt, Sarah wiped their mouths and whispered to them words of comfort. Words that were more for herself than for her boys.

Crimson streaks continued ripping through the sky. In a twisted marriage, another stream of trumpet horns came crashing down as well. On the fifth flash, the sky did not return to blue but stayed a harrowing red. It was like Heaven was now vacant and the new occupants were from Hell. Across the sky in yellow font appeared the time of 20:00. Again, there was an explosive horn that sent vibrations through Sarah's bones. Like a gunshot at a track meet, the sound gave permission for the numbers to begin moving, and with each passing second, the numbers fell lower and lower.

It was a timer.

Sarah watched in awe for longer than she could remember doing. Confusion set in immediately, but it wasn't until 19:20 that panic arrived and joined in. The numbers silently ticked away.

Sarah glanced back down at her two sons and again tried resuscitating their consciences. Her efforts remained futile. In an effort to figure out what was happening, Sarah ran through the dog park in search of anybody who could provide her with some answers. The back of her legs ached as she traveled from person to person, waving her arms frantically in front of their faces and screaming as loud as she could.

"Hello? What's going on here? Can you help me? Are we in danger?" Those were just a handful of the many questions that she screamed as she continued to search for that one person who could provide her with something...Anything. Unfortunately, they were all the same. Nothing more than vegetative beings with heads flipped back like tops to a pill bottle.

The timer was now rolling below fifteen minutes.

Initially, the fear that consumed Sarah was focused on the eeriness of the behavior of those around her. But as the timer continued winding down, another fear came along. The fear of what would actually happen once the clock struck zero, because this was no fairytale and a glass slipper would not be the solution to her problems. Around and around she ran until she could run no longer. Her lungs ached and her throat was dry.

It wouldn't make a difference, but Sarah wanted to scream. She wanted to scream so loud that it would shatter the sky and bring the clouds collapsing down to the Earth. Maybe that would be enough to snap these people out of their catatonic states; the weight of the world literally falling upon their shoulders.

Sarah bent over, placing her hands against her knees as she tried to regain her breath. As the timer reached ten minutes, a whinier more drawn out horn swept across the field. In less minutes than she had fingers, Sarah would be swept into the unknown that came along with the end of what she could only imagine may be time itself.

But why me? If Sarah couldn't get others to respond to her questions, her only logical solution was to begin asking them to herself. *Why am I the only one that can still freely move around? What is the meaning of all this?*

If this was the end of the world, Sarah knew that she would not be the one on God's list to be given extra time. Her relationship with the church had been broken many years ago; not to say that she didn't attempt to mend what was now fractured on various occasions. Or maybe that was just it! Maybe this was God's sick way of getting back at her. Forcing her to live her final moments on this Earth without the joy of her children or the interactions of others, but stuck with nothing more than her bruised and fragile mind. It was sick and she hated Him for it. But something within her knew that God wasn't behind what was going on. How could she possibly put the blame on a celestial being that she no longer believed existed?

A familiar set of brunette curls caught Sarah's eye. Sixty feet in front of her was the mother and son that she had seen earlier at the playground. They were still here. Sarah couldn't help but wonder if they could have escaped all of this. *Could they still be carelessly living their lives if they had gone directly home after leaving the playground? Was this paranormal event contained to Eleanor Grace Park or is it a global calamity?*

More questions did nothing but lead to even less answers.

There was a little less than five minutes remaining when Sarah returned to her boys. She wrapped them both in her arms and cried. The smell of their hair was as far gone as the shine in their eyes. The caramel pigment in their skin was fading, turning them into pale husks of their former selves.

3:00.

Everything about Rami and Roman were being erased right before her eyes. Strands of their hair were starting to fall out. Their skin was starting to loosely hang from their bones. In an instant, they had become geriatric versions of themselves; decrepit and nearly unrecognizable.

1:00.

All of a sudden, a surge of memories and emotions came flooding back into Sarah's mind. One by one, images of her life were being dropped into her brain like documents being uploaded to a flash drive. Her kids. Her parents. Her home. Her life. She remembered everything about them now.

It was hard to release them from her arms, but somehow, she did it. Sarah walked past Rami and Roman and laid down, her back against the ground on the blanket. "Twenty seconds," she whispered softly. Silently, she counted along while watching the time inch its way toward zero.

A static buzz pierced Sarah's eardrums as the countdown entered its final ten seconds.

Nine.

Eight.

Seven.

A white void came rushing toward the field from out of the horizon, swallowing everything that got in its path. The trees, the grass, the playgrounds, the tennis and basketball courts, the stream, the people and their dogs along with anything else that existed was officially turned to naught.

Six.

Five.

Four.

Sarah closed her eyes as the wave of white came crashing over her. If only for a split second, her mind was happy that the process didn't include pain.

Three.

Two.

One.

And just like that, the world was gone. Nothing remained but a blank canvas for the next user to paint on with their wants and wishes. Then, the light turned to darkness and a voice entered Sarah's mind.

"Disengage."

Sarah's eyes shot open. Her chest pumped forward above the bed as she gasped for air. What she inhaled tasted like spoiled milk and was filled with dust. The tiny particles stuck to the lining of her throat resulting in a string of coughs. Attached to her head was a heavy device that wrapped around the back of her neck and shielded her eyes. Sarah removed the headset and set it down on the ground next to her. She rapidly blinked and took a moment to gain her bearings. A single candle fluttered inside of an oil lamp on a wooden table before her.

Upon sitting up, Sarah could feel a painful stiffness in her lower back. There were sores across both of her arms that oozed with pus and blood. Connected to the cranial machine was an even larger machine that towered above the twin sized bed Sarah was laying on. Flashing on the screen of a monitor connected to the machine was a red drained battery icon.

Sarah's bones crackled and popped as she left the broken bed. Sharp springs poked through the thin mattress which were previously hidden beneath her dainty body. Shuffling towards the flame reminded Sarah of how much everything in her body hurt. From her neck to her toes, everything ached.

The oil lamp was heavy, then again, so was everything else. Any muscle that Sarah had ever managed to build was gone. A recent diet of insects, moldy bread, spoiled canned goods, and her own hair had left her body no choice but to begin eating away at itself in order to survive. To say that she weighed eighty-five pounds would have been farfetched, even upon adding the weight of the clothes that hung from her body; for her frame bore resemblance to that of a human shaped clothesline. Only two teeth still remained inside of her mouth, one on the top center shelf and one on the bottom back corner. And the top one wiggled around like a worm in the mud.

The illumination from the lamp provided Sarah with the guidance that she needed. For several months the bunker had been her home, yet she still found herself bumping into things if left to navigate in the dark. She picked up a long cord attached to the back of the headset and plugged it into a portable hand cranked generator that then connected to the larger machine with the blinking battery image. A small green light started flashing on top of the headset indicating that energy was being provided. As she lay the device down, Sarah could feel the bones in both of her knees pop. Sharp pain came with the sound, but pain was just a part of life at this point.

It would be a few hours before the headset was fully charged. Until then, she could go out and scavenge for some clothes. And if she was lucky, maybe stumble across some food. But the chances of that were nearly impossible. Even if there was any food left (and there wasn't), it wouldn't be edible. All it would do is make her sicker than she already was. Anything outside of a can was poisonous.

At the entryway, Sarah exchanged the lamp for a gas mask, a pair of gardening gloves too large for her hands, and a tattered windbreaker. The rubber suctioned itself to her face and her peripheral vision was lost. No matter how many times she put the mask on, she never got comfortable with how difficult it made breathing. Having to listen to her own wheezing was nightmarish, but it was minuscule in comparison to what waited for her outside. Sarah blew out the candle and placed her hands onto one of the rungs of the ladder. She would have to climb in darkness. Slowly, she ascended, until reaching the top, pushing open the metal hatch, and exiting to the outside world.

The world had been like this for months, yet the sight of a destroyed planet never became one that was easy to endure. Most of the buildings were nothing more than broken brick, dust, and glass.

The sky was a mustard haze, and beneath it was an everlasting radioactive storm that slowly ate away at anything that dared spend its time within it. Dead bodies lined the streets and the sidewalks; their flesh deteriorated and their organs melted. Cars were left abandoned, vandalism was commonplace, and the creatures that caused the fallout lived among it all.

Sarah shut the bunker hatch as quietly as she could. Making noise and getting caught would absolutely be the death of her. *They* were around. Listening. Watching. The challenge was making sure that she saw them before they saw her.

Even though she donned a gas mask, the rest of Sarah's body was not properly equipped to handle the extreme radiation. Large portions of her skin had already been eaten away, some areas nearly down to the bone. A flimsy windbreaker and a pair of jeans that she had to tie around her waist with yarn due to them being five sizes too large was all that she had. It didn't work well, but it would have to do.

She had a place in mind, but it was nearly half a mile away. Getting there and back alive would be a challenge, but the risk would be worth the reward. Not only would she have to be quick to minimize exposure, but even quicker to avoid Them.

With her head tucked low, Sarah scurried between the remains of what was once a strip mall. Limbs of mannequins had been thrown all over the place. Not a single one had an article of clothing attached to it. Broken shelves, cash registers, empty clothing racks, and a cornucopia of hangers littered the floor; some of which had been straightened and were stained with old blood.

Quietly, like a mouse, Sarah carried on; the gas mask pressing so tightly against her face that traces of blood were seeping onto one of the eye pieces. Not only had her bones become brittle, but her skin was thin enough to slice through with a butter knife.

Flashes of lightning lit up pockets of the sky warning of an impending storm. *That's not good,* Sarah thought. Add acid rain to the list of things that could kill her. Time wasn't on her side, and the window of opportunity was shrinking. Through a brief internal monologue, Sarah decided that she was going to continue. She had already travelled halfway to her destination. If she was quick, there shouldn't be any reason why she shouldn't make it back in time.

The Earth quaked beneath the thunder's drum. Sarah pressed her back against the crumbling foundation of a nearby building to catch her breath. She was hurting. The blood that had found its way from her nose to her left eye piece felt itchy against her face. She wanted nothing more than to remove the gas mask and scratch at the area, but she knew better. Breathing the air was hazardous.

To Sarah's surprise, she stood across the way from a shop that had great significance to her. Seeing the store's faded banner brought her back to one of the darkest moments of her life.

It was only a few days after the collapse of society as humanity had known it. Looting and murder had become commonplace. The abductions had begun and dismembered limbs would rain from the sky, falling out of disc shaped ships. Sarah had never seen anything like the chaos that ensued throughout the streets. She had seen post-apocalyptic films before, but they were nothing compared to the horrors that humanity was truly capable of.

Four days after discovering the bunker, Sarah ventured topside in an attempt to scavenge for food. The radiation was not yet an issue. There were other things that she had to be concerned with, such as the screams and gunshots that whizzed through the air. Not to mention the thieves and rapists. As well as the things that came from above.

The streets ran red with blood.

On the corner of Chester street and Church street sat a local grocery market. That was Sarah's destination. The likelihood of there being any food left was slim, but it was a chance that she would have to take. The next closest grocery outlet was a couple miles away and without a car she had no chance of making it there alive on foot.

Upon arriving, her prediction became a reality. The glass window in the front of the store had been smashed open. Carefully, she stepped inside and walked down the aisles. There was nothing. The smell of curdled dairy crept into her nose as she passed by the frozen section that was no longer frozen. The floor was littered with plastic and cardboard trash. There were even traces of animal and human waste spread along the shelves which added their own unique scents to the aroma of the ransacked building.

Sarah stepped out of the grocery story and had her attention caught by a colorful banner that swayed in the wind across the street. In bold yellow letters, the banner advertised a new virtual reality headset that could be purchased despite still being in it's alpha stages of development.

EXPERIENCE YOUR DREAM REALITY WITH THE LATEST AND GREATEST IN VR TECHNOLOGY! AVAILABLE NOW!

Sarah read the message on the tattered banner over a dozen times. A low growl escaped from the pit of her belly. It was a subtle reminder that she could distract her mind but not her stomach. She turned her head and gave the inside of the store one last good look. Calling it empty would be a disservice to those who looted it.

Out of habit, Sarah looked both ways before jogging across the street. The tech store had seen it's fair share of destruction, but the interest in technology was far lower than that of food. She pushed open the door. A bell hanging overhead chimed as she cautiously entered. The lack of smells compared to the grocery store was welcoming. To her surprise, there were still a lot of items left untouched. TV's. Phones. Laptops. But with the recent death of electrical power, what good would these devices do anybody? Lucky for her, the bunker had a generator.

Right in the center of the store was a single box. The last one. Sarah lifted it up and examined each side, studiously reading the small white print. Beside her was a tall advertisement promoting the VR headsets for 2499.99. The Dreamweaver it was called. Want it. Dream it. Live it. A simple, yet enticing slogan.

It wasn't going to stunt her hunger, but it may be able to satiate her appetite for a reality that was better than the one that she was living. Sarah hugged the box against herself. The sound of fast approaching footsteps came rushing up from behind. All of a sudden Sarah was on the ground and the VR box had been sent sliding across the floor. A pair of rugged hands turned her over onto her back. Then, one of those very same hands came flying across her cheek.

"Nobody told you that it's not safe for a pretty lady like yourself to be out walking the streets all alone? You might accidentally stumble across somebody who doesn't have the best intentions. We wouldn't want that, now would we?" The man licked his lips. He was equipped with violent eyes and a feral smile. Greasy locks of hair were tucked back behind his ears, wrapped tight in a shoulder length ponytail.

"Get off of me!" Sarah screamed. The man straddled her kicking legs and pinned her wrists to the ground. A must fell from off of his breath stinging Sarah's nose. "Get off!"

"Keep your dumbass mouth shut! Do you want Them to hear? Do you think that that would be good for either one of us?"

"Help me, please!" Another firm backhand whipped across her face. The taste of copper filled Sarah's mouth; a high-pitched ringing buzzed in her ears.

"Some of you broads don't listen too good. There are times when you just need to shut your mouths and follow directions. This is one of those times." Sarah continued to struggle as the man leaned forward and sniffed her hair. She recognized the sour smell of alcohol leaking from his pores. The fumes were strong enough to make Sarah's head feel fuzzy. Or maybe it was a residual effect of being smacked across the face.

"You don't have to do this. Just let me go." The man pulled his head back and revealed a black-toothed grin.

"You're right, I don't have to do this. But I want to." Again, the man leaned in and for the faintest second loosened the grip that he had on Sarah's right wrist. She lodged free and punched as hard as she could connecting with the side of his neck. The impact was enough to shift a majority of the man's weight to Sarah's left side. With a powerful shove, she sent him tumbling onto his side.

"You bitch!" He hissed. Keeping her eyes locked onto his, Sarah reached back and fumbled around in the side pocket of her backpack. The drunkard lunged forward. With a swift swing of her arm, Sarah took the box cutter that she brought along for protection and shoved it into his neck. His blood felt warm as it poured down the blade and across her hand. After a few gargled sounds, the man fell dead to the floor.

It was the only time that Sarah killed a man. Knowing that there could be more men out there like him, or worse, she snatched the VR box and hurried back to the bunker. Since then, it had become an object that made the little bit of her miserable life she had left worth living.

She was now coming up to the clothing store. Being lost in the visions of her past had left her subconsciously carrying forward to her destination. The sky was darkening and the howls of the creatures that roamed the streets were increasing.

In and out. In and out. It had become Sarah's mantra for whenever she had to come topside. The quicker the better. And the quicker the safer.

The lack of light inside of the store made it hard for Sarah to see. She wanted a pair of jackets; no more and no less. What once would have been a simple shopping trip was now like finding a needle in a haystack. Like most topside excursions, there was a good chance that she wouldn't find what she was looking for. But she had to try.

Sarah searched and searched. Seconds had become minutes. Light was becoming dark. And They were getting closer. They could hear her. Smell her. Still, she carried on.

The gas mask was pressing deep into her skin. The eye pieces were fogging from the heat of her breath. Sarah tried to wipe away the condensation from the outside of the glass but the moisture was all trapped inside.

In and out. In and out.

She needed to go. An internal clock had been developed during her previous topside visits and the alarm was sounding. Sarah had already circled the store once and had failed to find what she was looking for. But, she wanted to walk around one more time. She wanted to be thorough. Her vision was obstructed and it was possible that maybe she had overlooked them.

And she was right.

In the back corner we're a bunch of clothes that had been thrown around. The size of the clothing ranged from toddler to adult XXL but she was willing to make due with what was available. Sarah rummaged through the clothes, keeping her head on a swivel. The noises were so close now.

In and out.

"I got them." Sarah whispered to herself. With a swing of her shoulder, she allowed the backpack to slide onto the floor. She tucked the jackets into the largest pocket and zipped it shut. Now all she had to do was make it back to the bunker.

Night had fallen and it was Their favorite time to hunt. The fallen ones. The ones who caused all of this.

The aliens.

Sarah had only seen one once, but she had heard them often. They communicated with each other through croaks and high-pitched squeals. They were pale, tall, and lanky; they're knuckles dragging across the ground as they walked. Unlike humans, the aliens had no eyes, relying on their strong sense of smell and hearing to get around. They had jaws that could dislocate and open nearly a foot wide, and inside lay beds of dagger sharp teeth.

She had to be silent. If she could hear them, they could hear her.

It was impressive how quickly Sarah could move, despite her frailty and need to be quiet. This wasn't her first trip topside, and she hoped that it wouldn't be her last. By now, the world had gone black. The sun had retired for the day, and the aliens patrolled the land. Not only could she hear them, but she could see them as well. Nine foot silhouettes crept around in the darkness with their long, giraffe-like strides. They were even more horrid than she remembered.

With a little less than a quarter mile to go, Sarah found herself pressed against a building, listening to three of the aliens communicate with each other. The croaking and squealing was hair raising. Her skin was beginning to burn beneath the windbreaker. Time wasn't on her side. She needed to keep moving; and needed to do so without alerting the celestial invaders.

Peeking around the side of the building, Sarah noticed that the aliens would glow whenever they made noise. Greens, blues, purples, and yellows. They were bioluminescent. There was an unsettling beauty to the monsters.

The first step was the hardest. It was enough to suck all of the air from her lungs. A part of her wanted to collapse and give up. The sores were scathing and her head felt like a balloon on the verge of popping. But she had come this far.

She was in the open now. There were no buildings to hide behind. The only thing standing between Sarah and the bunker was an open road. Her strides hastened. With each step she was closer to safety.

All of a sudden, a chorus of high-pitched shrieks erupted from out of the aliens. A collage of colors flashed across their bodies. Sarah turned her head and felt her heart skip a beat as the three monstrosities were galloping towards her. Another set of foreign cries filled the air. Mustering up the rest of her strength, Sarah sprinted forward. Dozens of aliens filled the street now, joining in on the chase. Their primal screeches were ear splitting.

Sarah couldn't see it, but she knew that the hatch was nearby. It couldn't be more than a couple hundred feet away. Jolts of pain shot from her calves to her outer thighs. Her body was malnourished and in no condition to be running. Even something as lightweight as the three pound backpack strapped around her shoulders felt like carrying a bag of lead weights. Her breathing had become heavy and unrhythmic. The claustrophobic conditions created by the gas mask was making her hyperventilate.

The aliens were closing in on her. There were hundreds of them now, trampling through each other to catch the woman and rip her apart. Each of them glowing and screaming and clawing over one another to be the first one at the prize. The surface of the street lit up beneath the chaos; a visual fireworks display minus the booming explosions.

It was a tall tree with a bulbous trunk and no leaves that Sarah was looking for. Twenty yards behind it was the hatch that belonged to the owner of a nearby farmhouse. He, unfortunately, didn't make it beyond the first day of the invasion. Nearing seventy and having had multiple surgeries in his legs to remove blood clots had left him in a wheelchair. There was no surviving for him. At the first site of the alien ships, he took his shotgun and pulled the trigger beneath his chin. His body was still sitting in his favorite chair in the living room.

There was a loud whine as Sarah lifted the steel hatch. With all of her strength, she pulled and pulled until the lid flipped open. As carefully as time allowed her to be, Sarah stepped down onto a rung of the ladder and began her descent. The aliens were nearly on top of her. Their screams echoed off of the steel and flicked at her skull.

She reached up and grabbed onto the handle and pulled once more. Slowly, the lid to the hatch began to fall forward, but not before a glowing body reached down and slashed at her arm. Sarah released the handle and the lid slammed shut. Blood poured from out of the deep gash along her forearm. The aliens yelled and pounded against the top of the hatch.

Sarah took off the gas mask and removed the torn windbreaker, wrapping it around the wound. A well struck match created a tiny flame that was used to ignite the oil lamp. She lifted it and stepped inside.

The first thing she noticed as she entered into the bunker was the bright green battery symbol on display showing that the VR headset was fully charged. It was haunting to listen to the muffled croaks and squeals leaking in from the topside. They were persistent in their attempts to get inside.

Sarah twisted the latch on a thick steel door that separated the central area of the bunker and the bedroom. She stepped inside and allowed the flame to be her guide. They always were, but Sarah was relieved to see that they were right where she had left them. Rami and Roman. Her boys.

"Mommy's back." She whispered. "And look, I went out and got you both something." Sarah took off the backpack and dropped it onto the concrete floor. Two jackets. One for each boy. She lifted them out of the backpack and pushed the bag aside. "You guys each wanted one, remember? Rami, you wanted a yellow one and Roman asked for red. I did my best, but the only colors they had were green and black. I hope that's okay."

The boys were laying down in a bunk bed. The eldest on top and the younger down below. Sarah tucked her hand beneath Rami's left arm and slipped it into the sleeve of the black jacket. Then, she reached across his body and did the same with the other arm. The teeth on the jacket's zipper were bent.

Sarah lifted the lamp and placed it onto the top bunk. The light casted an orange glow against the wall that reflected onto Roman's face. His skin was green and his face sunken in. The surface of his lips were cracked from dehydration. Underneath, Rami looked even worse. Sores the size of craters covered both of his legs. Maggots had moved in, deciding to make the child's flesh their new home. The squirming larvae devoured the boy from the inside out.

By now, both of Sarah's sons had been dead for weeks, but she refused to live her life without them. For most of her adulthood, Sarah was on a journey to find somebody willing to love her in the same way that she loved them. It took years for her to finally come to the realization that what she was searching for was right in front of her all along;

hidden in plain sight behind the laughs, tears, wants, and needs of her children.

"Mommy loves you both so, so much." Sarah winced as she leaned forward. There was a scorching pain around the gash on her arm. Her vision grew hazy as tears welled inside her eyes. The aliens weren't letting up. They knew that she was inside and they weren't leaving until they had her.

But she wouldn't let them have her children.

Sarah kissed each of her sons on the forehead. Their skin felt like rubber. She fetched a bottle of lighter fluid and began dousing the bedroom and the furniture within it. The room became imbued with nauseating fumes.

Sarah took a piece of paper, rolled it into a tube, and allowed the flame from the lamp to catch on to the end. From there, the fire jumped from the paper onto the thin sheet on the bottom bunk. As the flame continued spreading, the room filled with a red radiance.

A wave of heat surged through the door as Sarah closed it. There was a loud click to confirm that the door was fully sealed. At the top of the ladder, the aliens continued to relentlessly pound against the steel.

Sarah unplugged the VR headset and strapped it around her head. She felt around until finding the table that she could lay on. The heat from the inferno in the bedroom was making its way into the central area. Beads of sweat soiled the inner frame of the tech. With the simple press of a button, the headset came alive. The familiar chime of the machine booting up brought peace to Sarah's mind, but another sound quickly spoiled the moment.

It was the sound of whining steel. The croaks and squeals of the aliens were no longer muffled. The hatch had been lifted. Like mindless zombies, the aliens came crashing down into the bunker. There was a collection of sickening wallops as their bodies smacked against the concrete.

"Press the power button once to engage, or press the power button two times simultaneously to shut down." The headset had given it's commands and was ready to be used. Sarah pressed the button once. The feeling of being surrounded and the noise of the aliens all faded away as she was pulled into an endless white light. "Engage."

Suddenly, the white turned to black, and there was nothing...

...It was the beautiful smell of lilacs and sunflowers that woke her. A floral sweetness hung in the air as a band of blue jays sang beneath the morning sun. Sarah slowly opened her eyes, and for a short time stared up at the white ceiling above her. The morning light sprayed against her chestnut skin and gave a glow to her dark hair. There was comfort in the sun's touch.